ABSALOM

Exit Hell

Kelly Coleman

Copyright © 2012 by Kelly Coleman.

Library of Congress Control Number:		2012910588
ISBN:	Hardcover	978-1-4771-2692-9
	Softcover	978-1-4771-2691-2
	Ebook	978-1-4771-2693-6

All rights reserved. No part of this book may be reproduced or transmitted in any form or by any means, electronic or mechanical, including photocopying, recording, or by any information storage and retrieval system, without permission in writing from the copyright owner.

This is a work of fiction. Names, characters, places and incidents either are the product of the author's imagination or are used fictitiously, and any resemblance to any actual persons, living or dead, events, or locales is entirely coincidental.

This book was printed in the United States of America.

To order additional copies of this book, contact:
Xlibris Corporation
1-888-795-4274
www.Xlibris.com
Orders@Xlibris.com
116049

The generosity of the human heart never fails to amaze me. Throughout the writing of *ABSALOM*, family, friends and acquaintances encouraged me. Many extended themselves, getting involved in the story emotionally and taking time out of their lives to critique, type and proofread. A special thanks is in order.

THANK YOU
Jan Walker McNiel
Chad Coleman
Kim Stapp
Ryan King
Hannah Keirsey
Barb Combs
Anneliese Homan

Mary Kerns
Julie Cook
Juris Jurjevics
Bill Bunch
Debbie Bunch
Lisa Shoemaker

The events and characters in this book are fictitious and any similarity to real persons, living or dead, is coincidental and not intended by the author.

For the fallen angels

Is there beauty in Sodom? Believe me, that for the immense mass of mankind beauty is found in Sodom. Did you know that secret? The awful thing is that beauty is mysterious as well as terrible. God and devil are fighting there, and the battlefield is the heart of man.

The Brothers Karamazov, III, 3

CHAPTER I

Climax Springs, MO, Spring 2001. Jinx isn't wearing any underwear. No panties and no bra . . . not on Friday nights. Has plenty of lingerie in her frameless backpack. And, prescriptions, deodorant, cosmetics, change of clothes, mace, spikes, stripper duds, cell phone and condoms too. But, no underwear under her Wrangler jeans, and these are hiked up enough to pull the seam between the folds of her vagina. Her nipples point out the black tank top. A blonde vixen for sure. Five and a half feet of sleek muscle shoved into cowgirl boots, ruled by fear and a winter heart.

    It's raining hard outside the backwoods shanty and, every once in a while, the second bulb in the strand around the porch ceiling flickers off and on. The wind's blowin' and the rain's coming down and the yellow lights are dancing around like marionettes. Open windows are rattling and the sound of water pouring out the ends of old gutters, wind chimes ringing and, every now and then, an oak branch scrapes across the tin roof. That one bulb keeps flickering, more off than on. The water is running in rivulets now and cutting across this driveway that comes back in here to her shanty castle, built on a bank over the Little Niangua River.

    Jinx hasn't much time, and she's in a hurry. Got her fake tattoos stuck on her twenty-five year young skin on the outsides of her shoulders, long hairpiece attached, and beauty mark penciled on her cheek. Wouldn't recognize her at the grocery store, and this is what she wants, and this is the way she does it every Friday night. This night, it's raining hard. She's got a low-slung '87 Vette to cross the low water bridge and the river's coming-up, and she knows this, and she is in a hurry.

Jinx takes a last look in the mirror attached behind the antique dressing table. Big thunder rolls overhead and the rain is pelting down and she can smell it. Except for the cat, she is alone. It's more than that. Like the cat, she is a nocturnal huntress, and her sleep comes in catnaps.

She fastens a small cross around her neck, steps over the books and clothes splayed out over the uneven pine floors, grabs her purse with the sharpened down screwdriver, banging the screen door behind. The silver-blue Vette with bleached canvas top is two steps off the porch, driver's side in. The rain and the lightning and the thunder and the wind don't matter. She's a harnessed nerve ending, reined in on ditch-weed doobers, and has a subterranean bead that keeps her tense . . . that is, sex.

The string of lights around the rim of the porch is bobbing in the wind, and she's jerking the door open, flinging the backpack and the purse into the Vette. She jumps in after, and leans back to check that her .38 special is still behind the passenger seat.

Lightning cuts a jagged fissure across the dark above, flicking over this vacant mutiny of geography. Steep, uneven, forest covered ridges shoved up all around her little shanty and grassy flats. Not a neighbor within a half-mile. In the darkness, not a dawn-to-dusk light anywhere.

Switching on her headlights and wipers, Jinx is in low gear, edging her way out the long driveway. Out to the country gravel road, she turns left and approaches the river crossing. She's too late, and the river is too high. Lots of turbulence and current. Couldn't get across in a pickup, much less the Vette. She backs up from the encroaching waters, around onto a yet hard gravel bar and heads back the other way.

It's slow going. The Vette has only a few inches clearance, and she's extremely cautious on gravel or rough roads. And, visibility is poor in the dark and sheets of rain. Her objective is Climax Springs.

Her 'day' job is west from Climax Springs, and her night world is east from Climax Springs. Highway Seven goes either way. In a manner of speaking, so does Jinx. There's a Jinx West and there's a Jinx East and the river divides them just as it does the land.

Tonight, she has to make it up to Seven, then east. She is slow going on the gravel towards Climax. Uncharacteristically, she leaves the radio off. Slung back in her seat, watching out through the downpour over the rain-splattered hood, Jinx is thinking about a 'joint'. Oddly enough, she's not a habitual cigarette smoker, but likes her doobers. Considerably more so than most stoners. They help to quiet the inner trembling.

She's picturing herself, like she's outside herself. She does this often. Her Vette and self, following her high beams up against the silvery onslaught of rain. Following the dull watery gravel strip ahead, squeezed on both sides by dark swaying timbers. She's thinking, she left early, and she'll make it to SHADOWS on time.

CHAPTER II

This same storm that causes the Little Niangua to flood stretches southwest. Catcher Riley lives east of Cross Timbers, and he's getting it too, sheets of rain pounding the hell out of everything. He hardly knows his neighbor, a widower named Hattie Gates, but he figures to check on her. His electricity is out and likely hers too. Besides, he likes getting out in turbulent weather—keeps his adrenaline up.

Headlights bouncing against the rainfall, splashing through mud holes and squishing over fallen branches, Catcher is wondering why the widow woman doesn't sell and move to town.

The old Ram 4x4 slops over a crest and grinds downward into a dark, rain slicked meadow. Then, lightning vibrates through the downpour and Catcher sees the bleary farmhouse and barns.

Through the watershed, on the porch, in the dim light leeching out the screen door, he's clinching a fist to knock . . .

"How 'ya doing, Colonel?"

Catcher jumps, jerks right, and in the instant, strobe lightning exposes Hattie sitting past the window, on the porch floor against the outside wall of the house. She's got her legs crossed out in front.

"Whew, you startled me, Hattie. Didn't see you when I pulled up."

Hattie is pushing herself up off the floor.

She comes up, barefoot and one side of a cotton dress stuck above her knee.

"Move over Colonel, so we can go in."

The two of them are in the house, in the candlelight, out here in the Ozark outskirt, and in a pounding rainstorm.

"I was driving by and thought I'd check on you." Now, he looks around, "Guess you're in good shape here?"

"Yes. No electricity. I'm without water. But, I've got some tea made. How about we have some tea?"

"You bet."

She pulls a decanter out of the dead fridge and pours two jars.

"It's still cold. Electricity hasn't been out long. You want sugar?"

"No thanks."

Waving her hand back towards the front, "Let's go back to the porch."

She gathers up a pack of unfiltered shorts with some wooden matches.

They're leaning back against the wall, sitting on the porch, listening to the rain, sipping tea from old jelly jars.

"You have a little time to kill, Colonel?"

"I've got lots of time. That's about all I do have . . . my power's off too."

The rain keeps on. Now and then lightning pulsates behind swirling black clouds, then thunder rolls over this hilly timberlands. Just sitting, legs stretched out in front, enjoying each other's presence, watching and listening and smelling the rain.

"You have anybody in this world, Colonel?"

"No. It's just me."

"No folks, ex-wives or children or brothers or sisters?"

"Nope."

"Me neither. Not since John died."

"How'd he die?"

"Tractor rolled over him coming out the back hollow. Seems a long time ago."

"John was your husband?"

"The one and only. And, a good one too."

"How long ago was the accident?"

"It's been three years. Just before you bought your place . . . . You didn't move-in after you bought. How come?"

"Wasn't retired yet."

"I heard your wife died after you bought?"

"That's right."

"Want a Camel?" shaking one out of the pack.

"No, thanks."

"I don't usually smoke . . . just on special occasions." Firing up a wooden match and holding it to the end of her cigarette.

Catcher twists his head, watching this ritual.

The rain and lightning and thunder maintain.

Hattie holds the Camel in her hand on her thigh. "Colonel is a pretty high rank, no?"

Catcher, looking ahead, "Depending on your perspective."

"It's a high rank. Right below General, I think."

"Call me Catcher, please. Or, Riley. We're neighbors . . . . We're Ozark neighbors."

Shaking another short out of the pack. "Catcher, then." The match flares, flickering over the intensity in her face . . . . "Ozark neighborliness is a matter of interpretation . . ."

"Yes?" Catcher is waiting.

"It's true, far as it goes, as to you and me," blowing smoke into the soggy pitch. "I can tell, you and me will be good neighbors . . . . You know, we're in the white, not the yoke, of the Ozarks. We're in the overrun foothills, developers dividing everything up, bringing in outsiders. The Missouri Ozarks gets more Ozarky down south, near the Arkansas line. Then, down in Arkansas, you've got the Ouchita Mountains." Stubbing her smoke out.

Catcher, not looking over, "We are inside the Ozark Plateau, here, geographically speaking."

"Seems the people, more than the geography, define neighborliness," looking out ahead, like catcher. "Right or wrong, down south in the yoke, those people pretty much understand how it is between them and what will fly and what won't. They got their own code or whatever, and most of 'm know what to expect. More likely to be tolerable neighbors . . . . Up here, people flocking in from K.C., Iowa, Nebraska and God knows where all . . . . You don't have a clue who your neighbor might be."

"C'mon now, you got a clue about me," stretching his arms up, over his head, staring out into the black rainfall.

"I'm lucky to have you as a neighbor, that's for sure. Hope I pan out as good for you . . . . What I'm say'n, however, there's a lot of 'someth'n else' scattered around in the hills out here. When you think Ozark neighbors, I wouldn't be too quick to drop my guard."

Catcher twisting to face her, holding his hands up. "You're scaring me," grinning in the wet darkness.

"You laugh," giving him the 'you'll see' tone . . . . Turning to face him, "What'd you do in the army?"

His head still facing her, "Special Operations mostly. In exotic places," murmuring, so she barely hears over the pounding rain.

"Hold your face there," she's scratching another match to flare. Holding the flame up, inches from Catcher's wary canine eyes. Taking a hard look, then shaking the match out; recalling a fleeting encounter with a soot wolf dog in the woods . . .

"Hey," Catcher leaning closer, "do I look scared?"

"I'm guess'n you're not scared of squat! I'm read'n what crosses you should be scared."

CHAPTER III

While Jinx is en route to SHADOWS, and Catcher Riley, COL USA RET, is cozied down on the porch with Hattie, there's another party appropriate to mention here. Erik Starr.

He's sitting here, at the slick-top table in the kitchen of the old house on October Mount Pontiac. The windows and front door are open. It's not raining, but lightning is playing off in the distance and dull thunder reaches here. The bullfrogs at the pond are in a deafening cacophony. Somewhere, out near the porch, a dog is making a low growl.

Erik puts two things on the table: a Smith & Wesson .44 Magnum revolver and a .44 Remington Magnum 240 Grain Jacketed Hollow Point bullet. He sets the bullet up on its end. This young man is in his early twenties. He's a shorter version of the Hulk, with thick reddish hair and freckles. That is to say . . . stocky with thick, bulging muscles. He's in a black, wife-beater net undershirt and button-up Levis. That's all he's wearing.

He's smirking and staring at this Dirty Harry pistol on the table. "I'm not going to call you again, Bugs. Get your ass out here."

Bugs comes out of the shadows surrounding the lit table. He's bare-chested and pulling on his Wranglers. Kind of puny looking. And, scared.

"Sit down across the table from me," Erik commands.

The dog's still growling and there's the thunder again.

Erik is looking Bugs in the eye. "You go into Osceola today?"

Bugs' eyes are bugged out and he's sitting in the chair half-sideways from Erik. His jeans are unzipped.

Bugs kind of stutters. "You, you already know I, I did Erik."

Erik picks-up the .44 MAG revolver and shakes the cylinder outward and loads the single bullet into a chamber. The dog is still growling at the thunder and the sharp croaking of the frogs is incessant.

Bugs is hanging on the rim of his seat with both hands. Kind of leaning back away from Erik. Sweat's beading on his brow and across his upper lip.

"Jeez, Erik. What of it?"

Erik spins the cylinder on the .44 and snaps it closed and points it directly at Bugs' face.

"Did I not order you to stay out of towns until after harvest?"

"Yeh. Yeh. Yeh . . . I mean yes. But, but I needed some lug nuts for . . ."

Erik pulls the trigger.

A solid metallic click. That's all.

"Guess you're lucky, Bugs. Next time, I'll load all the chambers except for one."

Bugs is speechless. He's holding his eyes tightly shut, sitting in his own pee, shivering like a maple leaf in the wind. Speaking of which, the wind is starting to pick up on the October Mount Pontiac.

Erik lays the pistol down on the table and pushes it towards Bugs.

"C'mon Bugzy Wugzy, you try it on me."

Nothing. Bugs is immobile.

"Watch this, Bugzy Wugzy," and Erik retrieves the pistol. He snaps open the cylinder and spins it and snaps it shut. He bends his arm up and points the end of the barrel at his temple. He's holding it butt end up and leaning his head away to accommodate the length of the barrel.

Erik pulls the trigger.

Again, a solid metallic click.

Erik drops the pistol and coolly unloads the one round. He lays the .44 back on the tabletop. Then, abruptly gets up, pulling a shirt off the back of his chair. He moves over and sits down on the sagging couch and slips on his cowboy boots over his bare feet.

"Fuck you, Bugs chickenshit. I'm going to R4. When I get back, you'd better be here. Stay alert, dickhead."

He's out the door. Bugs can hear him start the truck. Then, he hears the truck crunching down the gravel. The frogs are silent and so is the dog. It starts raining really hard.

CHAPTER IV

From Climax Springs, Jinx heads east on Seven Highway. She keeps the Vette at the highest speeds the tortuous, rain swept highway will allow. She moves through the darkened countryside, then the gradual build-up outside Greenview. Crossing the Niangua Branch Bridge, and, in the rainy blackness, she can see a few lights around the bleary edge of Lake of the Ozarks.

The SHADOWS is a glitzy, legal, non-alcoholic, totally nude strip club. The girls coming in or going out, on shift changes, pass between the stage and the tables in the customer pit. Behind the tables are the tinted glass lap dancing VIP rooms. The dressing room is behind the wall from whence the stage protrudes. As this night shift comes in, Mercedes, from day shift, is doing her last naked dance for chump change. Even if she spots one of her regulars, she may not stay past shift change. Not even for lap dances. Lap dances run twenty-five dollars per.

There are three chrome poles evenly spaced from the back to front stage. As Jinx passes by, Mercedes has fastened her legs around a pole and flopped backwards, upside down, hair dragging the stage, breasts outward, spinning herself by pushing off the stage floor with her hands. The guys around the stage barely notice night shift coming in. They are apprising the Mercedes family jewels to a song with a diesel beat all about 'can't be loving you while you be giving your stuff away.'

Then, Jinx is in the dressing room, with Mom's office at the far end. 'Mom' is here and watching the girls. Seems, even strippers want a mom around, but tonight, there's no fights, money mess-ups, or costume repairs required, and Mom keeps to herself in the office.

The dressing room has a long dressing 'table' in the center, with mirrors and lights to accommodate ten dancers per side and the girls' lockers are on the outside wall. Half-lockers for the new girls and full lockers for the veterans. These lockers are decorated inside with photos, magnetic and adhesive one-liners, and the normal kind of personal expression one might expect in a high-school locker. Maybe, there's a higher sexual content here. Jinx has no display inside her full length locker.

Now, seventy to eighty percent of these totally nude strippers are bisexual or lesbian. Make no mistake about it; these women are all about appealing to the prurient interest and are sex provocateurs.

Angel's on a stool turned away from the mirror and lights behind, legs spread open, displaying the new piercing in her clitoris. "I can get off anywhere, anytime, jus' walkin'."

"Where'd you get it done?"

"Dragon Tales Tattoo Parlor. Just slapped me back, like in a dentist chair, and held my clit with a clamp while they poked a hole through it using a slender punch and a mallet. Put a big cork underneath to stop the punch."

"Did it hurt?"

"Na. Windy said hers did, but I liked it. Kind of a bummer for two weeks, though. No sex without a condom. No cunnilingus either. I already used a dildo and the feeling was fantastic. Guy said about one out of seven girls getting their clit pierced will lose the feeling in the clit. Not happening here, just the opposite."

Phoenix is curious. "How come no sex for two weeks?"

"Got to let the pierce heal up. Don't want no semen or saliva on it till then." Angel spreads her legs a little wider and leans over pointing at the mini, silver colored barbell hanging on her clit. "This little feller keeps me wet all the time."

Out in front, the so-called D.J., who is really an announcer, is announcing, "Boston has arrived and is coming on stage for two dances. Get your dance tip ready, gentlemen."

Boston is coming forward from backstage, and hits a pedal for a puff of smoke and a blue spotlight on the ceiling. She's got sequins sprinkled on her body and these are radiating tiny flares and sparkles, and she's coming out of the smoke, and she's got a flashy royal blue dress 'glued' on her muscular, over-tanned body, and the men start laying dollars on the edge of the stage. She's got a catchy song going, and she's got the beat, and she's attracting interest. Boston's aware of the interest, and she's watching for the gentleman who might crave her company in a twenty-five dollar per dance VIP room. Her shallow platforms are her only plebian accoutrement. She's new at the

SHADOWS and can't afford the seventy some dollar platform shoes, till after tonight . . . . And, this is no guarantee. She's paid one hundred dollars for her spot here tonight, like all the other girls, and this is overhead, and she needs the lap dances to make this pay. Most the new girls don't have the money for the taller platforms till they've lasted awhile. And, a girl that will go out and strip naked lasts, unless she can't attract the dollars. If they're not too unattractive, they last and get the tall platforms and the little 'spanky' outfits too. To last, they must not get fired for prostitution or drugs at the SHADOWS. The SHADOWS will dump you for this and management won't take you back. For anything else, they will rehire.

While Boston is showing her pussy to an older gentleman with a stack of twenties, Jinx, who goes by 'Saxony' here, is engaging in chit chat with Calico, backstage, in the dressing room . . .

"You kick the deadbeat dad out yet?"

Calico, "Not yet." She leans over, stepping into a thong. "Says he's getting a job. Same old story. My mom's watching the kid. My man's not home, but says he's getting work soon. Same thing he always fucking says."

"You're pulling some good money out of here, right?"

"Yeah, but grinding my ass off to get it."

Jinx laughing, "Keeps us in totally good shape, sweetheart. What's your boyfriend's name?"

"Richard. I call him Dick. Suitcase Dick. He's always comin' or going or trying to."

"Sounds typical."

"Yeah. If you can't buy it, move it or screw it, who needs it? A fucking guy alright."

"At least you have someone."

"Uh-huh. And all he does is complain. A pencil dick with a nickel hard-on; and he complains about loose pussy."

"Maybe you need someone else. Get rid of dickhead."

"Someday. I'll have an old man who puts the bacon on the table. He may be out there now."

"If he is, it won't work," and Jinx leads out of the dressing room.

Boston has picked up a lap dance session, and Venus is on stage slapping her bare butt in another stripper's face, who responds by kissing her rump. Then, Venus is grabbing the vertical pole and swinging around it. The other girls are circulating, making themselves solicitous. Laughing to each other about body parts and sex. And, chatting with the patrons about both the patron's and the stripper's lives, usually adding some sexual innuendo. Gotta get the lap dance.

The announcer, "Get ready for this, gentlemen. You're going to Horn-dog Heaven now. Get your dollars out . . . here comes Saxony, our Friday Night Special Feature. She is here every Friday."

Now, Jinx, aka Saxony, is on stage, in spikes; the only girl to wear spikes. She's wearing a custom made dress from 'the city', and it clings to her body like wet silk. The music is louder and livelier and she's coming out of a smoke explosion and kaleidoscope of light.

Right here, in the get go of her dance routine, she spots a man who knows her from Warsaw. She turns her head directly towards him and fastens an unsmiling, unblinking stare on this man, all the while doing her statuesque, semi-bullfighter routine.

At first, the Warsaw man hints at recognition. This fades under Jinx's withering stare. He starts off thinking he's 'caught' her. Goes on to think this Saxony just has some uncanny resemblance to the girl in Benton County named Jinx. Ends up wondering if someone in the SHADOWS might recognize him.

Coming off stage, 'Saxony' has choices to make. Several dirt sooted construction guys are trying to sidetrack her with twenties in outreaching hands. She dismisses these 'gentlemen' and gets over to an empty side table. Winnie's up on stage struttin' her stuff.

While 'Saxony' is finishing dressing in her minimal outfit, she's watching an older man in an expensive sport coat watching her. She gets up and goes over to sit beside him. "Would you like for me to dance for you in private?"

She's up close to his face, leaning over so he can see down her narrow top.

"I've got the money for it," he answers.

"You can touch me anywhere, except under my thong. It's twenty-five dollars per dance."

"Show me the way, honey."

She's leading him back through the semi-naked girls and voyeur men (and women) to a corner VIP room.

The VIP rooms have tinted glass, so it's hard to see in. But, not impossible. 'Mom' has to check on the girls doing lap dances in the VIP rooms. A—She's watching for their safety. B—She's making sure the law and club rules are being followed, i.e. no penetrations and no touching the girl's vagina or her handling his penis. And, he can't take his penis out of his pants. Some voyeurs can turn into real flag wavers.

Besides the tinted glass, this VIP room has vinyl couches built around the walls with a mirror on the back wall, so the girl can get into her narcissism and mom can see reflected what she can't directly.

"My name is Saxony, what's yours," asks Jinx, as she strips down to a thong.

"Ross, Ross Keets."

"Well, Ross Keets, you need to pay me twenty-five dollars for the dance. I'll wait till this song is over . . . start on the next one, so we have the whole time."

Ross has sat down and stands back up. He pulls a roll of bills from his pocket, and a one hundred dollar bill from the roll, and gives it to Jinx.

"You want to prepay for a few dances Ross, before you've had a taste?"

"I trust it will be worth it." Ross sits back down.

The song begins, piped into the room from out in front.

"Just lean back, Ross," Jinx is pushing his legs apart so she can kneel between them. She's got her head tilted back watching Ross, and him her, as she rubs her shoulders up his inseams. Her chin is an inch or so from his crotch. Then, she's up on her bare feet, grabbing the metal handles on the wall behind Ross, on either side of his body. Her breasts are in his face.

"You can touch me anywhere you want Ross, just not under my thong."

Ross puts both hands on her breasts, but doesn't know exactly what he's supposed to do with them. Just sitting back, kind of like at the movies, 3D.

Jinx is holding on to the handles on either side of Ross, with one leg planted behind her and the other bent up so the knee is rubbing Ross's crotch.

"I've got to rotate now, Ross. We have to rotate our bodies from front to back a minimum of three times per dance." Then, 'Saxony' is turned around, with her back toward Ross. She pushes her buttocks back into his crotch, trying to catch his root in her crack. Now, arching backwards, hanging onto the wall handles, palms out, kind of covering Ross up.

At first, Ross isn't reacting. But, now, he's got his arms around Jinx and his hands on her stomach . . . then up to rub her nipples. Jinx relaxes most of her body onto Ross, except her legs and butt muscles are working to give Ross a hundred dollar ride.

Jinx likes it that Ross isn't talking much. She likes the men that let her do the pretend-sex dance and dispense with the small talk. This way, both of them, the man and Jinx, can simply enjoy the moment.

During the fourth dance, Ross asks Jinx if she's got a phone number where he can call. Says, he'd like to take her out.

"Can't give you my number, sweetie . . . that could be construed as solicitation . . . there's another way though."

"How?"

"Think about it, Ross." Jinx has a sweat film over her body from the workout. Mom's going by again, looking in, checking things out.

"I guess you've muddled my head, cause I don't know how I can reach you without a number."

The fourth song is over, and Jinx is standing back from Ross, and he has that wallowed disheveled look. He gives her another forty dollars for a tip and one last dance, still trying to figure a way he can contact 'Saxony'.

Jinx likes Ross, as far as it goes. "You in business, Ross?"

"I own a boat dealership."

"You have a business card?" Jinx is in front of him now, rubbing his crotch with her knee. "Why don't you give me your card."

"Don't call me, I'll call you," laughs Ross.

"Maybe."

"I think a call girl means the guy has her number and calls her?"

"Who said I was a call girl?" In a flash of contempt.

"Hey, I don't mean it badly. Call it wishful thinking. I see it, you're a call girl."

Jinx staring deadpan at Ross, "This call girl gets your number and she calls you."

"C'mon. Admit it. In the movies and novels, the guy has the number of the call girl and calls the call girl whenever he gets the urge . . . . That's the service . . . . He gets 'it' when he wants it."

"Well Ross, you don't make the rules. I do. And, this call girl calls you when, and if, she wants."

"But, I'm paying for it, so I should call you when I want the service, not the other way around."

"You want a service, do it with your hand. You want me, you can wait and see if I call." Jinx drawing back, intent on his face, "We going to argue over whether you call the call girl or the call girl calls you, or do you want to date me?"

"Alright. Alright. I want a date. I'll wait for the call girl to call, then I'll pay to do it her way. Is this the way it works?"

"That's the way it works, big guy," Jinx begins rubbing close to him. "We do it my way, or we don't do it."

"A call girl who has your number and calls you. That's a twist. I mean, which one of us is providing the service? . . . Is it me or you?"

"That's for me to know, and you to find out."

"Maybe when you call, I won't be in the mood," Ross looking perplexed.

"Really?"

When this song is over, Jinx puts her scanty outfit back on, and Ross gets up, waiting for her. He notices there is a black light overhead in the VIP room, and this details his pants in a different light. He hasn't messed himself. For a second, he wants to run out of the place. Then, when Mom isn't looking, he gives a business card to Jinx.

Out of the VIP room, Ross splits off to leave, and Jinx heads for a seat at the water bar. She's damp with sweat, and a little breathless. She's got Ross's card hidden in her top. While a girl dubbed Princess is showing the love canal to a few boys at stage front, Jinx walks to the dressing room to prepare to go back on stage. She takes Ross's card and puts it in her purse in her locker. She averages nearly eight hundred dollars per Friday night, and she's got a lot of bodies to press. She takes another swig off her bottled water, and goes back out front. The jukebox is playing some kind of rap, "I want it now, I want it now, do it to me baby, do it . . . ." All the dancer is wearing is her platforms, and she's squatting, spreading her legs, licking her finger before putting it on her clitoris.

Jinx has an individualized shift schedule with SHADOWS' management. At 12:30 a.m., she's done. Saturday morning, 12:30 a.m., and she is anxious to get her sweaty duds into her pack and the clean ones into her locker. Nine hundred dollars to the better (or worse), and three business cards for future solicitation.

She's back in the parking lot, in her Vette, removing the tattoos, beauty mark and hairpiece . . . dismantling 'Saxony' for a more complicated Jinx. The rain has stopped, and the overhanging oak branches are dripping water, and a diffused light spreads out over the lot. The SHADOWS' neon sign, like a little fallen star glowing from the bottom of Humidity Sea.

She starts her Vette and heads out for R4.

CHAPTER V

About the time Catcher and Hattie finish smoking on the porch, the lights come back on and the rain stops. The timelessness fades. A sense of time and 'in the now' reasserts itself. Getting up to their feet. Catcher is scratching the top of his head, holding his recon hat in his other hand.

"I enjoyed the evening. A lot. Thank you for check'n on me. You should do it more often." Hattie's smiling at him.

The lightning and thunder seems to have moved on, and the dark dampness is turning into a drizzle. Catcher, leaving down the porch steps, waving over his shoulder as he walks away . . . . Getting into the old 4x4 Ramcharger.

Turning left onto the county road, listening to his wipers, thump-thump back and forth, following his headlights. The road running with watery rivulets. Thinking. About Hattie Gates . . . . She perseveres, even as she watches the wilderness reclaim her pastures, acre-by-acre, year-by-year.

Catcher's thinking takes a different turn, kind of like dropping over a ridge into a hollow. In the early years, before his marriage, Catcher wanted to be the first to sleep with his sweetheart. In the later years, after their marriage, he wanted to be the last. She never failed him. He cherished her, and she him. Then, the cancer. 'Till death do us part. When the object of love dies, you're still stuck with the love. A lady to the end. She was well groomed and attractive to the end. Lying in bed, in their home on base. Planning her own funeral, saying and writing her goodbyes. Then, rotating the switch for an overdose of morphine. With him all his military career. The perfect military wife. Then, she dies. But, the love and respect do not die. He didn't stay in the army . . . . He might have made general.

Parking back in the barn, and trotting through the light rain for the house. It's the early hours of the next day as he fiddles for his key . . . out in front of the big, cedar sided tri-level, in the meadows, in the black drippiness, between the ragged Ozark ridges. Going through the door, the familiar void of loneliness engulfs Catcher. And, he's tired.

Thinking, he may be the last man standing . . . . He's not. North and east, on the east bank of the Little Niangua, the weekly all night Friday night party is shifting into overdrive. There's no way Catcher could know. He's not yet heard of R4.

CHAPTER VI

R4. Erik Starr is jittery after the 'conference' with Bugs. Fucking Bugs. He's a security risk, and Erik is on to him. The weak link in the chain is gonna get them all busted . . . . Erik has to slow the pickup down. The rain has stopped and the fog is thick as the center of a cloud . . . . But, by damn, Erik is going to R4 and shake his heebie-jeebies.

It's a forty-minute drive from the ranch to R4 when the Little Niangua is flooded. The drive down to Preston, then to Mack's Creek and back up to the river, takes forty minutes in clear conditions. In this fog, the trip is much longer. When Erik finally pulls into the R4 parking lot, it's around one a.m. Still, lots of cars and trucks.

He's heading across the lot towards the light seeping through the fog, listening to a muted country-rock tune. Mostly unaware, when The Hand reaches out of the drippy mist and grabs him on the shoulder. "What?"

Erik is leaning back and turning in the direction of The Hand. Wishing he had his .357.

As he comes around, Erik catches his balance about the same time as this giant Indian bumps into him. The giant has black braided hair down the sides of his face, big nose and bulbous protruding lips, and fire where each of his eyes should be. The Indian says, "Don't do it! Go back!"

He can't get the Indian's grip loose from his shoulder. "Get your fuckin' hands off me, motherfucker."

The Indian again, "Don't go in! Go back." The fires in his eyes burning into Erik.

"Fuck you."

"The woman inside will jinx you and bad fortune comes towards you." The fires subside in the Indian's eyes, and he lets loose of Erik and disappears into the fog. It's so surreal, Erik is reeling. 'What the fuck.' 'Drunken fucking

Indian.' 'Good thing I don't have my gun!' Then, he's turning back towards R4. 'Fuck The Hand.'

R4 is a private nightclub owned and operated by Jake Boss. He's a twenty-five year old local boy made good, financially speaking. Went all the way through school with Jinx and her twin sister Nicole, in a backwoods micro-school. He graduated, came and went till his grandfather died, leaving him this place on the river. It had been a twelve thousand square foot fishing lodge originally. After grampa died, Jake turned it into a nightclub.

The building is impressive. From the outside, it looks like an ancient flying saucer set down on a grassy knoll beside the river. A very large, primitive saucer; like an oaken space ship. The river on one side and parking on the other. Big oak trees are around this saucer-like building and scattered throughout the parking lot too. A narrow rock road, lined with oak, hickory, elm and cedar, comes into here and terminates at the parking lot. The building is an octagon. Inside, the roof rafters meet in the center, at a stone chimney. The chimney services a four hearth stone fireplace in the center of a central room below this oak canopy ceiling. Originally, this central room was ringed around the outside by a veranda style porch. But, after his grandfather died, Jake enclosed the porch around the central lodge room. He built living quarters, an office, a bar (that serves to the outside or inside), modern restrooms, designated drivers' lounge and storage around the outside of the central room. He also extended a party deck out towards the river. The porch was enclosed with vertical oak siding around the outside. Since the original lodge was built from logs, the inside central room has log walls with white chinking between them—all this beneath the aforedescribed oak ceiling draping down from the center, with the rafters and bracing showing. The effect is quite rustic. Added into this, is a large bandstand built on one side of the round, central room. This is where Jake's carefully selected bands play on Friday nights and Saturday mornings—from sunset on Friday till sunup on Saturday.

The R4 members and guests dance immediately in front of the bandstand or around the four-hearth fireplace in the center. Tables and chairs spread out from the sides of the bandstand around the outside edge of this inner sanctum. Smoke eaters, heating and cooling vents, mixed in with party lights, are mounted in the oak ceiling bracing, creating an inviting, rough hewn hodgepodge suitable for 'cutting loose.'

Jake keeps the bar and grill open during the week, but his 'money night' is Friday night. And, since he runs the place as a private club, he can stay open till he pleases, which is sun-up Saturday morning. And, back open again at noon on Saturday till midnight Saturday night. He will not open on Sunday. It is one of those anomalies about Jake the Rake; he will not operate this heathen den on the Lord's day. And, this really is the reason he does not open on Sunday.

Persons become members of this club by paying dues monthly, semi-annually or annually. This precludes the 'average bear' from holding a membership in R4. However, professionals, successful businessmen and government workers from small towns miles away, line up for a coveted membership card to R4. The way Jake works it, members bring the alcoholic beverages of their choice to the club, and Jake stocks the bar with their liquor or beer, catalogued on the huge back bar and coolers by name. Soft drinks and mix are on the house. It is a BYO establishment.

In the early days, Jake nearly ran through his inherited money before the concept caught on. But, he never wavered, and he paid for good bands, hi-tech sound systems, and charismatic bartenders and barmaids, when membership fees wouldn't cover such extravaganza. Then, when R4 became an 'item' and financially successful people began searching out R4 for some incognito hell raising, Jake boosted the membership fees. He stayed right 'in there' running this party colossus. And this took grit. Like, R4 was the kind of place where someone might dance naked or copulate on the deck overlooking the river. After dark, and when the party lights came on, and the band began to play, the only person in the world who could make sense of the operation was Jake. Jake made it his business to know all aspects of the operation and every one of his members.

This rainy, foggy night, R4 is rocking. The music is nuclear loud; the crowd is well under the influence of alcohol and mob-bonding. Who'd think Jake would notice Erik coming in to this honky-tonk bedlam. But, he does . . . . Then, he spies Jinx coming through the door. And, she cuts straight through the crowd to Jake, and the two of them get a table to themselves. Jinx is yelling at Jake, to be heard over the raucous pandemonium.

Now, remember what you got here! Two people, same age, opposite sex, that have been the 'closest' since kindergarten. Best friends, then fuck buddies, right on through high school graduation, and the seven hardscrabble years heretofore. Jinx in her rain-wet Wranglers, tank top and boots, minus the tattoos, hairpiece and beauty mark. The two of them yelling at one another, sitting at a table bordering hard country rocker mania. Jinx oozing sensuality through a thin scent of musk smelling sweat and peptic ozone brought in from outdoors, like a dazzling, sweaty Venus; a reined in orgasmic tour de force half-listening, half-watching, this black haired rake named Jake. He's nonchalant, keeping his eyes on the stompers. Velvet Jake, always was, always will be. And strobe lights, spotlights, colored lights and laser lights sweeping through the smoke, an eight piece band with three trumpets blasting over the dancing and boozing and smoking and chemical laced crowd . . . . Jinx wants the key to his quarters, so she can shower.

Jinx gets the key and leaves Jake to shepherd his unruly flock. She gets to the four inch thick, custom built, metal veneer door opening into Jake's eclectic pad. When she closes and locks the door, her demeanor sags.

She's in Jake's shower, standing here under the steaming water, holding her palms over her eyes, letting go. She's separating again, leaving the here and now, like maybe she's going to float right up out of the shower to the ceiling. She goes into something akin to a seizure as the backside of her brain lets go of a memory.

Bam! She hears the bathroom door bang against the inside wall. Papa's drunk again. He's yanking the shower curtain back, and she's a six year old girl backed up against the far wall of the shower holding her hands over her cookie. Papa's gonna want to play with her cookie. He's drunk and this means it may hurt and she's scared. No . . . no . . . he wants her to wash his dolly off. He's pulling her hands off her cookie, soaping them up and putting them on Dolly . . . showing her how to pet Dolly. She's scared. Her mama's gone. There's nowhere to run. She isn't doing it right and Papa's getting mad. He's grabbing her hair high up on the back of her head . . . wants her to kiss Dolly . . . . She slips in the tub . . . . She's not really in the shower anymore. She's floating, hovering up in the corner of the bathroom, watching this tormented little girl . . . then, it's more scary . . . . She's coming back down, going into the little girl . . .

Jinx is laying in the back of the tub in a fetal position when the hot water turns cold. She is getting herself up off the floor of the tub. Very tense. Focused on hanging onto immediate realities. Trying to control that spinning . . . that spinning that wants to take off up through the ceiling, right past the stars and comets and asteroids and moons and planets and into the black abyss of nothingness beyond. Her hands are trembling. She doesn't stop to dry or get a towel. Gets out of the bathroom to her purse. Shakes the Xanex out. She gets a doober going.

Hey, she can barely hang onto this disoriented existence. The floating towards the dark abyss beyond is scary. It's even scarier when she wants to go, can hardly keep from going. When her personal reality is intolerable, the flight outward to nothingness awaits her charter.

The marijuana is kicking-in now, and the Xanex is coming to the rescue. She's drying and getting dressed and fixing her hair. She's loving the music reaching here from beyond the door. Maybe she'll dance till she collapses.

Sifting through the revelers, looking to give Jake his key. She spots him, standing alone, near the end of the bar.

"Jake, Jake, over here."

Jake joins her at a table. "What took you so long?"

"I had another flashback while I was in the shower. 'Bout didn't come out of it," Jinx is looking around for a barmaid.

"You OK?"

"Yep. Just fine now." Jinx is straining around to see where Jake is looking. "What are you looking at?"

"I'm watching a guy, Erik Starr, from the OMP."

"The OMP?"

Jake looking back at Jinx, "October Mount Pontiac . . . or Ozark Mafia Posse, depending how you see it."

"October Mount Pontiac? Ozark Mafia Posse? This ought to be good," Jinx craning her head in the direction of Erik Starr. He's at the far end of the bar, gesturing and talking to some rough types.

"Yeah. Erik and his brother own a big place back towards Osceola. They call it the October Mount Pontiac. Cattle ranch. But, they do a little farming too."

"Farming?"

"They're growing weed and selling it up north. Lots of weed."

Jinx is really watching Erik now.

"I hear you better not stumble on any of their crops. No one has ever seen any of their fields and been around to tell it; least ways that's what I hear. So, us country boys call 'em the Ozark Mafia Posse, or OMP. The straight world may recognize the October Mount Pontiac as a cattle ranch. I've seen some of the cash they toss around here. I'd call 'em the Ozark Mafia Posse, but, not to their face. Especially not to that one." Jake jerks his head in Erik's direction, "He's a crazy motherfucker."

Jinx, still watching Erik, with a puzzled look, "What's he so excited about? He's really hollering and stomping around."

Jake, putting his attention back on Erik, "Before you came out, he was saying something about getting pushed around in the parking lot. Wished he had his gun . . . . I need a shooting here like a hole in the head."

"Must have got him pretty riled up."

Erik spots blonde-haired Jinx looking at him, and Jinx doesn't turn away. He lifts his beer in her direction, as to toast her, and drinks it down. Squinting at Jake, and back to Jinx. Reaching around for another beer, heading towards the blaring bandstand, still watching Jinx. Getting up to the bandstand, he's shouting something in the ear of a guitar player. Alright again, he's looking back at Jinx, holding his beer up in her direction, and toasting her again.

Jake leans over in Jinx's face, "What the hell is he doing?" Holds his hand up, signaling security to back off.

"Hold on a minute Jake, just wait . . ." Jinx has an amused smile and is still watching Erik.

Then, the band stops playing and Erik gets up on the stage behind the microphone. His hair is very red and his brutish muscles accentuated under the spotlights. The crowd noise is dropping an octave or so, and Erik is sweating as he takes his shirt off down to the wife-beater undershirt. He's throwing his shirt over the top of the crowd. Taking the microphone in hand and directing the crowd's attention towards Jinx. A roadie directs a spotlight onto Jake and Jinx. Most the folks know Jinx to see her and all the members know Jake. Erik's voice is loud and clear, "Folks, we're just country and we say it the way it is. I'm going to tell that blonde-headed beauty over there, with Jake, what I'm feeling in my heart, for her, tonight. Guess I've missed the 'flower' of R4 till now," leaning forward, squinting towards Jinx, "cause I've never seen you, beautiful lady, till just a moment ago."

The crowd is whooping and hollerin' and whistling and clapping.

"I fell in love with you beautiful woman, love at first sight. It's never happened to me before, but it sure did tonight. I want all these folks to know it. I dedicate this song to you." Turning back to the band, "Hit it, boys." And, Erik's back facing the dance floor, singing the Eagle's PEACEFUL EASY FEELING to the band's accompaniment. "I like the way your sparkling earrings lay, against your skin so brown, and I want to sleep with you in the desert tonight, with a billion stars all around, cause I got a peaceful, easy feeling, that I know you won't let me down . . ."

Jake's saying something to Jinx, but she's smoking another doober, and her whole attention is on this gutty, redheaded bull serenading her.

He's good. Erik knows the song, and he can sing it, and the band's enjoying this, and so is the crowd.

Jake is looking down, shaking his head. Jinx is taking a toke, studying Erik intently. Then, the song is over, and R4 roars with applause, and the spot comes off Jinx and Jake, and Erik is getting down from the bandstand.

Jake's trying to tell Jinx, "Watch yourself with this one, Jinx. He's dangerous."

Erik is nearly to their table now, and Jake is clamping his mouth shut.

"My name is Erik Starr. May I have the pleasure of yours?"

Jake is looking down at the tabletop. Jinx is holding her joint off to the side, looking up at Erik.

"Jinx is my name."

"Jinx?"

"Yes."

"Well, Jinx, that's the second time tonight I've heard that word . . . I think an omen."

Jinx interrupts, "Yes?"

"I'm not going to stay tonight. Was going to, but it's not going to work out. May I have your phone number?" Erik glances at Jake. "You don't care do you, Jake?"

Jake looks up. "I don't have a thing to say about what Jinx does."

Looking back at Jinx, "Well, Jinx, how about it? Can I have your phone number?"

Jinx motions to Jake for a pen. "How about you give me your number?"

"Will you call me?"

"Yes, I'll call you," and Jinx is pulling a scrap of paper from out of her purse on which to write.

"It's Erik Starr." He gives her his phone number.

"OK, Erik. I'll call you."

"Don't forget." And Erik is leaving.

While Jinx is getting the paper back in her purse, Jake is cautioning her, "Jinx, you don't know what you might get into there. Don't you think . . ."

Jinx cuts him off, "Jake, stay out of it." She pinches her joint out carefully, laying the butt in the ashtray. She gets up and goes out towards the dance floor, picking-up a partner on the way.

She stays on the dance floor till about sun-up. When the band finishes, she gets Jake's key and goes to his quarters. And, while he is closing the club, Jinx showers and gets into his bed.

Finally, all is quiet. Jake getting into bed with her, kissing her, and caressing her. Jake marvels at her breath . . . been up God knows how long . . . done God knows what . . . and still, there is life's fruity, ripe, youthful smell force.

Jake has no resolve where Jinx is concerned. Never had. Not since he was five years old. But, he knows he has to stop fucking her to get on with his life. Not this morning, however. This morning, after the storm, there is peace on the river. Outside, shafts of sunlight pierce the woods, and a mist hangs over the Little Niangua. The great oaken octagon building is quiet. The only sound is the rushing river and some crows. Jake needs to sleep. Come noon, he'll be reopening R4.

CHAPTER VII

Saturday morning, about the time Jake is closing up R4, Catcher Riley is laying in bed with a headache. It hurts across the back of his neck. He's already taken two coated aspirin and one aspirin free Excedrin, laying there in his bed waiting for the headache to recede. He's had them periodically since his wife got cancer. He's planning his day, as he watches the early morning light spread across the queen size bed.

As the diffused light turns to sharp shaft, he is up and into his fatigue cargo pants, hiking boots, and dark sweatshirt. Down to the kitchen, having an instant coffee. Before going out to the barn, he grabs a plat book, Truman Lake map, and binoculars.

At the barn, he hitches his twenty-two foot aluminum boat to the old Ramcharger, and double-checks the outboard motor, making sure it's in the up position. He starts the Ram and heads out the drive towards Hermitage. Since moving to the ranch, he's been taking coffee in Hermitage with some of the locals . . . .

He's sitting with a few acquaintances at the café here, and the sun's barely cresting the Hickory County Courthouse. Catcher's attire and 'high and tight' haircut distinguish him from his disheveled coffee mates. Lester's turning his coffee cup between his thumbs and inside fingers, "My daughter brought a friend home from the university and took her down to Springfield. She's a little spit of a girl; doubt she's five foot. From back east. Haley something. Heard'em talking when they got back to the house. Haley 'what's-her-name' was going on about how there's so many pickups and four wheel drive vehicles in Springfield. About the big heavy tires on'em. Said there's lots of BMWs, Volvos, Mercedes and such in Cos Cob, Connecticut. Anywho, I was tellin' her it's practical. It's practical. Don't guess she knew much about rock roads and dirt lanes and Missouri mud. Told her, a lot of these people need the vehicles for hauling mowers, cattle and such. And, I guess they don't get flats in Cos Cob. Told her, those big tread tires are less likely to take a hole from a rock."

"Michelin's got the best tire for field work," offers Cutter. He's tilting his head over so his face is in the shadow of a post. The sun is shootin' straight in through the front windows now, and cigarette smoke is swirling in the café. "Michelin's got a tough sidewall tire, I forget what they call it."

Mary's come over with the coffee, "Who wants another shot?" She fills the uncovered cups; tells Lester there's nothing wrong with the paved roads and Volvos. Then, she's getting back behind the counter, huddling down with a couple of the gals.

"What you up to this morning, Catcher?" Lefty is wanting to know.

Catcher is running his palm over his brown bristled head, "Going to take a look at Truman up near Osceola."

"You goin' fishing?" Lester is surprised. To him, Catcher doesn't look patient enough to fish. And, there was the storm. Fish won't be . . .

"No. Not fishing. Got my maps and just going to do a little exploring."

"What size boat you got?" Bill Covington is curious.

"A little twenty-two footer aluminum job," Catcher says. Raising his brown eyes up to meet Covington's, without raising his head.

"You're goin' to get beat to hell," Covington says.

"More whitecaps on the weekends too." Cutter's got a seed hat on and still wearing a winter flannel shirt.

"If you put 'er in at Osceola, you could go up the Osage or Sac, and it won't be as rough," says Covington.

"There a ramp at Osceola?" Catcher figuring there is.

"Kind of north of the courthouse there, up Second Street I think," says Lester.

Catcher's getting up and laying a few dollars on the table. "I think I'll try the ramp in Osceola."

"Water's real shallow up there at Osceola. With a little twenty-two footer, won't make any difference," concludes Lester.

Mary's heard Catcher, "Catcher, you want an egg sandwich to go? I got an extra one right here."

Catcher's going by her, headed for the front door, reaching in his pocket, "How much?"

"Don't be silly. Take it, take it and go," as she hands it over.

Driving along in his old Ram and pulling the boat on the trailer, cutting through the country for Osceola. The countryside is deep shades of green from the rain and the sun is spreading over the pastures and woods from a very blue sky. Catcher takes a deep breath, rare these days, and makes a conscious effort to block out Invisible Loneliness. Watching some turkey vultures up ahead, and thinking about the hardy character of the cattlemen scattered across the Bible belt. Hardy characters, in durable work clothes, supporting a family on thin returns eked out between summer droughts and winter ice storms. This is real cowboy country, with more cows per acre than any state in the union. But, the cowboys in the west get the attention, Catcher is thinking.... Come tomorrow morning, the men and women and children will be slicked up in yesterday's styles and sitting in simple wooden churches constructed all over the land.... Getting close to Osceola, the St. Clair county seat. His headache is gone.

The café on the Osceola square is open, and Catcher turns the corner onto Second Street. The street is nearly empty, and he parks the Ram and trailer parallel to the curb. Stretching, walking back around the corner, and going into the café. At the register, he asks for a large coffee to go.

The generals' table is crowded. He thinks of it as the generals' table because it's the table where the town's 'pillars' have their coffee. He can tell by the demeanor of these patrons that they're respected regulars. He and his wife noticed years before, in their visits to the Ozarks, that the small town cafes seem to have a table frequented by compatible gatherings of local leaders. They got where they could identify this table by the demeanor of the men therewith. In the military, one might say they had a certain command presence.

Catcher came to call these tables the generals' tables. Since moving to the Ozarks, he had an increased respect for the men at these tables. These were the guys who sustained their original marriages, managed nuclear families, did community service work, held leadership positions in a church and operated small businesses integral to local economic activity. They conducted themselves in a conservative manner, demonstrated mutual respect, and projected an understated purposefulness. Their wives often maintained gardens, served in the church, worked in the house and sustained the family organization.

While Catcher is waiting for his coffee to go, he hears snatches of conversation from the Osceola generals' table.

"Taxes are figured by pinhead bean counters so you can't get ahead."

"They've got it figured right down to the closest margin," answers a middle-aged man in a khaki shirt and pants with white socks and lace-up shoes.

Guy in a cotton button-up shirt says, "It don't matter how hard you work, or how much added income you manage, Uncle Sam will get the gravy. You c'ain't get ahead."

Man in a suit and tie says, "You can get ahead, but you gotta make more than Mel Gibson to do it."

"There's no incentive."

"Nope. The unemployed get all the perks, and the employer gets the penalties. I'm tell'n you, it's going to collapse some day, and, when it does, Katy bar the door."

"The problem is, they ever cut the checks to the unemployed, they will revolt. There's generations of dependency there, and it'd be a life and death matter overnight, if they lost their check."

"I'll tell you how it is, the federal government is the profit splitting partner so long as the employer is making money. But, you're an employer, and get in trouble, your partner ain't there to help you out."

"And, the next step is to take your gun away, so when the riff-raff rebel, you're defenseless."

"You don't have no rights anyway."

The senior man in the suit is looking for the coffee pot, "We could change it, but every time we send a new man to Washington, he gets the political correctness. Face it, the politicos have as many or more votes from the nonproductive sector, including government employees, as they do from the capitalists and entrepreneurs. The only way to change it, within the system, is to disenfranchise anyone getting a government check. Social security is not a government check; it's your money."

Guy in the khaki shirt, "I was going to build a new warehouse, but think I'll put a new roof on my old building instead."

Cigarette smoke is in the air. But, the smoke is not from the generals' table. Not many smokers here . . . . Then, Catcher has his coffee to go.

Down at the ramp, Catcher winches his boat in, parks the Ram and trailer, and trots back to the boat in the water.

Steering out of the shallow cove into the headwaters of Truman Lake. He heads westerly, against the current, over the choppy waters, and quickly faces a choice. He's approaching the point where the Osage River and

Sac River run together. Catcher doesn't care which river he goes up. Ends up taking the Sac River because it's alongside these big bluffs. The sun is warming things now. . . . He's seeing heron and eagles. . . . Now and then, a fish plops on the water. Sipping cold Osceola coffee and just sitting back in the boat, letting the motor vibration and swishing waters lull him into complacency. The bluffs have tapered off, and he's entering a flat area where the shore is nearly level with the river. Acres and acres of wild, flat, soggy bottoms. Catcher sees from his map, much of this land is government land. Up ahead, he sees a good place to beach and takes the boat into shore.

Securing the boat, he grabs the maps and hikes away. Winds up going over a hill, wherefrom he can see the river ahead and much of the bottomlands beyond. He's sitting here on a rock, in the sun, when a flash of reflected sunlight from the opposite shore catches his attention. On closer observation, he spots what appears to be the aft ends of two large boats up in the water grasses on the far shoreline. At first, he doesn't see any persons. Then, he thinks he spots someone up in the weeds beyond the boats. Instinctively, Catcher rearranges his position so that he is lying on the ground behind the rock where he was sitting, and he gets his binoculars focused on the far shore above the boats. Sure enough, there's about two, . . . three, men hard at work unloading boxes of plants . . . . He sees a fourth guy, off to the side, carrying a rifle with a scope. This man with the rifle appears to be a guard. Catcher is getting very interested. He hears the shrill cry of a hawk, and hacking crows. Then, he's back on surveillance, watching the three men moving these boxes onto shore. They've got boxes of seedlings spread out on shore . . . . Carrying the potted seedlings into the heavy vegetation, where they are apparently planting them.

Catcher pulls back behind the rock, out of sight from the river, and pulls his maps out of his cargo pants pocket. Leaning back against the rock, he is trying to figure out where he is on the Sac River. Gets his location figured by best guesstimate, and studies the map for nearest roads. He's wondering how he might reach the other side by roadways. Surprised how far away roads are from the opposite shoreline location. He doesn't have a pen, so he uses his pocketknife to punch a small hole in his map where he thinks the men are located. Gets his knife and maps back into his pockets and rolls over and pulls up his binoculars again. The men are still at it. Definitely a suspicious activity. Must be planting marijuana starts. What in the hell is the guy with the rifle supposed to do? Shoot witnesses? What an asinine stunt. Carrying a rifle around like you're going to shoot someone. Like a body won't draw attention? Catcher stands up and trains the binoculars on the man with the rifle. He is smoking now, and holding the rifle in his left hand, down by his leg.

Catcher watches the guard through the binoculars. Seeing the man spot him watching. The guard yells something to the others, drops his cigarette, and is pulling his rifle up. Sure enough, the man is taking aim at him.

Catcher drops to the ground, continuing to scan the area where the planters were working. The planters can't be seen now. He can't make out what the guard is yelling. Then, the guard drops the rifle to his side and is running down the shoreline, back towards a point opposite Catcher's boat. Catcher wiggles backwards till he is off the crest of the hill, gets up and trots back to the boat. The guard is on the opposite shoreline, raising the rifle. Catcher pushes the boat into the water and jumps in, wet to the crotch. He cranks up the Mercury motor, gets the boat turned downstream, and gives it the throttle. For a few seconds, he is blinded by the sunlight refracted off the river. He doesn't hear any rifle fire or boats behind.

What a bunch of nitwits. Planting pot on a Saturday morning, in broad daylight, and carrying around a high-powered rifle like they were in Central America. A vision of sleazy barbarians swarming over the streets and parks of America bounces off Catcher's mind. This isn't what the Ozarks is about. So incredibly juvenile. Catcher can't remember any newspaper articles about anyone being shot or bodies being found in desolate places. His resolve is not to make a report of the incident till he checks the area on the landward side. Soon!

Colonel Catcher Riley. From superpower national security, to nosin' around hillbilly pot fields. A pawn pilgrim in Outer Mongolia. Fact? What is the fact? These pot planting tumwads are not the Ozarks. They are free radicals in paradise . . . . Approaching Osceola now. As he's coming in, he's thinking about the old hotel here on the square. Where Jesse James and Cole Younger boozed and partied, one eye open for the law.

The idea of a dangerous criminal element operating in the present-day Ozarks is a newly minted coin for his mental purse. While he's getting his boat winched up on the trailer, the reality of local criminals starts to sink in . . . into his illusionary concept of the Ozarks. Catcher had always imagined the area as being in a primitive pre-pubescent state of innocence. But then again, he's never heard of the OMP.

CHAPTER VIII

The OMP. Jinx and Jake went to bed after dawn this Saturday. As we know, Catcher Riley took his boat up the Sac River. Erik Starr is up to something else. He's unusually 'vocational' this day. He's up early and directing the gang at the October Mount Pontiac . . . the OMP. Whispered around by some locals as the Ozark Mafia Posse.

Erik's still got the heebie jeebies. Yesterday, he had to straighten Bugs out. Then, on his way to relax at R4, he's assaulted by The Hand. The giant, fiery-eyed Indian soothsayer WHO WARNS HIM ABOUT A JINX. Then, he gets in the club and is mesmerized by a siren beauty like he's never seen before. HER NAME TURNS OUT TO BE JINX. No matter. He's going to have her and that's that, heebie jeebies or no heebie jeebies. If Jinx is a jinx, then he's Jack the fuckin' Ripper . . . . And, he's got his business to get underway. He's uptight about this. Hell bent on putting the 'pedal to the metal.' Keeping the goal in focus, right there on the forward cuspice of his frontal lobe—one million dollars net cash . . . his end. Gotta get those seedlings planted . . . all of 'em!

On the surface, the October Mount Pontiac is a sixteen hundred acre cattle ranch. What Erik and Ejay Starr really do is more like farming.

The ranch sprawls along a county gravel road in the middle of deep forests between Osceola and Warsaw, to the south of Truman Lake. The private lane comes out to the county road and overhead hangs the sign—OCTOBER MOUNT PONTIAC. ABSOLUTELY NO TRESPASSING signs are nailed on both sides of the entrance. There is a gate at the county road, but it is often open and a heavy-duty cattle guard serves to keep the stock inside. From here, the lane goes back a ways then drops out of sight over a hill. It continues down the hill, across a shallow stream, winds back up a hill between cedars to a wooded plateau. Usually, bunches of cattle are along the way, on the road, beside the road, back in the timbers or grazing in the meadows.

The big old house and dilapidated barn are back in a clearing on top of this plateau in the center of the ranch. The ranch is approximately half-timber and half-grass and rocky, like most ranches down here. There are numerous ponds and the aforementioned stream runs through the ranch from one end to the other. Hardly anyone visits the place, much less stay long enough to get the rhythm. Excepting Ejay, who is Erik's brother and partner.

The house is perched on a foundation of rock, many loose or falling out. To say the foundation needed tuck-pointing is an understatement. An old TV antenna sticks up from the roof at an odd angle and the shingles are multicolored. In places, shingles appear to be missing, and if you look around, you can see shingles out in the hog wire fence around the yard. There is a decorative aluminum ridge cap and lightning rods along the peak of the roof. The white paint is peeling off raw wood siding, and there are holes in the porch big enough to step through. The porch boards are worn and a lot of dog hair is stuck in the splinters. The mongrel dogs are big and moody and run loose. The yard is mostly worn to dirt from the dogs and guineas. Usually, there are two flat-bottomed boats with big Mercury outboards parked on trailers in the yard. But, not this Saturday morning; they are on the Sac River.

Inside is like an ill kept bunkhouse or barracks. Plaster walls with high ceilings and the laths showing through where the plaster has fallen off. Jack Daniels on the table, trash cans overfilled with beer cans; cigarette butts and empty packs and ashtrays brimming over. There is a big set of horns mounted over a smoke stained rock fireplace and stray bolts of wood and bark near the hearth. Pine floors wore to natural in the middle and unevenly stained where the edges butted up against baseboards. Lots of guns all over. Rifles and shotguns in the corners and one double barrel shotgun laying on a smoke-tar filmed TV set. Automatic and revolver pistols on the coffee and end tables. A Smith & Wesson .44 Magnum on the slick-top table in the kitchen; right where Erik left it after his Russian roulette with Bugs. Aerial maps of Truman Lake taped to the walls with duct tape. A dirty CD player is pouring out country tunes and CD's and empty cartridge boxes lay on the speakers. Bows, arrows and hunting knives and machetes. Camo shirts hang on the backs of chairs and cereal boxes are out. There is a saddle on a blanket slung over a sawhorse and a few bridles and odds and ends tools too. Flashlights and batteries mixed in with stacks of little plastic Ziploc

Baggies. A couple of cats are sifting through and an aluminum valve cover is lying beside the couch.

The disharmony continues down at the barn. There's an old snakeskin between some rocks around the dug well. There are horses and a water tank in a busted, faded corral and a few pieces of tin off the barn roof on the ground. You can see the rafters up where the sheets of tin have blown off.

The guys that live here are a hard bunch, living in a huge two-story house hidden from the road. One could get the creeps driving in here, and most God-fearing people didn't come here.

The two brothers own the OMP. Erik and Ejay. Ejay lives in Pontiac, Michigan and he's the distributor. Erik lives right here in the house, and he's the producer. Erik has a shifting number of 'hands', and they live in the house also. The number of hands varies from time to time. They are all from the Pontiac area, and their number on the OMP at any one time runs from five to ten. All of them with bad attitudes. Ejay comes down from Pontiac rarely, but when he does, he stays in the house too. He's a very serious guy . . . the older brother. Anyway, on average, there are about seven men around the place and that many 4x4 pickups or more. No cars, just pickups. Erik and Ejay both drive new, extended cab, three-quarter ton, V8 Fords. Erik a black one and Ejay a red one. Some of the older pickups are the brothers too, and some belong to the gang members. All of them are muddy, dusty or both, and bug splattered across the grills and windshields. All except Ejay's. When he's down, the clean, red Ford pickup with the Michigan plate is the lily among the thorns. Same cannot be said for Ejay. He's dangerously sharp, as a thorn.

Erik and Ejay came to the Ozarks from Pontiac, Michigan—in a big way. They bought the sixteen hundred acre ranch with cash. They wanted the cave. They moved down in October, a few years back. There were a lot of rumors and they have persisted. It's kind of like someone lays a 'handle' on you, others pick it up, and pretty soon it's common lingo. The rumor was that they were drug dealers in Michigan before coming down here. It is common knowledge that they bought the ranch and their herd with cash and hung a sign over the lane going in—OCTOBER MOUNT PONTIAC.

In the late 90's, Erik and Ejay made the decision to double their income by producing their own product. Expanding their marijuana business to include production and distribution. They had these criteria by which to select a piece of land suitable for a 'Starr brothers' cultivation project. The numerous criteria, by which they selected their land, was important to the success of their business; the sale, and now production, of marijuana.

Ejay first, and then Erik, had entered into 'dealing' in Pontiac, Michigan, after being driven from their parents' small farm outside the city. 'Driven' is the right word. After sixteen years, in a home dominated by a sadistic, autocratic father, each son was 'driven' off the home place. It went like this . . . . For sixteen years, the father provided minimum subsistence to his sons. The father prevented the mother from any display of affection towards the boys. Instead, she was the appointed choremaster. And, the boys had plenty of chores. Then, when Ejay woke-up on his sixteenth birthday, the father told him to come down to the barn. When Ejay got to the barn, his father was waiting for him with a baseball bat. The father told him to get off the place and never come back. When Ejay hesitated, unsure of exactly what this meant, the father hit him with the bat. As Ejay got up off the dirt floor, dear ole dad delivered him another blow, "Get out now. Run for the road, and don't ever come back. My job's over." Ejay ran for the county road, with no more belongings than he wore to the barn. It worked a little different for Erik. The night before his sixteenth birthday, he ran away from home, into Pontiac, where he linked up with Ejay. Over time, the two brothers were buying larger and larger quantities of pot, which they resold to dealers throughout Michigan.

They got older and wiser. Then, as their business grew, the supplier started increasing prices. Ejay ended up killing the contact man after the third price increase . . . . Outside a bar in Pontiac. Ejay had suggested to the contact man they talk prices in the alley. Out in the alley, Ejay pulled a handgun on this 'arrogant pissant,' and ordered him to his knees. He shot him through the top of his head . . . . Erik, the younger brother, surmised: you got a problem—shoot it.

After this incident, the boys got a new supplier, and this supplier kept the price constant. Then, demand started outrunning supply. That's when they began thinking about growing their own. They spent nights drinking beer in the bars up and down Blue Street, figuring how to do this. They agreed they needed a secret cave to grow seeds into seedlings. They needed generators in the cave to power the grow lights. Metered electricity wouldn't do, since the excessive use of electricity might raise suspicions.

Missouri has a lot of caves. And, Missouri has a lot of springs, streams, rivers and lakes, and water is important for irrigation of the plants in summer. And, Missouri has the right climate. The brothers' perception was that law enforcement was lax in the backcountry of Missouri. While looking at this sixteen hundred acre tract, which they eventually bought, the real estate agent spouted off about a hidden cave being on the property. Without the agent, the brothers camped on the vacated ranch and searched acre by acre for the reputed cave. They found it. Down in a cedar lined ravine. In the side of a short bluff. The opening was the size of a doorway laid sideways. Inside, the cave opened-up into a turkey barn size chamber. The brothers bought the ranch, and Erik assumed command of production, while Ejay remained in charge of distribution in Pontiac. Together, the brothers recruited different street dealers in Pontiac as hands in Missouri. The hands changed somewhat, as the dynamic processes of dealing pot in Pontiac made, or unmade, personnel available.

Sure enough, the OMP was Erik's kingdom. And, he was all business, when he was at his business. And, one better not get in his way or fuck with his operation, because Erik was going to 'do or die.' And, he wasn't afraid to die.

Erik is on the OMP this fine Saturday morning, and planting is starting, and he's got the heebie jeebies. In everything he's doing, he's dragging around this sexual charge administered sans Jinx the jinx. And he's got business to tend. His planting method is innovative and requires accurate reporting as to location of plots.

Innovative. That is to say, Erik does not plant the seedlings on the OMP. He feels secure enough, getting the seeds into seedlings under grow lights in the cave. But, there's no way he's going to get busted with the crop on the OMP. So, it's spring, and now he's moving the seedlings out of the cave to dispersed plots all around the county. Because of water requirements in summer and because of low detection probabilities, Erik is using boats to haul seedlings up the Sac and Osage rivers and around the coves of Truman Lake. This morning, his orders are the same as last year. Put the boats in Truman Lake at one of the dirt ramps up and down the brushy shore of Truman, and motor from here to different plot sites on the lake and up the rivers. (Thank the local yokels for their rough fashioned ramps back through the brush into the lake.) His orders this Saturday morning are the same as last year in another respect. Each boat is to include a sniper. And, if the planters are discovered, while planting the seedlings, the sniper is to put the witness down and hide the body where it won't be found. One more thing—the crews better have their plots marked accurately on the maps. During cultivation, and come harvest, the gang has to be able to find each plant in each plot. Once the harvested plant is back on the OMP, in fall, the stripping and packaging into Ziplocs begins. Ejay's got the ball from there!

Evening. Erik is sitting on the front porch with his legs hanging over the edge. Waiting. Waiting for the boats and crews to come in. Gunner's coming up from the cave, and sitting down on the other end of the porch, "They still aren't back?"

Erik keeps looking down the lane, "Nope. Not yet."

"Maybe they ran into trouble."

"It takes a long time to plant five hundred seedlings."

Some crows are hacking around in the trees and the guineas start up too. The sun's deep in the west, and one of the dogs lifts its leg to pee on a fescue tuft at the edge of what's left of the yard. Gunner leans back against the front of the house. "If I was back working for municipal, I wouldn't have a worry in the world."

Erik glances over at Gunner with disgust, "You'd be a parasite piece of government shit too . . . living off the money stole from working folks . . . . One year in Pontiac, I was a painter. The second half of the year, I worked a bunch of hours overtime. At the end of the year, I netted less than if I'd skipped the overtime. The increased wages moved me into a higher tax bracket. If you were working for the government, Gunner-man, I wouldn't piss on you if you were on fire . . . Jar Head."

Gunner keeps looking out ahead. He knows better than to argue. Then, he hears tires crunching on the rock lane. "I think they're coming in, Erik. I hear 'em."

"I hear 'em."

The pickups, with boats in tow, come into sight, and the guineas are cackling, and the dogs are running down the lane to meet the trucks. It's almost sunset.

Erik's going out to the first truck, talking to the driver.

"You got 'em all planted?"

"Yes."

"Any problems? How many separate patches? You mark 'em on the aerial?"

"Five patches, all up the Sac. I've got 'em marked on the map . . ."

Erik interrupts, "Park the trucks, and turn the fuckin' engines off."

The men are unloading out of the truck cabs, and heading for the house, a couple with high-powered rifles. But, Mark and the drivers don't go anywhere. They're waiting for Erik.

Erik says, "Let me see your maps."

The drivers give him their folded up maps, kind of soiled and wet. The driver of truck one says, "Erik, there was a little problem this morning."

Erik's head jerks up, and he's locked the truck one driver in an icy stare.

The driver continues, "We were planting on this site, here, this morning," and he points down to an X mark on the aerial map. "Some guy was watching us from the brush across the river. With binoculars. When Mark pulled his rifle up, the guy took off. . . . He had a boat. We heard him start it up and take off."

Emotionless, Erik looks behind the drivers, to Mark, "Why didn't you kill him?"

"I didn't see the guy at first. And, when I did, the guy took off fast. The guy didn't look like government, he was dressed more like a hunter."

"Fuck what he looked like. That doesn't mean a fuckin' thing. You didn't leave any seedlings at that location?"

"Nope. We put them back in the boats, and went on up the river to here," and the truck one driver points out a circle on the aerial map in Erik's hand.

Erik looks back at driver one, then to driver two. Then, back to Mark, "You aren't afraid to kill someone are you?"

Mark, shifting from one foot to another, "No. No way . . . . And, something else Erik. I got the registration number off his boat. I wrote it down," handing a scrap of paper to Erik. "I could read it clearly through the scope on my rifle."

Erik again, "You understand the policy, right? Some fucking lone wolf sees what we're doing, once the plants are in the ground, you kill him. Cut his hands and head off. Put them in a hole somewhere. Toss the body in some deep ravine out of the area. You'd never get a grave dug in these rocks . . . . If you can't hide a body in the Ozarks, you should work for the government." Looking at the number on the scrap of paper.

"Yes. Yes, Sir." Mark shifting his weight back to the other foot, jiggling the rifle held at his side.

Erik looking at the drivers and Mark. The sound of water draining from the boats onto the ground.

"Mark, you afraid to kill a witness?" Erik turns to one side, unbuttons his fly and starts to pee.

Mark, trying not to let Erik hear the fear, "I just didn't have a shot. And, the guy was across the river. Really, it was just simpler to pull the plants and go to the next location."

Erik is holding the maps in one hand and buttoning his 501's with the other. "You plant and unplant those fuckers, we'll lose some. They go into shock."

Driver two, "We were real careful, Erik. Mark hid up in a tree at our next location."

Erik stands here, tapping the maps in one hand against the palm of the other. It's getting dark, and they can see the lights in the house. Down on the pond, frogs are beginning to croak. One of the dogs is whining. The sun has dropped behind the timbered western horizon. It's the gloaming time of day.

Then, Boomer's out on the porch of the house. He's got an open can of tuna in one hand, and the cordless in the other, "You got a call, Erik. It's a Wo-o-o-o-man."

CHAPTER IX

Erik grabs the cordless out of Boomer's hand, and Boomer scats back in the house. Erik turns around to face outward, down the lane, "This is Erik." The drivers hasten past and into the house.
"This is Jinx."
"I've thought about you all last night and today."
"Did you think I wouldn't call?"
"I was thinking you would call!"
Pause. Jinx is putting her pre-paid phone card back in her purse. Not to be captured by Caller-ID. She lays back on Jake's bed, figuring Erik may hear the music coming from the other side of the door.
"I'm at R4."
"Maybe I'll come over?"
Jinx is kind-of thinking out loud, "Maybe we could meet somewhere in between."
"Any place you say, I'll go."
"You know where Crisco Crossing is?"
"North of Mack's Creek?"
"On the Little Niangua."
"Yes."
"I'll meet you there," Jinx can't find a doober.
"What time?"
"Say, nine-thirty."
"I'll bring a cooler."
"What I need is smoke." Pause.
Erik, "We're talking unfiltered?"
"Yes."
"I'll bring plenty."

"Nine-thirty then?"

"My serenade touched your heart?"

Jinx is getting off Jake's bed, "Let's say . . . curiosity killed the cat."

Erik, "But satisfaction brought her back."

"We'll see about that. I'll be on the east side of the river in an '87 Vette."

"I'll be driving a black Ford pickup."

"See you there, Erik."

Shortly, Erik is fussing around, getting ready for his Little Niangua appointment. He's showered, shaved, back into fresh 501s and a t-shirt.

He's wearing his better pair of boots. Pausing in the living room. It's dark now, and his guys are sitting around in here, watching TV, reading, drinking beer and smoking. None of them are saying much, not with Erik standing there looking them over. He says, "I'm going out. It's pleasure. I'll be back before dawn. You guys need to be getting up by then. We plant in the daytime, we'll harvest in the dark." Erik is looking around at the snipers. "You guards know your job. Someone sees the crews planting, they get shot. Then, you hide the head and hands the way I told you . . . the body too. This isn't hypothetical here. It's the real thing. I find out some witness got away from a field we put out, I'll show you how to shoot someone. We aren't fucking around. We're talking millions at stake here." Leaving his eyes on Mark. "I was easy today. Next time a witness doesn't die, you die."

Erik goes over to the fridge and pulls a beer out, and a baggy with several ounces of last year's production. The OMP call it 'Ozark Gold.'

Then, he's out the door. He knows the gang will 'cowboy up.' The money forthcoming after harvest holds them to the OMP. Like a set of leg irons. And, to the man, they fear him. With good cause. Gunning the pickup away from the 'ranch.'

He stops at a convenience store at a lonely blacktop intersection. Stocks the cooler with beer and ice. Before he gets back in the cab, shakes a quilt blanket out from behind the seat. Folds the blanket, throws it on the passenger side, pulls the tab on another beer, and heads out for Crisco Crossing. The radio's on, but the volume is down, and he's not listening to the country bards tonight. Trying to picture Jinx's body. Kind of got a vision of her hipbones and knees. He thinks about jamming . . . jerking the steering wheel, when a vixen darts onto the road. Corrects his steering and hits the vixen. Keeps on going. Back in the black, behind the big three-quarter ton truck, the young fox raises half-up off the blacktop toward the stars; some primitive cognition of it's own end. Then, falls back dead on the road.

Erik gets off the blacktop, onto gravel, and motors between the overhanging trees towards the river. Clots of dust behind, like lambent cotton fuzz under the newly rising moon. Coming up on Crisco Crossing. Sees the dry slab up ahead, and hears the current. The moon's starting to illuminate the open areas—the meadows off to the left, the taller timbers to the right, and the white slab crossing the river ahead and the surrounding gravel bars.

No '87 Vette. Erik creeps across the river looking down at the swirling waters running through the culverts under the slab. Gets turned around and motors back to the east side from whence he came. The gravel bars are showing bone white now, and he sees a fallen sycamore in the river downstream. Parks, gets a beer out of the cooler, resets the radio and waits. The truck engine is off, the music is low, and he can hear the river waters. Quiet enough to hear a vehicle on the gravel road. Looking at his watch. It's nine forty-five.... Now, he hears a car coming, and sees the distant headlights.

Jinx pulls up beside Erik, her radio playing, and shuts the Vette off. The top is down. The moonlight giving a dull gleam to the Vette and a brightness to her blonde head. She turns the radio off. They can hear the waters rushing down at the slab. And, there's the other sounds too. A creaking tree limb, some sparse frogs and insects.... The stars are stretched out overhead from the timber ridge to the far meadow's edge.

He reaches in his truck and turns his radio off. Takes a swig of beer and comes towards Jinx. Now, right off, Jinx is in the steel grip of forces unknown even to herself. She's down, he's up.

Like when she was in bed, as a kid. Like when daddy came through the doorway. Looming above her.

Erik leans on her car, and gets close enough to her face for her to really see him. "I'm super glad you called.... You want a beer?"

Jinx, just sitting in the driver's seat, head turned to study this stallion. There's a forcefulness there she's been trained to respect.

"No, not a beer. I'd like a smoke."

Erik's straightening-up, "I've got that too. You mean weed right?"

"Yes."

Erik gets a joint out of his pickup. Jinx is out of the Vette and just standing here beside her car.

Erik comes up and gives her the joint. She's leaning back against the Vette as he lights it with a Zippo. Clicks the Zippo shut, and puts it back in his pocket, "Perfect night, huh?"

"Yes," and Jinx is tilting her head back, looking up at the stars. She's got her Wranglers and boots on, and her nipples are pointing out the tank top.

Erik leaning back against the Vette beside her, taking another swig off his beer. "Jinx. That's a name to remember . . . . You've got the looks to go with it."

"Erik Starr isn't exactly a plebian handle."

"What kind of handle?"

"Plebian. It means common, your name isn't common."

"At least I have a last name. What's yours?"

"What difference does it make?"

Erik's excitement level jumps. "Guess that's right. We're not reporting to the government out here."

"What are we doing out here?" She's taking another toke, and turns her head towards Erik at a cute tilt, up towards his face. Some hair is spilling over her forehead. Erik can make out her blue eyes, very much as his own.

"We're getting to know each other."

"How well do you want to know me?"

"From inside out," pushing off the Vette, turning his body to face her. "You don't mess around do you?"

"Depends what you mean by mess around."

"I like it," Erik is grinning. "I haven't stopped thinking about you since last night."

Jinx is on another toke. Erik straightening up, "Why don't I get the cooler and a blanket. We'll go down by the river."

Jinx, noticeably seductive, "That suits me. Have you got some more weed?"

"All you want, princess."

Jinx drifts a little.

Princess, her daddy's little princess.

She heads down towards the slab, while Erik gathers up the cooler, weed and blanket.

When he gets down to the slab, Erik starts past Jinx as to cross the slab. "Hold up, big boy," she purrs.

Erik turns around, holding the cooler up. "What's so special about this side of the river?"

"It's the east side."

"Yeah. So what?" Erik is puzzled.

"Put the blanket over here," Jinx motioning out towards a sand bar. "We'll walk over the slab in a minute, Erik."

Erik gets the cooler down, thinking about sand fleas when Jinx softly touches his arm. He comes up in front of her. Out on the sandbar, in the moonlight, he leans over and kisses her. Can tell she's a little high, and starts to push his tongue in . . . . No go!

"Let's walk over the slab now," Jinx saying in a slow, silky tone.

They are walking across the slab holding hands, him with a beer in his outside hand and her with a joint in hers.

"There's a huge spring over here. There, in the bank, over there." She's pointing with her joint to the bank up ahead, at the end of the slab.

Erik sees and hears the water running into the river at the corner of the slab. Sees it pouring into the river like a fire engine hose stream.

"Shit. That is a spring."

Jinx lets go of his hand, kneels down and splashes water over her face, and Erik can see by the moonlight the veins of water running over her features.

He kneels down beside her, "Pretty neat."

"It's pure," she says. Cups her hand and takes a sip.

Erik stands up. "C'mon, we'll go back to the blanket."

"To the east side," she says. "Wonder what we'll do there."

"C'mon. I'll show you."

They're back by the blanket, kissing and Erik pushes her tank top up and gets on his knees so as to kiss her breasts. The joint is gone, and Jinx has her hands on his shoulders and his are on her waist.

Now, headlights and crunching gravel coming down the country road towards them. Jinx standing her ground, watching the upcoming vehicle, waiting for Erik to make a move. Erik keeps on kissing her breasts, and running his hands up and down the outsides of her thighs.

The old Ramcharger stops before going across the slab. Catcher Riley leaning across, yelling through the open passenger window, "Everything OK there?"

Erik pulling off Jinx's breasts, "None of your fucking business if you're lucky."

Jinx, glancing at the Ramcharger, yelling, "It's OK mister." She is standing here, with the hint of a smile, watching the old Ramcharger disappear as Erik unzips her Wranglers.

He's pushing her legs apart and licking the opening of her vagina. She's starting to squeeze his shoulders harder and her eyes are shut.

"Lay down over here on the blanket," he says.

She sits down on the blanket, "You lay back here Erik, and let me undress you."

"No way, honey. Just lay back and I'll do the driving," Erik is pushing her slightly backwards.

"Don't push me, big man," Jinx says in a voice not so silky. She's leaning back on one hand, and is motioning to stop with the other.

Without hesitating, Erik grabs this hand and pulls the other out behind her. She goes down on the blanket, face up, with him straddled over her.

"What are you going to do now, princess?"

"Whatever you make me," she says. "But, without my consent, I'll blow your brains out later."

"With no gun," Erik says, looking down at her face.

"Don't fuck with me, Erik. Ever," in a really serious tone. Doesn't seem like a stoner now.

"We going to take our pants off or not?"

"You asking or telling, Erik?"

Long pause. Erik is leaning over her, holding her wrists to the blanket, his unruly red hair glinting in the moonlight. She's lying limp as the dewy blanket.

"I'm asking."

"Saved your life," she says.

He lets go of her wrists and straightens up, sitting back on his calves, either side of her slender body. He can't see her eyes, but her hair is shining and the aquiline bridge of her nose, her cheekbones and chin are lit by the moon.

"I do the driving, or I don't take the ride," he says.

"You think so," she counters. "You have anymore weed?"

"I'll get you another joint," and Erik gets up and goes back towards the truck. Jinx sits up, pulls her boots off, wiggles out of her jeans and tank top, and lies back on the blanket, looking up at the stars and moon.

God? Could you love me a little?

Erik coming back down the sandbar, with a joint and lighter in one hand and a beer in the other. The river and animal night sounds. Seeing her laid out on the blanket. The perfect body. Five and one-half feet of gleaming white skin, with height-weight proportionate. Slender, well defined toes and fingers, with coltish ankles and wrists. He's thinking you can have anything you want with Ozark Gold.

He sets the joint, lighter and beer down on the blanket, and strips off his boots and clothes. Jinx has her eyes closed.

"Sit up baby, if you want a toke."

She sits up and he lights the joint and gives it to her. He's swigging beer and she's coughing after the first hit. Erik's used to this and waits. When she's done coughing, she hits it again. And, again.

When Erik finishes the beer, he takes the joint out of Jinx's hand and lays it over on the sand. Helping her back down to the blanket. She's clawing around over her head, pulling a condom out of her Wranglers. She gets it into his hand.

Kissing her neck and breasts and has his finger in her. Pushing her legs apart so he can get in.

"Can you get pregnant?" he asks.

"I'm coming out of my period, but I don't want an STD. Use a condom."

"No fucking way. I don't use condoms ever. It's unnatural, baby."

The Ozark Gold hits her like a Mack truck.

When he gets all the way in, she brings her knees up higher. He's got his fists in the blanket, pressed into the sand, either side of Jinx's shoulders, and he's watching her face. He never closes his eyes, and he gives Jinx a pumping like she can't remember last. She's stoned, and at first, isn't really thinking much about it. Then, it's like something dreadful coming-on. Getting pleasurable. He's getting more demanding and pumping harder and breathing like a stud stallion. He doesn't let up, and the pleasure syrup starts to run, and Jinx is into the sex. Oblivious to all else, past, present or future, she follows Erik to an atomic explosion. Atomic. A conversion of some mass into energy.

He's still in her. Giving her another toke. She wants him out, starting to get sick; but, he gives her another toke. And, another one. And, another one. Riding her again, whipping her to places she hates and loves to go.

Finally, it's over.

The moon has moved across the sky to the west. Jinx is laying on her back, and Erik on his back beside her.

"I gotta work in the morning.... Later this morning. I gotta go."

Jinx isn't talking.

"We gotta go," he says, getting up and starting to dress.

Eventually, she dresses too. First her tank top. Then, she's on her feet, pulling on her Wranglers. Falling back on her buttocks, pulling on her boots.

After he gets the blanket shook out, he picks up the cooler and carries this, with the blanket, off the sandbar. Jinx folds her arms across her breasts. Her clothes are damp from the river and dew. Walking along, a little behind.

Erik puts the cooler in the bed and the blanket in the cab of his pickup. Hears Jinx slam the door of her Vette. Reaches into the cab and pulls out the Ziploc baggy with the Ozark Gold. Back to Jinx's driver's side, he leans over to kiss her.

She pulls up a .38 special and cocks it, pointing it in his face.

"Does this mean you don't love me? What about the peaceful easy feeling?" Erik grinning, then holding the baggie up for her to see.

Her hair is ruffles and her face stern, looking slightly cockeyed from the pot. "This means I'm in control, Erik. Not you."

"OK . . . . Do you want the pot or not?"

Silence. He's dangling the pot in front of her, and she's steady holding the end of the barrel on his face.

She says, "Who is in control here." Struggling to maintain focus.

"You are," Erik still grinning.

"Good answer, Erik. I get an STD, you'll never know what killed you," un-cocking the revolver and bringing it back in the Vette. She reaches up and takes the bag of bliss. Lays it on the passenger seat and starts the Vette.

Erik standing up. Looking more serious now, "I want to see you again."

Jinx turning her head up to face him, both hands on the steering wheel, "You will, Erik. I'll call."

Backing the Vette up, pulling forward and crossing the slab to the west side of the river. Jinx is gone. Headed back towards her Ozark shanty castle. The loneliest and safest place in this world, as goes her soul.

Erik looking around. Getting in his truck. The bitch queen, and I own her, he's thinking, sitting here in his truck. Starting the engine. Pulling away from Crisco Crossing, back the way he came in. East. He's got crops to get out. Lots of Ozark Gold. It will get him anything and everything he wants. The crops. Ozark Gold. The money. His one and only necessity in this life. Is there any other?

CHAPTER X

Sunday morning. Sunny. Hawks. Lots of hawks. Woodpecker hitting an old hollow tree somewhere. Waters' Bible Church; on a gravel road in a grove of oaks; in a lapboard, one room church painted white; east of Cross Timbers. An ensemble who celebrate silver and gold anniversaries, clear brush from the fields, hay the cattle, care for disabled family members, tender money to relatives on hard times, live frugally, manage estates of the deceased, organize the weddings and funerals, raise the grandchildren in cases of dysfunctional children, solve their personal problems personally, get each other to the doctor, make hospital visits, attend school functions, hold local political offices, and, occasionally, go off to war. Local property owners concerned more with personal and community commitments than material or social success; given to the proposition that it shouldn't be offensive to anyone to read the Bible (the all time bestseller with over two billion copies sold or given away, and translated into over one thousand, two hundred fifty languages).

The program here is simple. A ninety-minute service, which consists entirely of a Bible reading taken-up where the last one left off the Sunday before. About eighty hours of reading gets the group through the entire Bible (fifty-two services a year). About twenty pages per week, read by volunteers. Through the narrative, then the poetry, then the prophecy.

In general, one might conclude that this congregation, and others like it in churches all through the area, represent many citizens which are the brick and mortar of law and order in the Ozarks. The police and sheriff's department perform a needed function, but on a daily basis, it's primarily the women and Christian ethic that keep folks 'in line.' The law is often distant. Red tape, haphazard ridge road grids, low population density and the absence of surveillance cameras give the population ample opportunity for clandestine activity. But, the influence of the kinder gender and the Christian ethic are positive behavior determinates. The economic necessity of gainful activity also helps occupy the citizenry's time. Brick and mortar of Ozark society; that's what most of these people are.

The only way you can tell the front from the rear of this primitive meeting place—A) An inscription is beautifully painted on the front plaster wall, GOD IS LOVE; B) there is a table and chair in front for the volunteer reader; C) the doorway is in the rear, D) the nine rows of pews face forward, E) the wood stove is in the front, and F) the coffee and tea is on a table in front. If someone needs the toilet, there are HIS and HER outhouses at the edge of the yard. Maintenance of the place is accomplished by volunteers.

This particular Sunday, Catcher can hardly wait to get out. He's studied his maps and has a route figured which should get him close to the spot on the Sac River where he'd been targeted.

Catcher sits on the back pew.

"Then went Samson to Gaza and saw there an harlot, and went in unto her. And it was told the Gazites saying, Samson is come hither, and they compassed him in, and laid wait for him all night in the gate of the city, and were quiet all the night, saying, in the morning, when it is day, we shall kill him . . . ."

Catcher can hear the hawk's shrill cry through the open windows and the occasional crunch of gravel as a vehicle passes. Then, he can smell the gravel dust. He's thinking about the maps in his Ramcharger. He's warm. Looks out the window a lot. Then, at the back of Hattie Gates' head . . . . Momentarily has a mental snapshot of the shadowy couple making-out down by the river . . . at Crisco Crossing.

Daydreaming. Thinking about an artwork he'd seen displayed by a vendor in Paris. It was poster size. The thirteenth century artist had applied reverse painting on Venetian crystal with hard enamels. It was hand painted, and the brush strokes accented by gold leaf, giving the piece an iridescent, metallic appearance. From a distance, the shiny gold on black looked to be the richer cousin of a painting on black velvet. In this picture, a church was represented in the upper left-hand corner, with the front doors open. A narrow line of people lined up to get in the church, and then broadened out to a crowd, which stretched across the bottom of the representation. The painting was a pictograph of how Catcher conceptualized mankind's different approaches to eternal life. In the painting, the people were represented in quick, undefined strokes, giving the impression they were different races, gender, occupations and persuasions . . . all working their way to His mansion. And, the doors were open, and people were getting in, and others were waiting to get in and would eventually.

He's thinking how these people came to his house after he moved to the Ozarks. Offered to help Catcher get settled, anyway they could. And, invited him to this barebones Sunday meeting. Since then, Catcher has attended most of the meetings, and helped with the maintenance of the property. He isn't a total lone wolf, and believes that the Bible, more or less, offers a contingency plan that works . . . not that some other plans don't work as well. But, there has to be a plan.

In his Ram, pulling away from Waters Bible Church, studying the open map in the passenger seat. Coming up over a hill, Catcher slams on his brakes to avoid hitting a tractor with brush hog stopped along the side.

Heading southwest out of Osceola on 82 highway. Shortly, he parks on a wide shoulder, grabs his maps and compass, exits the vehicle and crosses the pavement. Takes a compass reading, sights out ahead, then strides down the embankment into the bush. Into the bottoms, he's thinking the boots were a good idea. A bit informal for the Waters Bible Church meeting, but a good idea for chasing after the Sac River.

By his best calculation, Catcher has about a mile, maybe a little more, to reach the spot on the river where he'd seen the two boats the day before. It is rough going. The brush is thick, his footing unsure. In places, the ground is wet and soggy. In other places, so much underbrush that a measured step is impossible. It's getting hotter; the afternoon sun is turning into a sulfuric furnace.

Catcher keeps thinking about snakes. He figures there's only three poisonous snakes to watch for. There's only three in Missouri—Copperheads, Rattlers and Cottonmouths. While he's picking his way through a wild blackberry patch, he's thinking a copperhead would be his choice of bites . . . . Thought he was all done with this sort of thing when he left Central America.

He's in tall enough brush that he can't be seen from the highway, and he can't see out to get a compass bearing. What he's doing now is keeping his eye on the compass almost continually. He's got a certain sense about the direction of sunlight down here. Stays on a bearing that keeps the shadows and the location of the sun consistent, but this is largely a subconscious reckoning.

It takes him an hour to reach the river. The insects are virulent, and he's picked-up some of the first ticks of the season. But, he's found some high ground where he can study the opposing bank. After some jockeying around, another half-hour, he's in a location where he thinks he can see across the river to the rock he was at yesterday. Looking around now for anything unnatural. He finds a series of holes ringed round by footprints. Goes over this area closely. Moves to where the guard was standing and finds a filter from a cigarette. Can't make out the brand. He's figuring the crew must have removed the marijuana seedlings after spotting him.

Nothing. He's got nothing. And, he's hot and sticky. Thinking he should have brought some water, when he spots a scrap of paper lying on the ground. Picks it up. It reads R4, and a phone number. Catcher's never heard of R4. He folds the paper, with mud and all, and puts it in his wallet. Eighty-five minutes later, he's back on the highway about two hundred yards west of the Ram. Not bad for an old Ranger.

On the way home, he gets off the main road into a ratty community of old cabins on the river. The sagging, bullet-hole riddled sign reads ALGIERS.... 'Downtown' has one trashy café, a dozen or so old rusty car shells in the weeds behind. Catcher parks and goes in.

This place is a low down, home-style restaurant. Like, you have this woman with oily hair sitting back in a booth that has a roll of toilet paper and a jar of Vaseline on the table. There's polaroids of kids holding up big fish tacked to the wall and faded pictures of men with their turkey and deer kills. Another table has a tube of Preparation H and tweezers on it. One table has an unfinished jigsaw puzzle laid out. The 'waiter' is also the cook and cashier, and doesn't appear to wash his hands between functions, and has about a five-day beard going. One of the customers is smoking and she's visiting with a girlfriend about the Jerry Springer Show. The upper parts of the toebox on her tennis shoes are cut out so you can see her chartreuse toenails with little dirt lines up the sides. Both girls are blinking, relentlessly, and flashing rotten teeth.

Place smells like year-old grease and decaying wood, and the window glass is fly specked and dirt caked. Nobody but Catcher has any posture. Sagging is "in" here and droop they do . . . the shoulders, the bosoms, the heads, the backs.

Catcher's thinking a rock band could do a song here—*Droop, Droop de droop, I'm saggin de saggin, drooping all the way home, don't you say you're sorry, sorry, all the way home.*

Catcher gets his hot dog, leaves the meat and bun and skips the water in the plastic glass. Figures, he'll eat later. Trying to pay, but the business won't take a credit card, and they don't have change for a fifty, so he's writing a check. The bottom of the counter is wider than the top, and he's leaning over this in an awkward manner so as to keep his balance. The front of the counter is covered with narrow shelves cluttered with stuffed bears and cats. Catcher figures these are sopped with grease . . . . A guy with no shirt comes out of the kitchen and sits down at the end of the counter.

"We ain't takin' no check."

Catcher stops writing . . . . This younger guy is big and bulky. Could be a weight lifter. He's got grease or oil, something dirty, up and down his arms. Lots of tattoos and hasn't shaved for days. Looks like khaki trousers he's wearing and no lace tennis shoes without socks. Probably be over six feet tall, if he stood up straight.

"I don't have anything but a fifty, and you don't have the change," Catcher in an expressionless manner.

"That's yer problem, buddy. You c'n leave the Grant."

Catcher's putting his checkbook back in his pocket, and turning to face this grunge.

"I didn't eat your food, sir."

"That ain't nun 'uf my problemo. Leave the fifty."

"I'm not paying fifty dollars for a hot dog and bun mister. I'm not your buddy either."

"We served you a hot dog, buddy," the slob standing up. He's confusing Catcher's good manners with weakness. "Fuck'n giv' me the fifty, asshole," he's got a greasy hand out, palm up. "Yer bout to git yer ass kicked."

Catcher reaches in his pocket, eyeball to eyeball with sewer-plate. Places the fifty in the man's hand . . . grips the man's little finger and twists it back hard. "You want the fifty, Jack?"

Sewer-plate is backing up, trying to straighten his bent finger. He's hunched down grimacing in pain.

Catcher moving forward, keeping the finger back, "Still want the fifty?"

The sewer-plate is backed against a propane space heater and the stovepipe may fall out. "Take it! Take it!"

Catcher lets loose, and sewer-plate grabs his injured hand with the other, whimpering, "You broke m' finger! Fuck! Shit!" The fifty falls on the scuffed linoleum floor.

"Pick it up," Catcher sharply.

"Pick'et up yerself, asshole."

Catcher kicks sewer-plate's legs out from under him. Sewer-plate is flat on the floor. Groaning, handing up Catcher's fifty.

While he's putting the fifty in his pocket, Catcher's turning and taking a good look around. The folks here are staring, immobile zombies from Loserville Algiers, trapped between cigarette packs. The last pack, then the next. A bell on the door tinkles as Catcher exits.

Driving homeward on headlights. Itching from the ticks around his ankles. Hungry and thirsty and curious about the R4 telephone number. Catcher's got an itch, and he means to scratch it. He's going to find the outfit he saw on the river.

All in all, a good day . . . . Excepting the incident at the river rat's Road Kill Café, Shit Town Algiers, USA. Very different than the Officer's Club at Fort Knox, Kentucky . . . . Not so different from El Gato Negro Ristorante y Cantina on the coast of Nicaragua.

CHAPTER XI

Monday morning. Catcher's exercised and finished an oatmeal and toast breakfast. Sitting out on his front steps, drinking coffee and waiting for Marco. He's usually punctual. Marco, that is. Catcher's always punctual. The sun's coming up over the cedars in the east and the barn isn't getting fixed. C'mon Marco.

Now, here's a character for you. Marco. A thirty-something, drop out magician from the city, living in a bus full of books down the river at Camp White Cloud, doing odd jobs for a living. Used to be an electrician with a family in Kansas City. Bought an old house up there, rented it out on the investment plan where rent pays the house off. But, the hairdresser renter quit paying her rent, after month one. Marco couldn't get the rent out of her, but she wouldn't move out. She just went on with her life; except she wasn't paying her rent and she wouldn't let Marco or his wife in the house. Marco's paying the taxes, insurance and mortgage payment, then an attorney to get her out. This went on for months and Marco's wife started harping about how Marco was an ignoramus. Marco's thinking this is a hell of a way to live. You can't get in the house you bought and make mortgage payments on, and you can't evict a delinquent renter, even after six months. And, he's really a talented magician and musician, and he's pulling wiring for a disgruntled wife, and his kids could care less who he really is. So, Marco takes his money stashed from the weekend magic shows, buys an old bus, loads his favorite things, hooks his Suzuki 4X4 to the rear, and leaves Kansas City in the middle of the night. Now, he's camped out at White Cloud doing odd jobs in the Ozarks. And, he's happy about this, and a cheerful, cavalier, independent oddity in these parts. But, then, the Ozarks is full of just the sort. Marco. Catcher wonders if this is even his real name. Wondering what wild story of pending doom Marco has in store this fine Monday morning.

Marco is coming up the drive in the tattered Suzuki convertible 4X4. Getting out with a book in his hand, "You gotta hear this, Colonel. The end time is here." And, he's coming up to Catcher, proffering his book.

Catcher doesn't mind the book. He's smiling, "Marco, you ready to work?"

"You bet I am, but it's a waste of time, the world's getting ready to flip."

"Maybe, but we're going to be working on the barn when it does."

Down at the hundred-year-old barn, Catcher is directing Marco as to how they're going to pull the remaining siding and put it back up without empty spaces. The ladder is up and Catcher's got the crow and pinch bars, hammers and skill saw. A sack of sixteen-penny nails and an electric drill, just in case. It's humid as hell on the Amazon.

All the time Marco is prying boards working off the ladder, he's telling Catcher about the condition of the world.

"You're not getting it, Colonel. The world, as we know it, is finished. Anytime, it's going to tilt on its' axis, and when it does, there will be five hundred foot waves crashing inland from the coasts and five-hundred mile per hour winds. Like a nuclear blast, then a nuclear style winter from the dust and debris." Marco pauses to get down and move the ladder over, then he's back prying and talking again.

"We should be building a bomb shelter instead of doing the barn. You need a whole bunch of teenage wives to breed so we can maintain progeny. The salvation of the human race. Gotta survive the fifth cataclysmic end of civilization. That's what happened to Atlantis you know."

Catcher is cleaning the rusty nails out of the boards Marco is pulling off. Marco is talking on.

"If we're in bomb shelters with food and water, we can emerge after it's over with our wives and babies. Then, we can either stay here, or get on the Annanaki space ships that will be landing for rescue . . . you know, we are the descendents of an ape like creature and invitro fertilization with aliens don't you? You gotta know this!"

Catcher's laughing out loud. "Somehow I missed this in school."

"Hot damn right you did," Marco says. "The government doesn't want you to know. They depend on propaganda education to control us. They're suppressing all kinds of evidence about our alien space fathers. Hell, I know some by name. There's Enki . . . . Enlil . . . . You know Enlil was flying over the Earth, near present day Syria, way back in the beginning, and he saw several attractive female semi-humanoids. He landed and filled both their wombs with his life force."

Marco gets very respectful. "Enki loved us. Enlil was another story. If it hadn't been for Enki, Enlil would have partnered up with Princess Innana and eradicated the humanoids after being finished here."

Catcher is waiting for another board. "Finished doing what?"

"I can't believe you don't know this. Finished working the humanoids as slaves, and the cross breeds, who ended up looking like aliens. That's who we are. We were slaves, mining gold at the tip of what's now South Africa, so the Annanaki could transport the gold back to their planet. Back then, they had a problem with their atmosphere thinning. It was warming-up. Kind of like our own greenhouse effect. They were getting the gold into dust and spreading it around their planet to protect it from the sun. They also tipped their spacecraft with gold."

Catcher's laughing, "I swear Marco, you will become a lightning rod for every rum pot, crackpot in the western world. Give me another board there."

"Laugh all you want," and Marco stops, leaning back on the ladder to pull his pants up over his voluminous stomach. He pushes the bandana sweatband up into his brushy brown hair. "You'll be glad to see 'em when you come out of the bomb shelter with your wives and children. The Earth will be devastated. Your toilet could be stuck in the wall of the presidential palace at Baghdad. And, that under five hundred feet of silt."

Catcher is laughing again, shaking his head. "Where do you get this stuff, Marco," shaking his head.

"From translated Sumerian texts and late night talk radio. Where have you been, Colonel? Our brothers from Nibaru will be here to pick us up. You know, Enki prevailed over Enlil. And, these folks keep track of us, even now. They're already setting up buildings on Mars as way stations on the relay back to Nibaru. We've got satellite photos of these buildings and landing strips, but NASA and the National Security Council suppresses all this so the world won't panic. They'd rather have you washing your car and shopping at Wal-Mart than buying guns and building bomb shelters. You can bet they've got bomb shelters, they know e-x-a-c-t-l-y what's happening. It's an international conspiracy within the scientific community to keep the truth from us."

Marco's coming down off the ladder to rest his feet. They're getting sore standing on the rung.

"You got any hot tea, Colonel?"

"No. How about ice tea?"

"No way. The hot tea is a longevity builder. Creates enzymes that search down and kill radical protons in your body that cause cancer."

"Maybe I'll heat the tea up for you later, Marco," and Catcher is standing here watching Marco getting his hefty, sweat soaked body back up the ladder.

"You know, Colonel, they don't want the armed services community to know the truth. On either side. The deceivers own the big munitions industry and pharmaceutical and oil, and they want problems so they can enrich themselves off the deaths of their brethren. They started AIDS. So they could sell those high priced drugs made out of rat poison and formaldehyde. They've got it all figured out. But, the Annanaki won't communicate with them direct, cause they know their message will be misconstrued or suppressed. Our space brethren want their relationship with the common folk around the world. The waitresses that always have a warm word for you, even while their bunions are killing them . . . and the mechanics, that keep your car running, and the nurse's aides that take care of old folks deserted by their families, and the barbers and hairdressers and handymen."

Catcher smiles, "Like yourself."

"You betcha," and Marco is resting on the ladder. "You got any water, Colonel? If we aren't going to drink hot tea, let's drink some water," and Marco's coming back down the ladder.

"I'll bring some back," Catcher says as he's heading away toward the house. He almost steps on a copperhead, and jumps ahead and turns around to keep the snake in view. Looking around for something to kill it. There's a shovel against the barn, and he cuts the snake in half with it, and pitches it off to the side.

Bringing back a big thermos of water, glasses, and several peanut butter and jelly sandwiches. Probably more truth to Marco's ravings than a settled mind can deal with. Wondering what else he knows.

"Hey, Marco, I killed a copperhead by the end of the barn. Be careful where you're sitting."

"Snake bites me, it dies," as Marco gets settled against the barn. Hors'deuvres on the veranda, Ozark style.

They're sitting here eating and drinking their water, watching some turkey vultures and a hawk circle around.

"Marco, what do you know about marijuana growing around here?"

"I know the ancients used it. They've found frozen bodies of cave men in the mountains with a bag of weed on them . . . it grows wild around Missouri, but not the good stuff. The marketable pot is cultivated."

"By who?"

"By big and small growers. These guys don't make news releases. I think it's about twenty-five years in the brig, no parole, you get caught . . . . I know someone that probably knows the story on local marijuana farming. How come Colonel, you looking to become a stoner?"

"Not hardly . . . . Who do you know that would know?"

"One of the Annanaki no less. You know, the Annanaki are bigger than men. After the alien-human hybridization not all the Annanaki returned to Nibaru. The plumed serpent of Mexico, . . . Annanaki for sure . . . . The Osage Indian tribe was the tallest of all native American Indian tribes."

"Marco, who do you know?"

"I know this old Indian down by the river. Osage. Direct descendants of the Annanaki I figure. They were taller than their half-breed hybrids—that's you and I. Anyway, Big Track is his name. Big tall Osage. You know the Osage came from the sky. They know they came from the stars, their oral history,"

"Marco," Catcher interrupts, "how do you know this Big Track?"

"Well, Colonel, we aren't best friends or anything. We'll pay each other a social call occasionally. He lives down the river, in some cabin near R4. He gets paid to do maintenance."

"R4. What's R4?" Catcher's thinking of the slip of paper he found at the 'would-be' marijuana plot site on the river.

"A nightclub, Colonel." Marco raises his eyes up to Catcher's, "What you got here is a nightclub, private, bring your own bottle thing, lots of money to belong. Big Track maintains the place. I've gone there to do handiwork. Big Track sees a lot and hears a lot . . . . I don't try to kid myself. I know I'm out of the loop. So is Big Track. And, we've got other friends, you know, too, that are not establishment monkeys. No disrespect intended, sir." Marco stops to shift on his haunches. "You know, Big Track has a light of intelligence in his eyes that almost burns; like fires from his eyes."

"Marco, how would Big Track know anything?"

"He doesn't own a car. He doesn't drive. He travels his own path. He goes great distances, cross-country, hunting and such. He knows the land, and who's doing what thereon, you know. And, we talk when I'm doing repairs on R4. He observes things. Indians have a different kind of intelligence. How do you think Geronimo evaded the U.S. Cavalry for so long? Cause he knew about the cave tunnels running under the Continental Divide, under the Rocky Mountains, from Canada to Mexico. Indians."

"Marco, you think these pot growers are dangerous?"

"Some of them would be very dangerous. The big growers. They run a big risk for a lot of money."

"Is R4 a place they hangout?"

"I don't know. They could. You have to make good money to belong to R4. It's an unconventional place. Private. Stays open all night on Fridays. Wild. Yeah. It's a place outlaws would like."

Catcher's eating the last of his peanut butter and jelly sandwich, watching the squirrels jumping from branch to branch, thinking about the guy that aimed the high-powered rifle at him. Outlaws in the Ozarks.

Marco is sitting here watching the turkey vultures. "What do I know? I live in a bus in the woods, somewhere between a nervous breakdown and great genius. The essential truths are the omissions within the facts. It's a great sham. You gotta dig to find the truth."

The two of them finish their waters and resume work. And, as the sun traverses across the blue Ozark sky, Marco continues his theories to Catcher. In what seems a short time, evening is approaching and Marco is getting ready to go.

"Do you want your money now, or when we're finished, Marco?"

Marco isn't listening. He's looking up into an oak tree, "Dexter, Dexter, is that you? C'mon down, Dexter."

"What are you doing, Marco?"

"I think I saw Dexter."

"Who's Dexter?"

"My pet squirrel. I let him go out here awhile back. I think I just saw him."

"I swear Marco, you've got more friends," chuckles Catcher.

"You bet I do. You don't know who an animal was in his last life. Or, who he's going to be next," murmurs Marco as he squeezes his hulk into the Suzuki. "Could come back as a beautiful woman. Take Jinx. No telling what she was before."

Catcher, laughing, "Who's Jinx?"

"Just the prettiest woman in Missouri, mister. You haven't seen her buzzing around in that corvette? B-e-a-u-t-I-f-u-l. Works in Warsaw."

Then Marco is pulling off down the drive.

CHAPTER XII

Jinx has a 'day' job. She's the head teller at Warsaw Bank, Monday thru Friday. Today, she's two cats in a sack and her mind is on a razor thin blade going south. Her little girl wants out, and the nympho can't cum to distraction. Emotional shrapnel is worming its way out in welts across her stomach and inner thighs. BB size acne working up the undergrounders around her elegant face. Passing two hundred cash out the drive-thru window, "Thank you Rob, have a nice day." Peripheral vision blurs, "Here's your deposit slip, Mrs. Clemson. Have a nice day." Her hands got the Saint Vidus, and this backs up the parasympathetic highways of the autonomic nervous system . . . all the way back to the hypothalamus. She's got a rusty splinter in nerve central. Been there since she was six years old, the splinter. The trembles traveling her subways started after the breakdown her senior year. A dropout with a straight-A average, sub-zero self esteem and a boiling point well under 212 degrees Fahrenheit. An I.Q. over one hundred and fifty laced with anxiety and beggared by depression. "Hello, Annie. How are the kids? How much you want today . . . . Fifty dollars coming right up . . . Have a nice day, Annie."

This is Jinx west. She's got a river, which splits her in two. A sub-terrestrial trickle through her psyche, no less defining than the Little Niangua. She runs her fragile existence by it. West side of the river, she's impersonating the girl she could have been . . . the make believe adult extension of the little girl trapped inside.

She's also Jinx east. The magnum opus of her white trash father. Groovin' on the east side of the Little Niangua River.

Using geography to facilitate de facto segregation of her two selves has kept her alive to twenty-five. Interestingly to herself, she bought her shanty home on the west side. Close to the river, for easy transformations.

Most days, the west side bank job is a manageable function. But, there are those unpredictable days, when the rusty splinter in nerve central is tipping the panic button. This is one of 'em. "Two hundred fifty. Have a nice day."

She sees an old primered truck in the mirror. It's approaching her drive-up. Driver's got the baseball cap on, slouched over against his door. Looks . . . looks like 'Daddy.' Killer anger bolts up from her underlying panic . . . would break through the bulletproof glass to slash him up. "Mary, could you take over here . . . ." She's going to the ladies room.

Going in, she vomits across the tile floor before reaching the toilet. She changes direction to the adjoining stall. On her knees retching bile. There goes this morning's Xanex. Should've taken more. Gotta do a doober before I come in.

Cleaning up the floor with paper towels. Her navy blue suit is none the worse. Looking in the mirror without seeing herself, putting the face together. Gotta take another Xanex.

Coming out through the lobby, she's got an incoming phone call on hold.

"Jake? Is this you? God, what's wrong?"

"You OK?"

"Yes. OK, I guess."

"You left Saturday without saying anything."

"It's OK, Jake."

"Hey, I'm going to be in Warsaw anyway," he lies. "If you want to have lunch, I'll buy."

"Get it to go. I'll meet you at the dam, regular place."

Jinx is smiling and waving through the glass. There's the pervert in the Town Car. They're all pervs. Given the chance, they'll gore the bud before it's a flower. Fuck him. Cum jackals chasing the crannies for Little Red Riding Hood.

Outside the bank. The sun catharsis ratcheting down Jinx's tremorous sub-system in micro bits. But, her stomach is cramping and a new zit is running behind her ear. Feeling better in her Vette, got the Xanex. Feeling better with Jake.

"Fuck Jake," she's crying, "If I'm not curled-up, gone fetal, I'm down so low I could drown in the bathwater. Then, I make it through this, there's the manic phase. Working forty hours something straight on my kitchen." She's sitting across from Jake on a bolted down government picnic table below Truman dam. The park is empty. Except for her and Jake. "I'm fucked."

Jake's looking at her fries, "You gonna eat anymore?"

"Fuck no, I'm not eating anymore. I was throwing-up this morning. Saw a guy coming through the drive-thru with a truck like my father's."

Jake's getting up. He looks tired and has bags under his eyes . . . the late Dean Martin, without the show. "C'mon. Let's take a walk."

They're walking south, down the headwater shoreline of Lake of the Ozarks, below the dam backing Truman up behind Lake of the Ozarks. All the water here just came through the Truman Lake dam. This is the meeting place of the two waters . . . . Truman and Lake of the Ozarks.

"Jinx, you're going to have to get a little discipline in your life. You can't work at SHADOWS and go around screwing everybody, and expect to feel good . . ."

"Guess I ought to quit screwing you too, then," Jinx says sarcastically.

"Yeah. Maybe. Maybe no one for a while. Wait for Mr. Right. Truth be known, intimacy should follow affection."

Jinx hugs Jake's arm, "I love you, Jake. I always have."

"I know. But that's different. Really, we're friends that got a little too friendly."

"Way back," she says.

"Probably a good reason for that. Remember what was happening then. My dad was drinking himself into an early grave. Your dad was molesting you and your sister."

"Yes. Where were our mamas?"

Jake's walking along, looking at the ground, "Mine was smart enough to run-off. Yours might as well have . . . . Remember when Pop died? Five yards from the porch, face down in a rut? In his own vom . . ."

"I remember, Jake."

"That was probably the best thing that happened to me. My grandfather kinda got me straightened up."

"I remember."

"I remember too. When you had a breakdown. Best friends all those years, and I never knew till then, what was going on. You never begged, crawled or cried, that anyone could see."

Jinx, looking across the lake at the weathered backside of downtown Warsaw. "I didn't. You go into denial. You go through lots of things. For a long time, I was like a girl playing in the woods. Sees a big bear moving around her, just starts going on whistling and playing with her doll, like the bear isn't there. Denial."

Jinx's eyes are watery now, "Later, I was enjoying it. With my own dad. Even flirting with him sometimes . . . . Fucking glad I took my Xanex."

"You didn't know it was inappropriate. How would you know? Both of us living down there in the drizzling shits . . . . It was a good day when I got out of there."

"At least you graduated."

"You have to go back to work, Jinx?"

"No, I told 'em I'd see 'em in the morning."

"Nice to be the head cheese."

"I can't do that very often. I answer to someone."

"You know Jinx, you are not defined by your pussy!"

Jinx glances over at Jake, surprised, "Nice talk from one who loves to go there. You've been chipping a piece off whenever you wanted."

"Yeah, and that isn't right either. We're never going to get married. I'm not marriage material. We're best friends having sport sex together. This cheapens our friendship. Like now. I'm trying to help . . . I've got a sixth sense about you . . . I know when you're having a rough time. And, I can't get my point across, cause my own behavior weakens my argument. Nonetheless, it's true; your pussy is not the center of who you are. It's your heart. Your heart is the center."

Jinx, kicking a piece of gravel, "You bet. Everyone is just sitting around waiting for love."

"No. They're into professional pursuits . . . vocations and avocations, cause everything isn't about sex."

"How old are you, Jake?" looking over at him. "You've been having sex with me, off and on, for the last eight years. I didn't see you putting it on the back-burner."

"I am now."

"You're kidding. Right?"

"No. I'm not kidding. You got sexualized the wrong way. I did not. I'll be your best friend till one of us dies, but I'm done contributing to the problem. That's what it is, sex is your problem."

Jinx is crying, and Jake is letting her. She gets out, "But I've always come to you, Jake."

"You still can. I'm counting on it. But, you can sleep on my couch. Or, I will."

They're approaching the highway. Turning now to go back.

Jake taking his shirt off and tying it around his neck. He's got a logo t-shirt on that says, 'GOOD GUYS FINISH LAST.' "You saw Erik Starr Saturday night, didn't you? I know you Jinx. Couldn't pass it by."

"You're not my keeper, Jake."

"Nope. You never had one. But, I love you, and I don't want you getting hurt. Erik Starr could kill someone. You've got enough problems without compounding them."

Jinx is thinking about the pot. This is her secret from Jake. He knows she smokes, but has no clue as to how much. And, he doesn't know she solicits out of SHADOWS.

Jake is still talking. "You've got to keep more regular hours. What about your medication. You ever go back to see the psychiatrist, get updated on your prescriptions? You gotta keep these coming in, in the right amounts. And, you've gotta give up the idea of you being a sex object. You've got a lot of other things going for you."

"Like what, Jake?"

"Hell. You're smart. You're personable when you're not in a funk or on drugs. You've probably read more good books than most college graduates. You can work like the devil, if you want."

"In fact, Jake, if I'm in the manic phase, I can work non-stop for an indeterminate number of hours . . . maybe talking machine gun fast."

"The doctor said you were not manic-depressive. You fear it, so you exaggerate the tendency. You're not on lithium and don't need to be. You suffer from anxiety and depression. You don't have any boundaries because your dad wiped 'em out. If you worked on self-improvement as much as you chase after your sexual inclinations, you'd feel better."

Jinx is getting tired walking in her suit skirt. Looking up to where her Vette and Jake's El Dorado is parked. "I'm not going to be giving you anymore, Jake."

"Good. Maybe I can get a girlfriend now."

"You don't know what it's like. If I can't stand myself, who do you think will love me?"

"Someone can love someone who doesn't love themselves."

"Yeah, but I'd never know it."

They're at the vehicles now. Jake leaning over Jinx in her Vette.

"You still love me?"

"Yes, Jake. You are my best friend."

"You call me if you want . . . need to . . . right?"

"Yes."

"Don't make me come driving down to your place to see if you're OK."

"I'll call, Jake."

"I love you, Jinx. I wish you knew how good you really are. You were more ready to help an unfortunate than anyone in school."

"You really have business in Warsaw today?"

"No, I knew you were having a rough day. ESP my dear," as Jake taps the side of his head.

Then, they're going out of this place, leaving the birds flitting over the frothy waters below the dam, Jinx following Jake's El Dorado.

She leaves off at Wal-Mart.

Jinx is back home to her shanty. Surrounded by dirty laundry, stacks of books, and pictures of herself as a little girl. She's on her broken-down couch. Got the dim light on the end table, reading Shakespeare this month. Romeo and Juliet. This is her habit. To read, before going to bed.

During her sleep this night, she's having a dream. She's an Eskimo or woman like this. And, she's got some kind of fur coat on with the hood laid back. She's got her arm around the shoulders of a little girl in a coat like hers. The girl is an Eskimo or someone like this too. They're crossing a steppe or high plains under a dark sky with foreboding low lying clouds, and there's volcanoes or some such belching smoke in the horizon. It's a treeless land and cold and very gray. Then, she's in a bed of some foreign design. Like leather straps stretching across for a mattress, kind of hammock like. She's inside a hut or shack, and the wind's blowing, and it's cold, and she's covered with a heavy fur skin of some kind. The little girl is playing on a fur rug on the floor beside her bed. The little girl is making friendly gurgling noises and trying to get her toys to sit upright on the rug. Without warning, there's a huge scruffy giant in fur clothes and coat and in heavy leather pants and boots coming through the door. His face is hairy, and his hood is up. Jinx is pulling the fur blanket up around her chin, bracing for an attack. The giant stops and turns away from her bed and goes over above the little Eskimo girl. She can't see the giant's face, but knows he's evil. The giant is kneeling down in front of the little girl, putting her toys in his pocket. Jinx is trying to get out of this sagging strap bed, but can't pull herself up. Somehow, the bed has magnified the pull of gravity, and she's getting panicky, real panicky, and the giant is lifting the little girl up and making to carry her away, and Jinx can't, cannot, get out of this strap bed . . . . *Then, she's in the body of a naked, chalk white savage huntress, animated by instinct and pure animal drive. She treads barefoot on this narrow mountain trail, in a totally amoral condition.*

CHAPTER XIII

M is the thirteenth letter in the alphabet. In the sixties, seventies and into the eighties, the number thirteen, and the letter 'M' were code for marijuana. Number thirteen commercial growers are engaged in a risky enterprise. And, anyone that thinks raising marijuana is an easy way to make big money hasn't done it . . . . Erik's life is hard . . . . He does make big money.

Today, his brother Ejay is flying into Kansas City. To check on his supply. Erik drives up to K.C. for the meet.

Not hard to pick Ejay out. He's the tall, lean, serious one coming down the tarmac.

Erik's in 501s with a wide leather belt and buckle and a bright yellow t-shirt and got his better boots on, "How was the trip bro?"

"Uneventful," smiles Ejay. He's wearing 501s, a pullover, short sleeve, blue polo shirt, thin leather belt and small buckle, and cowboy boots.

"You didn't bring a suitcase?"

"Nope. Just this carry-on. Have to go back tomorrow," looking for an exit.

They don't shake hands or swap spit.

Out in the pickup, and threading their way out of the airport, and Erik's doing most the talking.

"Want a J?"

"Got one," as Ejay pokes a doober between thin lips and lights it.

"Primo," he says, smoke swirling around.

Wouldn't guess they were brothers, except for the coloring. Both have reddish hair and freckled white skin. But, Erik's got a tan. He calls it that. Really, he's just red. The sun brings out the color of his freckles. After this, the brothers' resemblance ends. Erik is about five foot, ten inches, and Ejay is about six foot, two inches. Erik is built like a brick shithouse, and Ejay is lean and wiry. Erik looks like he might do anything anytime, and Ejay more thoughtful, or cautious. Both got the air of soldiers of fortune and neither a suggestion they would ever know their age.

Ejay's wondering, "You bring a piece? I'm naked."

"Got a couple revolvers behind the seat . . . a .357 and a .45 Colt."

"I feel naked without my .44," says Ejay. He looks a little like Dirty Harry.

Erik, "Guess the only gun I'll need is the one between my legs. Mine's hard enough, a cat couldn't scratch it."

Ejay's smiling, "What's new?"

Checking into their rooms in a downtown hotel; each has his own, but the two rooms are adjoining.

Erik has come over to Ejay's room, waiting for Ejay to pee, shower and dress. Erik enjoys this time. His older brother is here and the camaraderie loosens him up. Fancies watching out the window as nighttime comes over Kansas City. He can see the yellow and white streetlights popping on and the various colored lights on signs, buildings, towers, and across the bridge. Strings of headlights, like beads moving along their strings.

Posthaste, Ejay is ready to go. He's got his jeans and boots on and a fresh red polo shirt. Smoking a Pall Mall, no filter, as he closes the door behind them.

Erik's saying, "I'll drive us to the Plaza."

Ejay asking Erik if everything's going 'copasetic' at the OMP.

"We got our little headaches, but nothing I'm not handling," replies Erik.

Having beers down on the Plaza. Erik raises his mug, making a toast. "Here's to younger women, faster horses, and stronger whiskey." Ejay's wanting to know about the production routine.

"We raised the seedlings in the cave."

Ejay's lighting a Pall Mall with the logo free Zippo, "How many starts you have?"

"Over three thousand. Course, that's male and female plants. Right now, seven men and two boats to put them out."

"Still using the rivers?"

"Fuckin' A. I'm marking the patches on my maps. I even know how many plants at each patch."

"You wouldn't want those maps where anyone could find them," Ejay says, sitting back studying his younger brother through the cigarette smoke.

"I've got two sets of maps. I don't mark the patches on the 'fishing' maps up on the walls. The working maps are hidden, and scattered out too. I don't hide them together. You find one map; you only find one or two patches. No computer, so there's no . . . incriminating . . . hard drive.

This is tough fuckin' work. I mean planting the three thousand seedlings takes forever. But, I had good seeds. That'll make-up for any sloppiness. I'm camo-ing some collapsies on some patches. Other patches, we'll water at night by pumping out the lake. The collapsy tanks and lines and valves are a hassle."

Ejay is smiling, "I'll have a good supply?"

"Not just quantity. It'll be good stuff. Good size, good shape and smell. Good smoke. Good stone. But, it's not easy. The fucking ticks and mosquitoes are a bitch. The guys are planting under trees. Not so many trees we don't get the sunlight, but enough to hide the plants from aerial detection. The boats will be running all night, every night. Gotta water, gotta fertilize, gotta switch guards."

Ejay asks Erik if he's hungry yet. It's after 10pm and Ejay eats dinner earlier in Pontiac. He's married. And, his wife likes to come home from her school teaching job, get dinner over and the dishes done before any 10pm.

During their steaks, the two brothers converse about the same things most non-family Missouri growers talk about: Drugs, guns, sex and 4X4s.

Erik is saying, "Busts worry me the most. Fuck, my guards can't be shootin' the law. The law finds a patch; they're going to burn it. My guards can't do anything about this. We aren't going to waste the law . . . . No problem about poachers. We get poachers, they get dead. My guards are watching the patches nearly fifty per cent of the time.

"I had fence put out around some patches. It works for the deer. Won't help with the rats, but it works for the deer," as he mops up steak juice with a roll.

Ejay, "You're a commercial grower using guerilla growing techniques. Sinsemilla is a harder go than ditch weed, but it's worth the trouble considering what we get for it."

The waitress is back. She's given up flirting with Ejay, and concentrating on Erik. As she walks away, Erik's smiling at Ejay, "Nice ass."

"I'll send you a couple more guys down. You're going to need more help."

"Only if they know what they're doing. I could use another sniper for guard duty."

"No pirates going to get over on the OMP . . . Right?"

"Right," Erik cavalier like.

Ejay pays for dinner from his cash roll.

They're walking around the Plaza, looking for another bar. All different colored lights around and inside the cameo Moroccan storefronts. A horse drawn buggy is coming past with a seemingly mainstream yuppie couple smiling and laughing on the bench seat behind the driver.

Erik's telling Ejay, "It won't be the cleanest pot in town. Harvest is a critical time. We have to dry, strip and package fast. Then, I need it off the OMP. I'm very fucking vulnerable during harvest. We'd lose the ranch, if I get busted then."

Ejay's walking along, looking out at the sidewalk ahead, "I'll move it north when you say."

"You know, the crown cola on these plants will be longer than my forearm. Unfuckin' believable."

"The THC content is our selling point back home," Ejay musing out loud. "After a J, our customers can count their own chromosomes. They can't get enough of it."

Erik laughing, "Sex is magnifico after a couple of tokes . . . . I can take my own sperm count."

"You have a girl?" Ejay's eyes narrow.

"I've been fucking a girl named Jinx. Looks like Ellen Barkin in the movie SEA OF LOVE, with shorter hair. She loves her fuckin' doobers."

"How much does she know?"

"She doesn't know jack shit. She's never been on the OMP, and I don't talk about my work."

"Better keep it that way," Ejay's tone on the frosty side.

"Don't worry bro, she's cool."

They're in the pick-up, headed north towards their downtown hotel. Erik parks and Ejay sticks the .45 in his pants under his shirt. Erik does the same with the .357 Magnum.

Going through the lobby, Erik is studying the desk clerk . . . . nice fucking chickarito. He drops behind Ejay, still smiling towards this southern neighbor come north. Mexican, he's thinking, maybe Indian or half-breed or something. One fine looking chickarito, fuckin' A.

Ejay turns back over his shoulder, looking from Erik to the Chickarito, smiling, "See you in the morning, Romeo." The elevator door closes behind him.

Erik going over to the hotel desk, pulling his cash roll out. He's holding this, resting his hand on the hotel desk, checking her nametag. Addressing the chickarito with the dangly earrings, "Know where I can find a date and a beer, Mary?"

She's looking at this cash roll. Leaning over towards him, resting her forearms on the desktop, hands folded together.

"What room are you in?" Smiling.

"327."

"Give me a few minutes, and I'll have a friend come down," still smiling.

"How long?"

"Ten, fifteen minutes."

"Why don't you come up and party, Mary?"

"Could be I'll have her watch the desk," Mary grinning, standing up and reaching for the phone. "What's your name, cowboy?"

"Erik, sweetheart."

"Room service will be extra this late."

Erik pulls out a hundred dollar bill and gives it to her. "I'll give you another hundred after you deliver." He is smiling, his blue eyes squinting into her brown. Red hair falling over his forehead and ears.

Maybe it's the beer, but Erik is very full-faced tonight. Almost puffy. And his bulky muscles are showing through the bright yellow t-shirt.

She says, "You a boxer?"

"No sweetheart, I'm a rancher come off the back forty."

She laughs, "I'll bet."

"You coming up or not?"

"Two hundred more for the room service."

"You got it, honey," and Erik's straightening up, shoving the roll back in his pocket. "Room 327." Then he's crossing the red-carpeted lobby, back towards the elevators.

A little bowlegged, she notices. Hindquarters like a bull.

Downtown Kansas City is noisy. There's a jackhammer banging against the concrete, sirens, traffic whooshing by and a lot of people moving on the sidewalks. Erik and Ejay are sitting inside the front window having breakfast.

"You pickup the desk clerk last night, bro?" Ejay casually, between mouthfuls of hash browns and toast.

"Got it done."

"Nice?"

"Kinda on the rough side. I paid her too much. But, what the hell, we're having a good time, right?"

"Whatever floats your boat, bro."

Ejay's lighting a Pall Mall and leaning back holding his coffee. "You wish you were cookin' meth instead of growin' weed?"

"Fuck no. All that's good for is to shove up your nose and fuck all day. I don't need crank for that . . . . But, I'll tell you sumpthin', I'm down there in the crank capital of the Midwest."

"May be, brother," making to get out of his chair. "But, yer farming the nectar of the gods. Sinsemilla's up there next to stem cells."

Ejay making a few last minute suggestions to Erik at KCI. "Don't wait too long to pull the short, male plants. Keep your patches guarded; forget the patch if the law finds it; eliminate poachers and hide their bodies well. Debrief your guards every time they come in. Always ask them about low-flying aircraft. Be prepared to lose a lot of plants through the hot summer months. Come harvest and drying, do it as fast as possible, but keep the product as clean as possible and pack it in quarter pound bricks."

Ejay pauses to light another Pall Mall. Looking on Erik with a 'do-you-get-it' face. "Don't forget the math, Erik. You're starting with three thousand starts. After you get rid of the male plants, you will have fifteen hundred plants. Mark five hundred plants off as loss to weather, animals, mold and county Mounties. If you can pull one thousand plants through, with a yield of two pounds per plant, you have done it. I'll pay you cash, two thousand dollars per pound. Two pounds per plant, with one thousand plants, is two thousand pounds. That, times two thousand dollars, is about four million dollars. I expect my dope dried, manicured, and packaged right. If you don't pull a thousand plants through, you make less money.

"Be careful around this Jinx. Loose lips sink ships. There's no way you'd know who all she knows."

Shaking hands, "I hope Jinx isn't a . . ."

Erik finishes the sentence simultaneously with Ejay, "A bad omen."

Erik is standing back smiling, with his hands shoved into his 501s, "Jinx, you owe me some coke."

"Better than meth."

"But, we do,"

Simultaneously, "Sinsemilla."

CHAPTER XIV

Catcher Riley is America's son. Reared, molded, sculptured and manicured a la Midwest, Main Street, U.S.A. Grew up, should say r-a-i-s-e-d, in the heartland. Champaign-Urbana, Illinois. A programmed conformist, per contra intense achievement training.

His father hit it big in the construction business. This was a hands-on, twenty-four seven, don't-drop-your-guard business. And, Mr. Riley postulated any sober, sane man worth his salt must necessarily work and construct his life on Mr. Riley's model or he would fail. Mr. and Mrs. Riley were God-fearing Lutherans and didn't speculate regarding alternate plans for eternal life. Extending his religious beliefs into example, Mr. Riley was honest and hard working. Central to his belief system was the idea that ninety percent of success in life was due to showing up, and completing jobs no one else wanted. If Mr. Riley's business came too easily, he started to get suspicious, began double-checking things. The business didn't allow much so-called quality time, and Catcher's dad relied on Mrs. Riley to raise Catcher a winner.

Mrs. Riley was sufficiently socially 'engaged' to know what 'programs' and extracurricular activities were character builders. If she overlooked one, Mr. Riley pointed it out, "Why isn't Catcher in wrestling?" "Why isn't Catcher working?" "When does track season start?" "Why isn't Catcher in church this morning?"

Catcher was raised according to a fifties style paradigm. Christian. Patriotic. And, self-reliant, self-responsible and conforming.

When Catcher moved over to the University, he didn't shake-the-shackles, go wild or start humping the girls. He went with one girl, applied himself and was promoted rapidly in R.O.T.C. The Riley family paradigm was extended by a similar, however less personal, community paradigm. Graduating from

University of Illinois into the Officer Corps, United States Army, was a move into a national paradigm, like the community paradigm, which was like the family paradigm. Catcher was like the plant inside an eight ounce pot, moved into a sixteen ounce pot, then moved into a thirty two ounce pot, all with the same soil. Family values prepared him for successful community living, prepared him for successful national citizenship.

Growing up, Catcher had enough activities and challenges placed before him to preclude a detrimental deviation. Catcher's behavior and perceptions were crafted by one idea, then another, then another, so on and so forth. Take his brain—tabla rosa. Add:

> *God's commandment—Thou shalt not have no other gods before me; Cub Scout motto—Do your best; God's commandment—Thou shalt not worship any graven image; Cub Scout Promise—I, Catcher Riley, promise to DO MY BEST to do my DUTY to God and MY COUNTRY, to BE SQUARE, and to OBEY the Law of the Pack; God's commandment—Thou shalt not take God's name in vain; Boy Scout Motto—Be Prepared; God's commandment—Remember the Sabbath to keep it holy; A scout is Trustworthy; Honor your father and mother; A scout is Loyal; God's commandment—Thou shalt not kill; A scout is Helpful; God's commandment—Thou shalt not commit adultery; A scout is Friendly; God's commandment—Thou shalt not bear false witness; A scout is Kind; God's commandment—Thou shalt not covet; A scout is Obedient; A deadly sin—Avarice; A scout is Cheerful; A deadly sin—Pride; A scout is Thrifty; A deadly sin—Envy; A scout is Brave; A deadly sin—Wrath; A scout is Clean; A deadly sin—Lust; A scout is Reverent; A deadly sin—Gluttony; A cardinal virtue—Prudence; Football Maxim—No Pain, No Gain; A cardinal virtue—Fortitude; A cardinal virtue—Justice; A cardinal virtue—Fortitude . . .*

And so on and so forth, the tabla rosa being etched with the values of his family, then community, then country; each successive set of values a consistent extension of the values that came before.

Catcher Riley's niche in this paradigm was all the more secure for having a privileged life, uninterrupted by events or experience impugning the paradigm . . . . Until his wife got the cancer. Forty-two years young. The perfect wife. Inside the paradigm, inside the box. God's will—have faith . . .

this was Catcher Riley's programming. But, underneath this rote response, there began the stirring of some rebel sentiments.

All his military career, Catcher honored the principle of no PDA. No personal display of affection. The last time he saw his wife alive was in the presence of General Stamps and his wife, come to pay their respects. Catcher had to leave for headquarters, and when he looked at her, propped up against her pillows, his wife gazed upon him longingly. Catcher thought, waiting to be kissed. Catcher did not kiss her. Instead he patted her hand, because of the Stamps' presence.

As Catcher turned to leave, she had said, "Goodbye, S.C." S.C. was a nickname she normally reserved for their private times. She had taken to calling him S.C. at the University of Illinois, even before they were married. She claimed he looked and talked like Sean Connery. This romantic notion was preserved over time by this nickname. She called him S.C.

When he returned, Catcher found her asleep, and he retired to the couch in the adjoining family room. During the night, she had awakened and twisted the lever on the morphine so as to administer a fatal dosage. He had missed his opportunity to kiss her goodbye, because in his paradigm, there was no PDA. But, this was just the conscious tip of the iceberg submerged in his psyche.

Other rebel sentiments were churning around beneath the conscious surface; sentiments stemming from guilt and precognizant inclinations heretofore undetected. It was like a super-storm was coming up from within. But mental or emotional, from whence or where, he could not tell. His sense was that a lifetime of convenient denials protected his superior paradigm and his superior position therein. And that he played the denial card conveniently to escape the discomfort of introspection and critical analysis. He was closer to casting off his whole system of beliefs and thinking than he knew, debunking each and every idea ever recorded until his paradigm was turned to dust. Leaving a desert.

He had accomplished little towards setting up a cattle operation. Mowing grass, trimming trees, working on the old barn, etc. But, no moving on a mission with any sense of urgency. Really, Catcher liked driving around in his Ramcharger best of all. Exploring the area. This kept the interconnected series of mental tumblers from clicking into an autonomous reconfiguration, thereby converting Col. Catcher Riley into a Mick Jagger, Malcolm X, Gandhi, Timothy Leary, or somebody different. Maybe his natural self. Driving around in the Ramcharger, getting the lay of things in his new Ozark home . . . this kept the tumblers on ice.

He's sitting on a stump down by the old barn he's repairing. Thinking about all this . . . particularly about the last time he saw his wife alive. He's figuring he'll fire-up the Ramcharger. Do some errands in Warsaw. It's cloudy, looks like it might rain, and the BIG LONESOME is heavy on his land today.

Standing up, off the stump, still studying the old barn. Knows he needs to do something. Looking out past the barn, into the woods invading this pasture, thinking. Colonel, U.S. Army Retired . . . the distillate of about two thousand five hundred years of Western civilization . . . from the Greek city-states, through the Roman Empire, through Feudalism and the Middle Ages, through the Renaissance and into an officership in the most powerful modern-day nation-state in the world. And, here he is, standing between the stump and barn, under low lying clouds, in the Ozark Mountains, deliberating whether to put some boards on the barn or go to Warsaw on errands. He's going to lock the house. He's going to Warsaw.

Driving this nineteen seventy-nine Ramcharger. It's twenty-two years old, has a three sixty cubic inch engine and runs like a top. It's a 4x4, and one can put it in four-wheel drive without stopping. Same for taking it out. It's all brown, some oxidized over time, but without rust . . . . Catcher usually wears these camo-fatigue cargo trousers and black boots, and cotton pullovers. He knocks around like this most of the time. The Ramcharger fits. He leaves old coffee cups rolling around on the floor; and, newspapers, bottle water, tools, etc. lay around on the passenger seats. Behind the back seat, there is a spare tire, jack, sleeping bags, ground cloth, and even a pre-packed overnight bag. These simple accoutrements, stashed around inside the old Ramcharger, provide a degree of comfort for Catcher. It's a very simple environ; mobile and escape at the ready.

He's driving north on 65 Highway; can't get around a tractor-trailer rig blowing black caustic exhaust from out pipes that are poked-up like chrome chimneys behind each corner of the cab. Each time Catcher tries to pass, a vehicle is coming his way. So, this is the way he travels, breathing the toxic exhaust belching from the diesel rig in front. He takes the first exit off 65 Highway after crossing Lake-of-the-Ozarks.

Catcher's got a lot of money in 'his' bank. Since the F.D.I.C. does not insure a customer over the regulated maximum, per bank, the total monies Catcher has in this bank are not federally insured. So, this cloudy day, he's going to a new bank to open a checking account.

Jinx has been smoking a doober and taking half of a 0.5 MG tablet of Xanex first thing out of bed in the morning. So, she's under control at her day job . . . head teller at Warsaw Bank. Working the drive-thru window. This is where she meets Catcher Riley. The concatenation . . . the nexus between two lives, two incongruous paradigms. At the Warsaw Bank, Warsaw, Missouri.

He pulls up to her window. "Hi, my name is Catcher Riley. Can I open a checking account from out here?"

Jinx is amused at this uncommonly well-groomed man in the old Ramcharger. She's smiling, "You should come inside for that, Mr. Riley. You can park over there," pointing through the glass at the parking area. "I'll meet you inside."

"Yes Ma'am. That'll work," and Catcher pulls ahead into a parking space.

Inside the bank, she has replaced herself at the drive-thru window, and the other tellers watch Jinx come around the counter, meeting Catcher coming through the door. She's leading him over to one of the desks in the outer lobby.

"What can I do for you, Catcher Riley?"

Catcher is taken back by her beauty. She's got a sleeveless, navy-blue suit on, and this accelerates the effect of her electric blue eyes.

"I'd like to open a checking account." But his mind is frizzy, veered off, unfocused. He's taking in this young lady's broad shoulders and unblemished, harmonious biceps and forearms. Her hands and nails are clean and feminine. She wears no rings. Her shoes are a series of straps that leave most of her foot exposed. And this, with the delicate ankles, is very feminine. There is a hint of cologne.

"Business or personal?" as she's pulling the paperwork out of the middle drawer. She's sucking in her mid-section as she opens this middle drawer, and the medium length blonde hair is like a splattered sunspot over the navy top.

"Personal," Catcher shifting in his chair. Leaning back with his legs crossed out in front, hands interlocked in his lap.

From here on, if you ask Catcher what transpired, he'd have a rather fuzzy recollection. He'd remember writing a check to open the account. He'd remember her name is Jinx. And, he'd remember her asking, "Anybody ever tell you, you look like Sean Connery?" And, he'd remember she didn't wear a wedding ring.

Catcher Riley, meet Jinx the Minx. The girl that's fucking the guy, that's paying the gang, that's planting the pot, that has a guard, that aimed a high-powered rifle at you.

Entranced.

He's back out in the Ramcharger, sitting here, putting the several counter checks in his old checkbook. For use until his new checks come in. Trying to recollect his equilibrium. Feels like he's in a cup of tapioca, right next to the cinnamon stick.

On the way home, Catcher's thinking the lifestyle of a monk is going nowhere. Makes him crotchety. And, Jinx is exquisite.

Back at Warsaw Bank, Jinx is studying Catcher's address. Trying to figure where the Cross Timbers' rural route places Catcher. She concludes he lives east of Cross Timbers. The way he spoke, the way he moved, the constrained sharpness and his clean-cut good looks put a bee in her bonnet. A colonel in the Army, she's thinking . . . comes from far away. Wishing they could have visited longer. Decides she'll call Catcher when his new checks arrive . . . maybe he'll want to come in and pick them up. There was a softness in his brown eyes. Maybe a wound.

She can spot a wound in a micro-molecule given a half-second glimpse. In man or beast.

CHAPTER XV

Speaking of the beast. Erik's seen Jinx six nights in the last two weeks. Been banging the bejesus out of her. With this, and planting the M, he's averaging about four hours sleep a day.

Tonight, he's going to give her some more boo. Almost all buds. A couple of tokes, and she'll know every rivet in his DNA.

She called him after Crisco Crossing. This second time, they met at Miller Cemetery. And, this rendezvous was better than the first. Whoever said you can't teach an old dog new tricks, didn't know Jinx. Every orifice in her body, and he still had a chromium erectus. Before separating at Miller Cemetery, they set a third meet. Excuse me, should we say, they made a date. Next time they did it the same way. Not the sex; setting the date. Wouldn't see him Friday night. Won't give him her fuckin' phone number. But, shows up at the appointed place and time to receive her deposit from the jolly red giant. Using a condom now. Going to order some X-Large, from the World Health Organization, don't you know . . . . Well, he didn't always use one. Sometimes, Jinx is so fucked-up from the whack, she doesn't know the difference. She's a stoner looking for a boner.

And, he's giving her both—a major league stone, and bone. He's figuring she's gone through the Mary-J he gave her at Crisco Crossing. So, he's got more Ozark Gold for her. The mother lode. All bud. A la Carte. He's betting, five to ten times stronger than anything she's ever smoked.

Going to put her on Jupiter and keep her out there. Fuckin' bitch. She wants to hassle about control; he'll show her The Force, coming in on the A-Train from October Mount Pontiac.

So, here he is, leaning back against his black pickup, parked down by a busted bridge on a closed gravel road, outside Edwards. She's late and he doesn't have a phone number or know where the wench lives.

The moon is up, over the eastern horizon, and there's a shining off the creek rushing around the broken concrete slabs. Stems of rebar sticking out at odd angles, and clumps and stalks of weeds pushing up out of the creek bank around the haphazard slabs. The old gravel road just stops where the concrete has collapsed into the creek. He's next to a bottomland farm field planted with soybeans, and he can see horizontal sheets of mist stretching out over the beans. On the opposite shore of the creek, there's a steep ridge covered with timber, mostly cedar. The bullfrogs, tree locusts, katydids and owls are in their evening harmony. Now he's thinking he hears a car coming down the gravel.

Jinx is in the Vette with the top down. Always in a tank top, Wranglers and cowgirl boots. She's parking alongside the truck and getting out.

"You bring some weed? The Sinsemilla?"

"No weed, sweet thing. I got the partridge in the pear tree. Over an ounce of bud."

"Got any paper?"

"Already rolled you one," Erik offers, handing a doober to her. Then, he lights it. After a toke, she hands it to Erik, and he takes a drag. Alright already, he's seeing Jinx like she was translucent, right through her to the bean field behind.

He ends up doing her from behind while she's leaned over the side of her Vette.

"That's all it's going to be tonight," she's saying, as she pulls her Wranglers up.

She gets turned around facing him. Erik's finishing buttoning his fly. They fire up the doober. Smoking this. Mostly Jinx, that is. And, she's getting very stoned.

"This is good stuff," she gets out.

"Don't get too whacked out. I gotta go. I got men working."

"Doing what?"

"None of your business."

"OK. Be that way . . . Hey. Where's my baggy? My Sinsemilla?"

"I'll get it for you, it's in the truck." Erik is opening the door, and pulling out her supply.

"Whew-w-w-w. I think I heard my brain short-out for a minute."

"What'd it sound like, Jinx?"

"It went Z-e-u-t. When I lean over . . . this stuff is great."

"You're not going to be able to drive."

"I'll sit right here," she says, getting into her Vette.

"That's what you'll have to do. I can't waste anymore fuckin' time. I gotta go," and Erik hands her the baggy. "How about meeting here tomorrow night?"

"I'll call you, Dude," Jinx says in a languid way.

Erik's thinking about the dope he gives her, "I know you will baby." Starting the truck and driving out the gravel road through the mists. Jinx eventually does the same.

She makes the Little Niangua crossing and finds the lane into her shanty. Coming in through the mists, hearing the drum of river night sounds, when she gets a start. There's a car at her place. It's Jake's El Dorado.

Coming up to her porch, clutching her baggy of ganja bud, she spots Jake sitting here leaning against a post. No lights on in the house, and it's dark, except for the moonlight. Damp too.

"Wondering when you'd get home," Jake saying without getting up.

Jinx opening the screen door and putting the pot inside, coming back out on the porch and sitting down beside Jake. Putting her hand on his knee.

"You been here long?"

"Long enough to watch the moon pass over to above that ridge," Jake says, raising a finger towards the west.

"You startled me."

"Didn't mean to."

"What's wrong?"

"Nothing's wrong. I've been worried about you. You don't answer your phone, haven't been over to R4. What's going on Jinx?"

Putting her arm around him, pulling him in, putting her face in his, "I'll be over soon, Jake. What's wrong?"

"You smell like pot."

"Yes. So?"

"So, you are turning into a first-class stoner."

"Even if it's true, so what? I'd rather be dead than give up pot."

"So, you'll end up a pothead . . . if you live long enough."

"What's that supposed to mean," taking her arm off his back and straightening up, looking out towards the moon.

"You're seeing Erik Starr aren't you?"

"Maybe."

"Fuck, Jinx. You want to die? That guy is an accident going somewhere to happen. You still dancing at SHADOWS?"

Jinx is getting-up. "You want a J?" opening the screen door.

"No. I do not want a J."

She's sitting on the porch again, taking a toke. She's got a back-to-back stoner going and Pope Paul couldn't stop it.

"You know, Jake . . . what the hell difference does it make to you . . . what I do?"

Jake leans away from her and cranks his head back looking at her, "What is this? Why do you think? I care about you. We've been the closest friends since I was five years old. That's about twenty years. Fuck, you're so stoned, you wouldn't get it if I gave it to you in longhand."

Jinx leaning back, watching the moon, listening to an owl. In dreamland now.

Jake's getting up to go. Turning around towards Jinx, "Erik Starr is no good. He's a dead-end for sure. Get off the fucking dope, quit the SHADOWS and hang on to your bank job. You can't stay up all night and do the bank job justice." He's gesturing with his hand, "Drop Erik . . . . How you going to meet a decent guy if you're hooked-up with Erik? You need medicating, go to a doctor. No one decent is going to take a pothead libertine . . . . Period. End of story."

Jinx looks over at Jake. "Want to bet?"

CHAPTER XVI

Here's the deal with Catcher. For the last twenty-six years of his life, he's only had two real interests. His wife, who he dated during his University years, and the U.S. Army, with which he was associated in R.O.T.C., during his University years, and twenty-two years thence. A straight arrow, one-woman man and a spit and shine, gung-ho soldier. Now, he's without his wife and out of the Army. Before his wife died, their plan was to have a cattle ranch here in the Ozarks. After her death, and his retirement, he moved here, thinking he'd go ahead with the cattle ranch. Trouble is, he didn't factor in the ambivalence that goes with culture shock and depression. He's going through both. Face it, a lone civilian newcomer living in the Ozark hills and hollers is in a different culture than a field grade officer, U.S. Army, on active duty. This cultural (or paradigm) transition, following the death of his wife, has Catcher feeling low. He's having to make an effort to get up in the morning and get mobile. Consequently, he's taking longer than he would normally, to 'get things ready.' No doubt, he'll eventually go to a sale barn and buy cattle, but in the meantime, he procrastinates. He's got enough money in savings and retirement income to do this.

This morning, he wakes up thinking about Jinx. Figures, he'll shop for a few household goods, then swing by the bank. See if his checks are in. Say hello to Jinx.

He's in the line at the drive-up window at Warsaw bank. And, when he finally gets up to this window, Jinx is here.
She is very friendly, "Mr. Riley, I've missed you."
"Hi, Jinx. I'm wondering if my checks came in yet?"
"I've been watching for them, but . . ." and another woman is up behind Jinx, waiting to take her place.

Jinx, pointing Catcher over to the parking area, "Pull over there, Mr. Riley. I'm coming out."

Catcher pulls ahead, and into a parking slot. He's sitting here, with the window down, enjoying the sunshine and listening to the car wash next door, when Jinx comes out. She's wearing a sleeveless suit top with slacks and pumps to match, and a little-kid mischievous smile. Coming across the lot to Catcher's Ram.

"What kind of truck are you driving, Mr. Riley?"

Catcher's getting out, "It's a Dodge Ramcharger. They quit making them in the early nineties." He shakes her hand.

"You want to get something to eat?"

Catcher's got his hands in his cargo pants pockets, "Sounds good. You want to ride with me?"

"Surely do." She's going around and getting into the Ram; Catcher slamming the door behind her.

Pulling out of the parking lot, "Where do you want to eat, Jinx?"

"Let's go to McDonald's."

When they get their burgers and fries, and a table, Jinx asks, "You want a straw for your drink?"

Catcher doesn't want one. He's got the plastic lid off, drinking directly from the cup. Watching Jinx sip from her straw. Setting his cup down.

"Are you single, Jinx?"

"Absolutely. Never been married."

"Are you really single? No fiancé or boyfriend?"

"No sir," smiling I-know-what-you're-thinking . . . keep it coming. Yes?

"How did the guys miss you," biting into his burger.

Jinx looks down abruptly. Seems to be picking the pickles off her burger. "I didn't get around much. Fact is, I've had very few dates," putting the bun back on top her Quarter-Pounder. "Never saw a man I'd go for."

"You're beautiful."

"Thank-you."

"No. Really. You are very beautiful."

Jinx studying Catcher's face, "I think that means something coming from you."

"Why's that?"

Without breaking eye contact, "You know Catcher, there are three kinds of men. There is the lady's man, the man's man and his own man. His own man doesn't lie much. For better or for worse, he usually says and does what he wants. And, he means it. This is you, I think. The lady's man says and does what *she* wants. The man's man says and does what other men want."

"Yes?"

"A lady's man wants them all, and he says or does anything to have them all. A man's man doesn't really want any women, he just wants sex. He starts out, vis-a-vis the woman, having to prevaricate so she won't know this . . . . His 'own man' hasn't got a spin. You can take him or leave him. That's you." Jinx takes a bite. With half a mouthful she mumbles, "All he wants is his 'own' woman. One woman . . . . Exclusive."

Catcher is smiling at her. She smiles back, looking down to brush some crumbs off her suit.

"How much time you have for lunch, Jinx?"

"Thirty minutes. Not near enough with you."

"Thank you. I'm ready when you are."

Back in the parking lot at the bank, Jinx sits in the Ram for a few seconds without saying a word. The two of them looking out the windshield at the carwash. Catcher's got his arm out his window. He's looking over at Jinx. He can't keep his eyes off her.

Jinx, grimacing, "I have to go." Squeezing his hand, looking over at him, moving her eyes back and forth between his. She looks . . . sad. Stress, Xanex, sex and doobers keep their bags packed under her eyes. This makes her more . . . sultry.

Before going back into the bank, telling Catcher, she'll call him when his checks arrive. "Probably be Saturday."

CHAPTER XVII

Erik's in a foul humor. Three thousand plants are a lot of plants to plant. Fuck. It's all illegal and you have to be careful, and you got boats out all day and part of the night. Depending on Boomer, Mark, Bugs or one of the others to mark the location of the patches correctly. Betting the crews won't get caught in the act. Living on a few hours sleep a night. Where are they now? He's stomping upstairs to get'em going. Fuck, it's after seven, the sun's up and these guys are still sleeping.

He hears music and some of his men laughing in one of the bedrooms, and swings this door open. He's engulfed with marijuana smoke. They've got the windows closed and are hot-boxing . . . smoking pot with all the windows closed, toking and breathing the second hand smoke, not to waste a waff. Sun's early rays shining through dirty windows and into the streaks of smoke.

"What the fuck," Erik is looking around at them. "You know what time it is?"

"We've been hitting it pretty hard, Erik. We're ready," Mark says as he picks up his rifle.

"Yeah Erik, we're coming," Boomer says, sliding past Erik into the hall. The others are heading downstairs. Erik goes down after them; what the fuck?!

Outside in the seven-thirty a.m. sun, the men are loading the last of the starts off the front porch into the boats, and covering them with canvas and plastic and weighing this down with fishing poles and nets. Erik's reckoning the trauma will kill a number of the seedlings.

Then, the gang is hauling out the OMP drive. It's a beautiful day. The sun is rising into a clear blue sky and the turkey vultures are riding the thermals. There's the slightest of breeze. But, Erik isn't seeing any of this. He's thinking about the potential of his boys getting stopped. Fuck. The other day he was coming back from Osceola, and the Smokies had a registration checkpoint set up. He got through all right, but they stop his crews, and the jig's up. He's thinking he wouldn't be worried about hypothetical situations if Jinx had called him. Been days since he saw her at the broken bridges. She wasn't all that fuckin' horny then. Figuring, he should give her less pot at any one time. And, he's standing out here in this threadbare yard in front of the old porch, wondering who else she might be fucking. Kinda finds this amusing, but something he needs to know. He's thinking, he can't get silencers for his snipers from any class three dealers. All the fuckin' paperwork going into the feds would be bullshit. Nope. The snipers could go without. Who's going to pay any attention to a lone shot in the woods in the Ozarks anyway? If he knew a good machinist . . . . Doesn't need silencers. What he needs is Jinx. Thinking of going to R4 . . . talk to Jake what's-his-name. He might know how to find her. This is fuckin' Friday and he'll go to R4 tonight. Right now, he's got to feed the dogs.

This could be a long day. Takes a hit or two off an old doober, drinks and listens to the radio while he's got his several maps spread out on the floor of the old house. Figuring patches and plants and his plans for watering and fertilizing. Mostly drinking beer. And, wondering who the hell this Jinx is anyway . . . . Wondering who spotted his crew planting on the Sac River. Decides to identify this asshole by using the boat registration number supplied by Mark . . . his so-called sniper.

Pacing around the disheveled living room of the old house, sucking on a beer, Erik formulates a rough plan for getting the boat registration number into an ID with an address. It goes like this . . . . Get in the truck. Go get a ton of quarters. Locate a pay phone in one of the old pissant subdivisions on Lake of the Ozarks. Use the quarters in the pay phone to call Motor Vehicle Drivers and Marine Licensing in Jefferson City. The pay phone eliminates any danger of a Caller ID or phone trace leading back to him. Pretend to be a volunteer fireman calling in an emergency, to find out who owns the boat with such and such registration number. You know, give 'em some bullshit story about a fire on the boat docks at the marina, about a cable-lock on the boat, and how the boat is going to explode unless 'we' get it moved . . . . Give'm the good ole boy twang, etc., etc., etc. Then, if he's lucky enough to get this restricted information (boat owner's name, address and phone number), get the hell out of that immediate area. If the address is rural, some box number or route number, go to another pay phone and call the postmaster, postmistress or what-the-fuck, and find out where on the ground that address actually is. Then, he can deal with this asshole, Starr family style . . . . In somewhat of a nervous twit, Erik guns his truck off the OMP, carrying cash for quarters . . . .

It works like a dream, due largely to pure luck. The dicey part of the plan, getting Motor Vehicle Drivers and Marine Licensing to give up the name and address associated with this boat registration number, only works because the government employee in Jefferson City was new and feared for what might happen (and her liability) consequent to a large explosion in a marina with gas and diesel storage tanks . . . . By the end of the day, Erik not only has Catcher Riley's name, but he also knows where he is located. Out in the county, east of Cross Timbers . . . . Not bad for a fornicating, out of state transplant with a large scale dope growing operation and a penchant for tax evasion . . . . Face it. He can work with just about anybody, even the fucking government.

Erik's back on the OMP before the crews come in, discharging the leftover quarters into an empty coffee can . . . . Can't wait to pay this turkey, Catcher Riley, an 'after hours' visit.

The crews come in after dark. Mark is giving him another map showing the locations of new patches. The rest are refilling the boat motors with gasoline. And, pretty soon, Erik's showering and dressing for his visit to R4.

This trip to R4 seems shorter than before. He gets the truck parked in the parking lot, under a clear moon and a spangle of stars. Kind of looking around. Don't want no fucking Indian sneaking up on him. Hearing the music drifting out of the Octagon. He heads for the door.

Security is there, and waves him into the party. Erik's got a hangover going and goes directly to the bar. Needs to get a few beers going.

The place is crowded, and the rock music is loud and the lights splaying their magic. All this is hurting his head, but he's determined to find Jake and asks the bartender where Jake is in this rock-a-box. The bartender's pointing at a table beside the front door.

Jake's sitting alone, smoking a cigar, and watching Erik weave his way past the dancers towards his table. Damn it. The redheaded hulk is pulling a chair up at his table.

Leaning over so Jake can hear him, "What's happening, Jake?"

Jake gives the appropriate smile, "Doing Friday night, Erik."

"Yeah. I imagine that gets fucking old," looking back over his shoulder at the flashing lights and bobbing dancers.

Jake's leaning back in his chair against the wall, smoking that cigar, and watching Erik. He scans the room looking for security. He sees Tom is watching. Then, he's blowing a smoke ring, watching Erik.

Erik turns back around facing Jake, "Jinx here tonight?"

Just moving his mouth, "No, I don't think she is." Thinking Erik is hyper tense.

"Well, I've got to get a hold of her."

"Good luck," raising his cigar for another draw.

"You have a number for her?"

"I can't give out that kind of info, Erik. This is a private club . . . just like I can't give out any info on you," and Jake's saying this loud, so Erik can hear over the acoustics.

Drains his beer, and sets the can down on the table. He leans over, closer to Jake's face, "Well, I gotta have her number. This is important."

"If I had it Erik, I couldn't give it to you." Jake's leaning back still, holding the cigar down on the edge of the table . . . looks over to see where Tom is. Tom's moving in closer.

"Look Jake, I don't want to argue about it. Give me her number or tell me where she lives. She'll be alright with that," and Erik is studying Jake with a caged intensity.

"Sorry Erik. I can't do that."

"What the fuck you mean you can't do that? I'm not going to tell her you gave it to me."

"Can't do it," and Jake takes another draw off the cigar.

"You sure as hell can fuckin' do it," and Erik is looking real angry.

Tom, the security guard, is moving closer to their table.

Jake smiles towards Erik, "I'll tell her you're looking for her if I see her."

The band is doing a pretty fair rendition of Clarence Carter/ Dr. C.C.'s STROKIN'. The volume is way up, and the crowd is really getting into it.

"Have you ever made love in the back seat of a car . . . I be stroking . . . ."

Erik reaching across the table and grabbing the front of Jake's Guess shirt, "Give me her fuckin' number asshole, or . . ."

Tom moving in from the side and giving Erik a hard pop on the side of his neck. Erik letting go of Jake, and nearly tipping over his chair. As he's raising up to meet Tom, Tom pushing him down in his chair, "Hold it big boy, hold it."

Erik making as to rub his neck, but as Tom is releasing his grip, Erik raising up in an all out assault on Tom.

"I be stroking, that's what I be doing. I stroke it to the east, I stroke it to the west . . ."

Jake's leaning back from the table, but he's staying seated.

Tom going over with Erik's hard assault, but rolling right up on top of Erik, and putting him in a headlock, and he's got Erik where he can't move.

Jake's standing up now, "Get him out of here, Tom."

"You hear that dumb-fuck," Tom's saying.

Erik isn't moving or talking.

Through heavy breathing, Tom's saying, "I'm going to let you up. When I do, you'd better scram. You don't beat it, we're gonna mess you up good."

Another security guard coming up, and a few rockers are watching this . . . most are still dancing to STROKIN.

Tom's panting, "I'm going to let you up now. You be good, and get out quick." Then, Tom's letting loose. He's getting up off Erik, and Erik is just lying there on his side.

Finally, Erik is pushing himself up. He's standing here between the security guards, looking at Jake. Jake's standing behind the table, smoking that cigar.

Erik jabbing his finger towards Jake, nodding his head, not saying a word. Turning to go . . .

"Hey, Erik," Jake loud, so Erik can hear over the din.

Erik pausing, and glaring back.

"You don't come back here for a while. I mean it."

Snarling, "Fuck you." And, Erik leaves.

Jinx is a no-show at R4 this Friday night.

Jake is wondering. Wondering if she's finished at the SHADOWS . . . .

She is. Jinx, a.k.a. Saxony, is. Done for the night. Stripped, danced, collected the cash and blew the joint; homeward bound.

CHAPTER XVIII

Saturday.

The phone rings.

Catcher's wondering. He doesn't get many phone calls.

"Catcher Riley."

"Hello, Mr. Riley. This is Jinx from Warsaw Bank. Your checks are here. You want me to hold them or mail them," lilting, in a honey purr, direct from the square root of feminine sexuality.

"Hi, Jinx . . . . I ought to pick them up. I'm out of counter checks."

"Are you going to come in today?" the thinnest suggestion of recklessness thru the fiber optics.

"What time does the bank close, Jinx?" Catcher's breathing is a little shallow.

"Three on the lobby, but not until six-o-clock at the drive-up." Here's the ball mister, and don't drop it . . .

"I'm in the middle of something at the moment . . . I might make it in before six," ransacking for the option to see her.

"Don't you live east of Cross Timbers?" An oily suggestion, custom cut, Jinx the Lynx.

"Yes, not far from Jordan, if you know where that is," Catcher's got a three click respiratory flat line.

"I could drop them off if you'd like. I live out that way," a juicy golden arrow loosed from Calypso's bow.

"I'd like that," from Truth Summit. And, Catcher is giving directions to Jinx. When he's off the phone, he's taking a close look at his front room.

There's camping gear spread out over the living room floor. It's part of an emerging trend. When he first retired and moved to this Ozark 'ranch,' he set the rustic tri-level house up much as his wife would have done.

Like, the Chippendale Settee, end tables, coffee table, bookshelves, stereo, antique china cabinet, lamps and paintings, situated in a traditional manner. Then, as he's lived here, he's started leaving things around the house in the locations he preferred. So, now, the living room has his boots about, there's a handgun in a sheepskin case on the end table, ball caps, and books and newspapers strewn around. True-life adventure books like Peter Hathaway Capstick's THE AFRICAN ADVENTURERS, Collins' and LaPierre's OR I'LL DRESS YOU IN THE MOURNING and Fernando, Fournier and Aubry's DON FERNANDO. Around the stereo, in the open oak cabinet, there's a pile of CDs. There's a box of bullets on the coffee table for the .45 Colt. The .45 Colt is the same as officers are issued in the army. It's an old friend.

There's a picture of his wife on the lower shelf of the antique china cabinet. Taken in some distant time, a gallery product. She's got a V-neck dress on with her shoulders pointed one way and her face towards the camera. A blonde, very wholesome and attractive looking, with the slightest of smiles. A square shaped face, with shoulder length hair. Looks like the kind of woman that would be behind the proverbial good man.

She's coming, and Catcher's got this camping gear spread all around. He's got a rolled up plastic ground cloth. Rolled up sleeping bag. Several thermos jugs. U.S. Marine-style hunting knife. Pump shotgun and shells. A couple pair of jock shorts and t-shirts, camo cargo pants and socks. Matches inside a waterproof cylinder. Aerial and topographical maps. A can of tick spray. Compass. Machete. English pack frame and . . .

He's ferreted out a Rolling Stones' C.D. and has this on high-rise volume, and he's counting the two beers in his refrigerator. This is a clear shortfall. Needs to crank up the Ram for a beer-run. Yippie o, yippie ki ay A.

Having a beer on the front porch, with his shades on, watching this hawk circling above the barn. Very blue sky mottled with a few cumulus clouds; the hawk circles closer. Then, the Jinx comes rolling up in the '87 Vette.

Inside, the Rolling Stones:

"Yes, you could be mine, tonight and every night, I want to be your knight in shining armor, coming to your emotional rescue, you will be mine, you will be mine, all mine . . ."

She's got the top down, and her 'goldie locks' are mussed, and she has a calibrated stone going. Not that Catcher could tell . . . the calibrated stone.

He's seeing golden threads coming in on a silver blue needle. Coming towards his house . . . towards him. Got those thin strap shoes on, and is a little off balance on the gravel.

"Hey there, Mr. Riley. Nice place you have," looking past him toward the house.

"Want to come in and see it?" Catcher's received his checks and holding her elbow, assisting her across the gravel.

"I'd love to," comes the honey again.

Leaving his can of beer outside, holding the door open for the Lynx, "It's messy."

"Very nice," she's cooing, while he's rolling the Stones to a comfortable volume.

Going through the house like a pleasant draft. Catcher is smelling the hint of her perfume, and noticing she has on zero jewelry. They end up back in the living room with the camping gear.

"Would you like something to drink?"

"Do you have a beer?"

While he's going to the fridge, she's asking about his CDs.

"Put on what you like," from the kitchen.

Handing Jinx a beer to "*Under my thumb, under my thumb . . . .*"

Holding the beer up, "To the Rolling Stones and rock n roll," she's toasting, smiling.

Catcher is smiling. "Why not," tipping his can towards her.

She's looking at his wife's picture.

"Is this your ex-wife?"

"She died."

"Uh-oh. I'm sorry," Jinx withdrawing from the photo. "How long have you lived here?"

"Under a year."

Jinx is bobbing her head and shoulders slightly and tapping her foot to the Stones. "Didn't figure you for a Rolling Stones man."

"What did you figure," Catcher's grinning at her, and she's still keeping beat to the Stones.

Tilting her head to the side, smiling back, "Maybe ABBA."

"I've got them too. If you have the time, we'll play it next."

"I've got the time."

"I'll get us another beer."

She's raised her voice to reach him in the kitchen, "Alright if I take my shoes off?"

"Throw 'em over by the pack rack," Catcher bringing back the beer. "How long can you stay?"

"Till you run me off," tossing her shoes over towards the pack rack.

"That won't happen," handing her a beer. "Where do you live, Jinx?"

"In a little place on the Little Niangua River east of here . . . . What's the camping gear for?"

"I was going camping."

"Why?"

"Two-fold," Catcher says.

"Yes?"

"I spent a lot of time outdoors the early years in the army. I like it. And, there's a remote area I wanted to check out," staring at her. He's confounded how this beautiful creature is here.

"What kind of remote area?" the Jinx says, still keeping beat with the Stones.

"A place over by the Sac River. West of Osceola. I was going up the river a while back, and some guy on shore pointed a rifle at me." Watching to see how she receives this.

"I know the area. Lots of stuff goes on on the river. You mean you're looking for him?" She's still got the beat.

"Maybe. He and some guys with him were up to something. Didn't want me around. It would be a pretty place to camp out; maybe look around. Where there's smoke, there's fire. Never know . . ."

"What'd you do if you found them?" She's grinning in his face, keeping the beat.

Draining his can, "Oh, I thought at least to give them the finger," teasingly.

"Some of those river rats'll shoot you," moving harder to the Stones. Still smiling, "Can I have another beer?"

"On the way," Catcher taking the empties back toward the kitchen.

"Can I turn the lights on?" Jinx raising her voice to him.

"Go ahead."

She's turning the volume up on the music. Catcher coming out with the beers. She's taking these out of his hands, putting them on a newspaper on the coffee table.

She's poking him in the stomach with the tips of her fingers, and starts dancing in front of him. Staring at him with an impish grin.

"C'mon, Mr. Riley."

"Catcher."

"C'mon, Catcher."

He's smiling, but he's not moving.

"You snooze, you lose," and dancing more *for* him now than *with* him.

Catcher's tossing the beer back.

Jinx is letting go, and she's squinting, dancing up to Catcher.

" . . . *been sleeping all alone . . . cause I miss . . . I been . . .*" the head Stone is saying, " . . . *waiting at home . . . what's the matter man . . . walkin in Central Park . . . shuffling through the street . . . what's the matter with you boy . . .*"

"Can I use your bathroom, Catcher?"

"It's at the top of the stairs."

Getting her purse and going upstairs, and Catcher's going towards the bookshelf. Removing the framed photo of his wife from the shelf, and carrying it upstairs into his bedroom. Setting it atop the bedside table on the far side of his bed. "Sweet sleep," he murmurs.

Jinx turns on the exhaust fan and fishes a doober out of her purse. While she's peeing, she's smoking steamroller weight ganja. Leaving the fan on and spraying perfume around.

Catcher's back in the living room.

Now, the Jinx is back.

"Does your family live around here, Jinx?"

"I have a sister. She lives in Oklahoma City," sucking her beer. "I was born and raised in a little community in Saint Clair County."

"You go to college?"

"No. Had the grades for it. Didn't go. I've read every book on the Harvard reading list. R-e-a-l-l-y read them," finishing her beer.

Catcher's bringing more beer, "How long have you been at the bank?"

"Seven years. I'm head teller. At the highest wage the bank pays," moving to the music again. "Where are you from?"

"I was born and raised in Champaign, Illinois."

The Stones are doing a slow one, and Jinx is pulling Catcher in to dance. Her hair has a strawberry smell, and the perfume is like an opium.

He is getting into this. Jinx is really close, and she can feel him responding.

"*C'mon baby dry your eyes . . . ain't it good to be alive . . .*"

"You turn me on," she whispers.

"You, me too," Catcher, barely audible.

She's pressing tight to his front side, weaving together with the Stones. It's dark now.

The Stones are done with this one and Jinx is leaning back, "Are you hungry, Catcher?"

"Not really. I'd rather have a beer."

"And dance," laughing, already shaking to the Stones' next rocker.

"And dance," he repeats.

"This is new for you?" Jinx asks as she's wagging to the music.

"Yes. You could even say strange," picking up the cans and heading for the kitchen.

They're back drinking on the settee.

"How long has it been since you've been with a woman, Catcher?"

"A long time."

"Do you like me?" the Jinx says.

"Yes," Catcher replies plainly.

"I can make it good for you," seriously to him.

Catcher, "Probably."

"You want, I'll go all out . . . . You want?"

"You're scaring me," holding his hands up.

"You want both barrels!"

"I'm strapped in."

"You have a t-shirt I could wear?"

"Yes," Catcher getting up . . . . When he comes back, he's got a black, cotton t-shirt, and hands this to her.

"Why don't you get your boots and socks off. Take your belt off and pull this shirt out," as she tugs on his t-shirt.

While Catcher is doing this, Jinx takes her pants suit, panty hose and bra off, and pulls the t-shirt over her head.

Catcher is finishing another beer, "How 'bout a brew?"

"Sure," going over to replay the Rolling Stones.

She's still at the stereo when Catcher gets back with the beers. He sets hers on the coffee table and sits back on the settee, really seeing her legs. For a second, wonders if this is real. The Stones are rolling again, and Jinx is swigging from her can of beer.

"Forgive me Catcher, if I let loose? Promise?"

"Promise," smiling. "I'm going to take a pee. I'll be right back." He's not gone long.

She's put Catcher on the settee. She's straddling him. Looking at his eyes while she's doing this. When he's raising his hands to put them on her waist, she lays them back, palms up. "Relax."

Backing off him, and up and roaming around the room, adjusting the lamps. Dim. Pulling the coffee table back into the center of the living room. Throwing the camping gear to the edges of the room. "This is for you, Catcher Riley."

She turns the volume up, "I've never done this before."

So, here's this rustic, modern tri-level home, down in a crease of the Ozark mountains; Vette with top down in the drive; half finished old barn in some trees past the house, with the old Ram parked beside; with a moon just over the eastern ridge, and stars all above, and the Rolling Stones' tunes floating out across the misty meadow and into the timbers.

"*I can't get no . . . satisfaction . . . no, no, no . . .*"

This is pounding out, and Jinx fixing Catcher with a stare. Her right forearm over her face and hand spread over her blonde head, and her left hand gripping the inside of her left crotch under the bottom of the t-shirt. She's barefooted and the t-shirt is all she's wearing. Then she's spinning hard on the toe of her left foot, all the way around . . .

"*Get no . . . satisfaction . . . no, no, no . . .*"

Spreading her legs a little, and weaving her hips back and forth in rhythm to the music . . . .

"*I can't get no satisfaction, I can't get no satisfaction . . .*"

Head down, eyes up on Catcher, hair spilling over her forehead.

Now, both her hands are on her hips, and she's sideways, head turned to Catcher. Moving like a drummer's wrist.

Her hands are up, above her head, tilting her body left and right, back and forth, in front of Catcher, her face always toward him. Dropping her arms. She's got the bottom of her t-shirt knotted up in both hands at her crotch, the insides of her thighs jiggling.

"*Well I've told you once and I've told you twice, but you never listen to my advice . . . this could be the last time . . . maybe the last time, I don't know . . .*"

Swaying her shoulders back and forth to the beat, her head tilting up now, eyes closed.

"*This could be the last time . . . baby the last time, I don't know . . .*"

Her hands are on her hips, and she's locking Catcher in a serious stare, mouth set in a provocative pout. Her wrists are limp, hands hanging with the index fingers pointing downward, and her head and body bobbing.

"*A glass of wine in her hand . . . connection . . . you can't always get what you want . . . But, if you try sometime . . .*"

Her eyes are shut, and she's posing forward now, body weaving like a cobra coming out of a basket with a tick to the beat.

"... *you can't always get what you want* ..."

Hiking her t-shirt up to her crotch again, legs glistening like wet marble....

A sexy woman, dancing like this for a man, privately... melodramatic from a spectator's self-conscious point of view.... On the receiving end, it can 'go down' differently. For Catcher, it does.

The last self-conscious thought Catcher's had was over an hour ago. He thought of his house out here in the semi-wilderness, and it being just her and him. This was personal, and in a very private place.

Jinx stooping to clear off the top of the coffee table, hardly missing a beat.

"I wanna tell ya how it's going to be ... you're going to give your love to me ... I'm going to love you night and day ..."

Her whole body's a shimmy, and she's slowly turning on the table. The t-shirt is wet, and her body is glistening with sweat.

"What a drag it is getting old ... things are different today ..."

She's out of the shimmy, got her index finger up in front of her face, curling it open and shut to Catcher, and now she's laughing out loud. Teasing. Catcher's watching this, then gazing down her body to her feet. Her toenails are pink, like her fingernails.

A slow Stones' is on now, and Jinx is stepping down off the table. Pulling Catcher up to dance. Goodbye Mission Control...

After this dance, she goes to the bathroom, coming back down and clinking beer cans with Catcher on the settee. Leaning over and kissing him on the neck. "How about some slow music?" He puts this on and turns the volume down. Turns the lamp further down.

Somewhere in this time, the 'no beginning and no end time,' Catcher spreads his sleeping bag out. And, this is where they lay. During the wee morning hours, Jinx puts ABBA in and this replays till dawn.

Finally, Catcher falls to sleep.

As Jinx is getting dressed, a star catches her eye. A silver star about the size of a quarter. It is inset in black velvet, under glass, in a large wooden frame with a gold strip routed around the edge. The frame is about one foot wide and two feet tall, and is leaning against the wall next to the china cabinet. She gets closer to see. The Silver Star is centered at the top. Below the star is a burgundy scroll pressed against the black velvet backing. She squats down so she can see this better while buttoning her suit jacket. Written in gold ink on the burgundy parchment paper:

CITATION
THE ARMY SILVER STAR MEDAL
is awarded to
CAPTAIN CATCHER P. RILEY
For Valor

Half a league, half a league
Half a league onward,
All in the valley of Death
Rode the six hundred
"Forward, the Light Brigade!
Charge the guns!," he said:
Into the valley of death
Rode the six hundred.

Forward, the Light Brigade!"
Was there a man dismayed?
Not tho' the soldiers knew
Someone had blundered:
Theirs not to make reply,
Theirs not to reason why,
Theirs but to do and die:
Into the valley of death
Rode the six hundred.

Cannon to the right of them,
Cannon to the left of them,
Cannon in front of them
Volleyed and thunder'd;
Storm'd at with shot and shell,
Boldly they rode and well,
Into the jaws of Death,
Into the mouth of Hell,
Rode the six hundred.

Flashed all their sabers bare,
Flashed as they turned in air,
Sab'ring the gunners there,
Charging an army, while
All the world wondered:
Plunged in the battery smoke,
Right through the line they broke;
Cossack and Russian
Reeled from the saber-stroke
Shattered and sundered.
Then they rode back, but not—
Not the six hundred.

Cannon to the right of them,
Cannon to the left of them,
Cannon behind them
Volleyed and thundered;
Stormed at with shot and shell,
While horse and hero fell,
They had fought so well
Came thro' the jaws of Death,
Back from the mouth of Hell,
All that was left of them,
Left of six hundred.

When can their glory fade?
Oh, the wild charge they made!
All the world wondered.
Honor the charge they made!
Honor the Light Brigade,
Noble Six Hundred

Charge of the Light Brigade By Alfred Tennyson (First Baron)

Stuck into the corner of the frame is an old black and white photo of three men in recon hats, dark t-shirts and camo pants, all heavily armed. Appears to have been taken in a jungle. She's guessing, the one in sunglasses is Catcher.

Jinx stands up in the pallid light, and looks over at Catcher asleep on the floor. She collects her purse and keys, leaving out the front door.

The sun's early tentacles are yellowing the eastern walls of distant cumulus clouds. Some birds are chirping. Jinx sees a vulture high in the eastern sky. The sun hasn't yet crested. She lights up a doober, swings her Vette around, and goes out the gravel driveway.

CHAPTER XIX

Sunday is like any other day on the OMP, between March and October. Erik's business is time intensive, like 24-7, from March through October. From planting through harvest. The pleasant side of this is four months off, November through February, with good size pocket money. This is when exotic travel becomes a topic of conversation, along with the topics of drugs, guns, sex and trucks. If you're the gardener, course, you're shorted on the four 'off' months, as you have seeds to turn into starts, in the cave.

The OMP is at the beginning of the work cycle (planting), not the end (harvest), and Erik's trying to keep the big picture in mind this morning. The boys have finished planting and they're sleeping-in, permission granted per se Erik Starr. But, he's not sleeping-in. He's got a feather up his ass. His neck hurts from the R4 eviction Friday night, he still hasn't heard from Jinx, he's got to get his irrigation plan operational, and his in-grown toenail hurts like a bitch. This latter, he's working on as he thinks, out on the front porch where the morning light is good. He's sitting in a chair out here, with his bare foot up on an opposite chair, with his open pocketknife. Got some open alcohol here too. He's fired the knife blade to get it sterile, and he's prying the point of the blade under his big toe nail, from the inside. Carefully attempting to pull the nail out of the overgrown skin and tissue. Hurts like a bitch. Fucking pointed-toe cowboy boots cause this, he's thinking, and the knifepoint pops up without the nail. Back in he digs, trying to push the point into the quick, underneath the nail. Now, he's got it. The edge of the nail comes out and breaks, but not loose. He's having to tear this broken portion of his nail off, pulling it loose from the quick. Finished, he's dousing the toe with alcohol.

Thinking, he's got to get a pump that will draw water out of the river and discharge out a hose for watering the plants. These pumps can't be electrical and they can't be manual, and Erik's no technological wizard, so he's going to have to go shopping around. Then, when he finds the pump, he can only get one pump per retailer. Like, you go in and buy a bunch of these pumps, someone could get suspicious. So, he's going to have to drive all around Springfield, buying a single pump at each stop. As soon as he determines what type of pump it is he needs. He's pouring more alcohol on the toe. Hears the guineas making the African sound, and some crows behind the house. The eastern sunlight is coming across the OMP like the dawning of a new age. How's that for P.M.A. (Positive Mental Attitude). Douses the toe with more alcohol. Fucking A. The dawning of a new age. The pumps will probably work off gasoline engines. Noisy. Not good. Probably can't be helped. Last year was a lot easier. Did it with buckets. But, last year, they didn't plant any three thousand plants either.

This is a unique situation. Three thousand fucking plants. Erik's pulling his boot back on. And, his neck hurts doing this. Fucking R4 will get theirs! And, where the fuck is Jinx? This is the day to fuck her. He's standing up, and his toe hurts in the boot, but he can tell he got the ingrown nail out. A day or two, his toe will be good as new.

The guineas are still squalling. The dogs are laying around the porch, and out ahead, he can see some cattle on the lane. Big fucking cattle rancher. That's him. He fishes a doober out of his t-shirt pocket. Lights it. Takes a couple of hits and flicks the ash off the end of the joint with the tip of his left-hand index finger. She'll be calling. Got her hooked good on the Sinsemilla. She's going to need his Ozark Gold. Also, he's got the crotch rocket. She'll need some more of this. He's figuring, she'll call.

Erik is sitting in the living room, laying it out for the gang. There's eight of these guys now; Boomer, Bugs, Mark, Swede, Sarge, Jack, Trace and Steve. Of late, a few men went back to Pontiac and a few more came down. All in all, Erik's thinking a pretty good bunch. Ex-military rednecks, black sheep hippies and one loser.

Bugs. Erik doesn't like Bugs. Figures he may have to spray him with 'Kills-On-Contact' Raid. Exterminate him. He's the weak link. Yeah. You get busted or something, you can't have a guy that will talk. Worst-case scenario: they'd have to stonewall the Jar Head government estabulary. Got to hang together, then . . . or hang separately. Erik's thinking Bugs is a snitch waiting to happen. A loser.

"We're basically doing water patrol and guard duty the next few weeks," Sarge says before taking another swig of beer.

"You got it," Erik just sitting here.

"We gonna set-up our own shifts, or you doing that, Erik?" Mark wants to know.

"You guys do it, then tell me," says Erik. "For now, I want guards on half the patches every other day . . . for now."

"We'll take the boats out before first light and move the guards around, then pick 'em up after dark," Swede says.

"All the guards need to stay hidden. Take your water and lunch and rifle or shotgun," Sarge says, throwing his empty at an already full trash can.

"You want us to shoot someone if they gets into the patch?" Boomer looking at Erik. He's been toking and nearly stoned.

"That's what you got your firearm for, Boomer. Fuckin' A. I want everyone that stumbles on a patch killed. And, the body hidden the way I told you." Erik shifts in his chair, scanning the group with a pointed finger, "This does not include the law. If you're a guard, and you see the law find a patch, you should skedaddle. Get down on the riverbank away from there. If you don't show up for the boat pickup, we'll pick you up the next day."

Erik gets up, heading to the fridge for a beer, "Don't be shooting anybody unless you know they've identified our patch. Just cause some fucking guy is hiking or fishing near a patch, doesn't mean he's found it."

"Don't get caught out there," Sarge adds. "We don't pick you up, you ditch your rifle and make your way back here."

Erik's sucked a long drink off his beer, "Look. We shouldn't have any trouble right now. The plants are small."

"The reason we're patrollin' and guardin' is to make sure nobody has discovered us, isn't that right," Mark is asking Sarge.

Sarge, getting up for another beer, "Affirmative. And, for general intelligence. Maybe the river gets-up and washes some plants out, or something. We ought to know this."

"What about rigging booby traps around the patches," Boomer's asking Erik.

"Not this early . . . if ever," Erik says, finishing his beer, standing by the fridge.

"We're just keeping an eye on things," says Jack.

"Like riding herd," says Trace. He's smoking a doober.

Erik pulls another beer out of the fridge and limps back to his chair, "Yeah. We're ridin' the fuckin' herd, Trace."

Sarge looking at Erik, "I know what to do, Erik. How about me and the crew load up and take a boat ride up the river? Before it gets dark.

Sorta double check the patch locations, then in the morning start the patrolling?"

"You guys get to it. Don't fucking run out of gas out there. Take plenty of gas, and don't get stupid. No fucking around in the boats or speeding bullshit." Erik's up out of his chair signaling the meeting is over.

Some are going outside, and some going upstairs for personal items. Bugs comes up to Erik. He's wearing a black t-shirt with a big green marijuana leaf screen-printed on the front.

"What do you want?" Erik's eyes narrow and the hinge area of his jaw is oscillating under the skin.

"Erik, I was wondering if we're ever going to have time-off to go into a town. Sometime," and Bugs looks nervous.

"Not you, Bugs. You're mine till harvest is done. Then, I'll pay you, and you can beat it." Erik has his beer can in one hand and the other on his hip. "And, what the fuck you wearing a marijuana t-shirt off the ranch for? You advertising or what?"

"I'll get rid of it, Erik," and Bugs heads upstairs.

Bugs is fucking stupid, Erik's thinking. I'm going to kill him someday.

Erik's sitting out on the porch drinking another beer. Crews are gone. The dogs are gone. Hunting or something. He knows he should've gone with them. Taken the maps and oriented himself from the river to the location of each patch. That fuckin' bitch still hasn't called, he's thinking. He doesn't want to miss her call. He's got the patches marked on his maps. Still, he should fuckin' check them out. That fucking bitch. She's why his neck hurts. And, the cowboy boots are why his toe hurts. He's never giving up his cowboy boots.

The phone rings. It's fucking six o'clock.

"OMP," he says into the phone.

"Miss me?" she says.

"Hell yes, I've missed you. Where are you?"

"I'm on a phone talking to you."

"Why don't you meet me somewhere?"

"That works for me."

"Where?"

"There's a cabin boarded up on blacktop M, on the east side of the road, about four miles south of seven highway."

"Wait a minute, Jinx. Wait a minute. What county?"

"In Camden county."

"What's the cabin look like?"

"It's a log cabin. All the windows are boarded up. A dirt road runs behind the cabin to an old barn."

"Are we trespassing?"

"I know the owner. He's out of state right now."

"What time?"

"Eight."

"Eight o'clock. OK. I'll be there."

"I'll park behind the cabin," like she's making a promise.

"I'll find you."

"I can't stay out too late."

"Why not?"

"Cause I said so."

"OK. OK. I'll see you at eight o'clock."

"Answer my question . . . again."

"What question?"

"Have you missed me?"

"Well, fuck. Let me see . . . . Yeah, I've missed you."

CHAPTER XX

Sunday, mid-morning, Catcher is waking up wrapped in the sleeping bag on his living room floor. He doesn't get up immediately. He has no headache and is engulfed in a pleasantness he is reluctant to give up. Studying the sun streaming through the living room windows and listening to the birds outside. He's naked and can see his clothes scattered around on the floor. Vaguely remembers Jinx closing the door when she left earlier.

He's laying back on the floor looking up at the ceiling. His sense is that he's undergone an epiphany; that the iceberg locked inside has surfaced. The rebel sentiment, the super storm broiling within, has materialized into a strong spring breeze.

He's up; starting for his clothes, then changes direction, goes to his front door and opens it. He steps out into the sun on the front porch. Naked. Like, hello world, this is Catcher Riley, without forty-four years of social conditioning. A powerful, self-possessed energy pack, bred straight out of the original protozoa. So many mental tumblers are moving; Catcher's not sure where to start this first day of the rest of his life.

He is back in the house; shaved, showered, dressed and picking up the living room. Thinking of Jinx, and her supernatural magnetism . . . an agency of Pan, or the Philistines. An angelic Calypso postmarked the Ozarks. A virtual Venus. Yep . . . unleashed.

Straightening up the living room and looking around to see if she left a note. Hoping for a phone number, but finds none. Still slightly unbalanced, from this epiphany thing. It's as if he's become a nomad . . . in his own home . . . an outsider enjoying a host's hospitality. No ownership responsibility. Before, he imagined the dissolution of his old self would leave a wasteland or desert. Instead, it's as if he's a nomad. Grounded in the desert, maybe bonded to the desert. A part of its freedom. Like a Bedouin tribal chief.

He's up in his bedroom seeing his wife's photograph. Laying this inside his steamer trunk with his folded dress blues and metals and military bric-a-brac. "A quarter century together . . . you, me, the army and the mainstream mentality," and he gently closes the lid.

Returning to the living room, doing a mental synopsis of the lovemaking. Notes, she had the condom, and he used it and put it in the trash. Wondered what it would be like without a condom. If they were a couple.

Bam, bam, bam! Marco is pounding on the front door, "You in there, Colonel? . . . Hello?"

Opening the door, "Marco, what's happening?" The sun heat hits Catcher, and is radiating off the door.

"Hi, Colonel. Can I work on the barn today? I thought you might be in church, but I saw the Ram . . ."

"I missed church today, Marco."

"Yes sir. I can see that. What do you say? Work or no work," and Marco's sticking his hands in the pockets of his bib overalls. Got a t-shirt on underneath, and black high-top tennis shoes. Catcher doubts he's wearing any socks.

"We'll work, Marco. I'll meet you at the barn."

Marco is turning to go down the steps; already has beads of perspiration glistening below his bushy hairline. "Saw Hattie out on the road . . . said she might see you at church."

"No. Not today, Marco. I'll see you at the barn," and Catcher closes the door.

Marco's sitting on a stump in the shade when Catcher gets to the barn.

"What do you think Marco, we going to hang some boards or not?"

"I dunno, Colonel. I was just sitting here wondering why the old barn's back here and the new house is up by the road," he's got his arms across his front with his hands in his armpits.

"I think the old home place was over there," and Catcher's pointing to a clump of thorn trees around some stones.

"Hey, I've got an idea, Colonel. Instead of doin' the boards, let's look around the old homestead," and Marco is getting to his feet.

"We need a chainsaw to get the locust trees out of the way. I've got that," Catcher's eyeing the thorn trees.

"If you'll get the chainsaw, I'll get my metal detector." Marco's pointing back towards the Suzuki.

They're down by the old foundation with the chainsaw and metal detector. Catcher's cutting the trees down and Marco's pulling them back in a pile of sorts. He's dodging thorns and trying to get the limbs to lay on top one another. Catcher and Marco are both sweating and go back to sit in the shade by the barn.

"I tell you Colonel about that young pilot that's going to fly his helicopter through the center of the Earth?"

"No, Marco. You didn't."

"It was on talk radio last night. This young guy was on the show, and says they've found a huge hole in the arctic. I guess it's the general consensus of the scientific community that this hole goes clear through the Earth and comes out the other side," and Marco's sitting down with his wrists resting on his upstanding knees.

"You want some water, Marco," and Catcher's heading towards the house.

"I do, I do Colonel."

Catcher gets back with two thermoses of ice water. After their drinks, Marco is back to his story.

"You know about this hole, Colonel. They dropped a microphone seven miles down into the hole and recorded traffic sounds and people talking some queer language. Every once in a while, someone was screaming."

"What?"

"Screaming. But, the pilot says he's taking his helicopter in."

"I wonder which way he'll go in—prop up or prop down?" Catcher smiling.

Marco shrugs and shakes his head, "Dunno. Pilot says he can do it no sweat. He's going to attempt it as soon as he's off his medicine."

"What medicine?"

"I guess he's been mistakenly diagnosed as a schizophrenic, and he's trying to straighten this out before he leaves . . . you know Colonel, if you're a far sighted missionary, people think you're crazy."

"Well, if this is the only problem he's got, he should be OK," lifting his thermos with both hands to drink again, so Marco can't see him chuckling.

"It isn't. He's also partially blind," Marco's shaking his head and looking down at the ground. "He says this won't make any difference, cause once you get down in the hole, no one could see . . ."

Catcher's laughing out loud . . . getting up. "C'mon Marco. If a blind crazy man can fly his helicopter through the center of the Earth, we can clear thorn trees."

"It's more than just flying through the center of the Earth," and Marco is getting to his feet. "There's whole civilizations down there. Very dangerous to cross through I think. He won't know the lang . . ."

Catcher's started the chainsaw. Not long, and Marco is pulling thorn trees away from the old foundation. About an hour later, the foundation is quite apparent and very accessible.

Marco has his metal detector on and he's scanning the area. Looks like Pooh Bear with a hockey stick.

A few spoons and old pennies later, Marco gets excited. "I'm showing silver about one foot deep!" His machine's giving off that high pitch static.

Catcher puts down his thermos and starts digging, with Marco standing off to the side. Using a shovel, then picking at the dirt and rock with an old hunting knife. Pulls up a clod. Marco scans the clod and the static jumps.

"That's it. That's it."

Catcher's pouring water from the thermos over the clod, and using his thumb to break the clod up. When he's finished rinsing the dirt away, there's a silver pendant with two fish intertwined. About one inch long. Marco has it now, and he's holding it in the afternoon sun, up close to his face, really scrutinizing it.

"It's some kind of charm I think."

"Two sharks isn't it," Catcher offers from the side.

"They're not the same," Marco says, turning the piece around. "Look at the nose on this one, then look at this one. And look at the two different tails."

"This one's a shark," Catcher's pointing at one. "This other one looks more like a dolphin."

"Strange," Marco murmurs. "Yeah. One's got the bottlenose and smaller tail fins . . . must be a dolphin. But, look at the fin, nose and big tail fins on this one . . . and it's a lot longer. It's definitely a shark."

"The Ozarks is a strange home for this," Catcher shaking his head.

"Here you are, Colonel. A good luck silver piece from long ago," and Marco drops it in Catcher's hand.

"We done for the day, Marco?" Catcher smiling bemusedly.

"I need ten dollars, if you got it, Colonel," and Marco is facing Catcher, with a thin film of sweat covering his face.

Catcher giving him a twenty as they walk back up to the Suzuki, carrying the chainsaw and metal detector.

"You know Colonel, there's a guy in Switzerland who's been abducted more times than he can remember. He's starting to share his stories with us now. And, the aliens have been giving him warnings to pass on to the world . . ."

"Yes, Marco. I didn't know."

"Well, I've been staying up listening to the interviews. This old guy says beware of a dark stranger coming bearing gifts. And . . ."

"Marco."

"And, if we don't listen to his message, the world is going to have a cataclysmic upheaval and wars with terrible casualties."

"Marco."

"Now wait a minute, Colonel. They've got an alien in Area 51, and he's saying the same thing. He's the survivor from the Roswell incident . . ."

"Marco. Hold it. Stop. I know this is important, but we'll talk about it the next time. OK?"

"You got it, Colonel." Marco is starting the Suzuki.

"You see anymore of the Jinx girl?"

"You know, Colonel, I haven't. Wish I did though. She's beautiful. If I had a different body, I'd take her on an expedition to find Atlantis. We'd . . ."

"You don't know anything about her?"

"Yes I do . . . She's from around here. Country girl. Drives that Vette and works in Warsaw."

"Where's she live?"

"Down the river from Camp White Cloud, I think. From where I live. I dunno exactly where." He's revving the Suzuki up and trying to slide his seat back for more stomach room, but it's already back. "Got to boogie, Colonel. Got my alien interview tapes I have to listen to," as he's starting to back up. "I'll be back in a few days."

Catcher has showered and watched the news. It's night, and he's got the shark/dolphin pendant out on the kitchen table, cleaning it with an old toothbrush and baking soda. Listening to the radio . . . . Discovering an engraving to the front of the shark's tail fin. TAHITI. He's got a box of old jewelry pieces and chains on the kitchen table. Eventually fashioning a necklace with a sterling silver chain that barely slips over the head. "Outside Cross Timbers, Missouri—A little bit of Tahiti," he says out loud. Absentmindedly carries it outside.

He is looking at the stars from the front porch. Admiring the old 4X4 Ram down at the barn. Walks down and checks to see if his windows are up. While he's here, he opens the door and gets in behind the steering wheel. Thinking about going somewhere, maybe Tahiti! Still holding the pendant. Hangs this over his rearview mirror and gets out. He's standing here, studying the night sky. 'Forty-four years old is not too old. You are never too old to fall in love.' There's a falling star. He thinks of Jinx. Wondering if . . . wishing . . . maybe the two of them . . . . Going back towards the house, he's surprised at himself. He's never been a dreamer before. How does the ode go?

We are the music makers,
And we are the dreamers of dreams,
Wandering by lone sea breakers,
And sitting by desolate streams
World losers and world forsakers
Upon whom the pale moon gleams;
Yet we are the movers
And shakers of the world forever.

CHAPTER XXI

As usual, Erik is waiting for Jinx. He's found the boarded-up cabin, and pulled around behind. Sitting here in the shadow of the cabin, looking east down a long flat valley between timbered ridges. He can see the dirt road leaving here and twisting out across the fescue meadow to a distant, faded, wood barn with a steep metal roof. He's turned the radio off and sitting here thinking about Jinx. She's a looker, but he doesn't know much else. She drives an old Vette, is a great piece of ass and a full-fledged stoner. Well, she's an independent cuss, too. He's smoking a little doob, watching the sky getting dark, and listening to the meadowlarks, and dreaming of possessing Jinx.

Now, he's hearing a car coming down the blacktop. It goes by. He's alright though. Cool. Except for his toe. It's hot and it hurts. And, his neck still hurts. There's another car coming down the blacktop. This time it's pulling-in. He's thinking it's a little cooler tonight. He and Jinx need to get to know each other better. Maybe they could sleep together at her house or fuck all day and night. She's coming around the cabin in her silver blue Vette. She's got the top up tonight.

Out of the truck, standing here waiting for Jinx. She's getting out of the Vette. In her Wranglers and boots, and has a sweatshirt on. Coming towards him, smiling, "Long time no see," soft and sweet.

"Whose fault is that," and Erik gives her a one-arm hug.

"What's that about?"

"The hug?"

"Yeah, I thought you'd be pulling my pants down."

"I missed you," and Erik's grinning down at her, still has his arm around her.

"Above the waist or below?"

"Ouch. You're fucking with me."

"Not yet . . . you've got goose bumps."

"It's chilly tonight."

"You have a jacket?"

"No . . . I've got the blanket. We going to drive out to that barn?"

"Let's walk."

"Too cold, Jinx."

"Get the blanket. Wrap it around your shoulders."

He's going over to the truck, getting the blanket, opening it up some, and draping it over his shoulders. Now, he's limping back to Jinx. Holds his hand up, "How! I'm Chief Big Dick."

"Why are you limping?"

"No big deal. Worked on an ingrown toenail."

"Feel like walking to the barn," amused at Erik's softer demeanor.

"Yeah. Let's go."

"Got some doobers?"

"Sure do."

Taking off down the old road, heading for the barn. He's limping, holding this blanket over his shoulders, and she's walking along with her hands shoved in her front pockets. Something about the encroaching darkness makes her blonde hair like it was just rinsed with lightener. Erik's noticed the little bags under her eyes, and finds them sexy. Look sexy at twenty-five and old at fifty. She's twenty-five. Erik finding her hot as ever, but something has tempered his desire. Maybe the experience at R4; his neck; his toe; or the realization of responsibility at the OMP. Or, the lapse of time since he's seen her last. Or the beer and doobers this day. Maybe, a combination of the above.

"Where do you live, Jinx," shuffling along between the fescue clumps holding this blanket together in front.

The whippoorwills are communicating out in the darkening meadow, and the stars forming a great dome overhead.

"Why do you want to know?"

"I'd like to visit you."

"Well, I don't want any visitors."

He laughs, "You're so hard."

"Yeah. You're not."

"I've got a soft side."

"It isn't below the waist."

"That's because I love you," Erik's got a tight-lipped smile.

"What the . . . what's wrong with you? You eat some catnip or something? All you want to do is fuck me," and Jinx is looking up at the stars, still has her hands jammed in her pockets.

"Maybe we got off on the wrong start."

"Yeah right, what other kind is there?"

Neither says anything for some seconds.

"I ran away from home at fifteen," he's saying.

"What do you do now? For a living?"

"I'm a cattle rancher."

"Yes. And what else?"

"I sell grass . . . . What do you do for a living?"

"None of your business."

"How are we going to progress if this is how you are?"

"We aren't."

"Jinx."

"I'm a dancer."

"A dancer? . . . You mean a stripper?" Erik laughing. "That figures. No wonder you give the Blue Ribbon Pump Job. I love it."

"Really."

"Yeah. Really."

"I do a little hooking on the side. How do you like that?"

Erik laughing loudly. It carries across the meadow, and echoes off the ridges. "A match made in hell. I love it. A whore and a dealer."

"You think it's funny?" Jinx is walking along looking outward at the stars.

"I think we're two peas in a pod . . . you pay taxes?"

"What?"

"You pay taxes?"

"Why? . . . I pay some on the dancing."

"That's a bitch."

"What?"

"Paying taxes. The fucking government reaching out to the dispossessed."

"What are you talking about?"

"The fucking government. They've never done a thing for me. A collection of parasites living off the misery of their neighbors. Jar Head parasites, holding people up at the end of a barrel . . ."

"What are you on this for?"

"Think about it. The fucking government would put me in prison if they caught me meeting demand with supply. And, on top of this, taxing the proceeds from a stripper."

"You sound like an outsider. You're an outlaw, Erik."

"You fuckin' bet I am," Erik says. "What do you think you are? Joan of Arc?"

"Take it easy big guy."

"I'll take it anyway I can get it. What's all the secrecy about?"

"Secrecy?"

"Yeah. I've got no phone number and no address. Where do you dance?"

"In my line of work, it pays to be private."

"Mine too! But, we've got a personal thing going."

"You stickin' your dick in me and handing me an ounce of dope?"

"Yes, that's fucking personal. Fuck, I've missed you."

"You and the one-eyed snake."

"No, really. I've missed you. You're not getting it."

"Getting what?"

"You and me. We're alike."

They're at the barn now, and Erik's limping around, looking for a place to sit.

"You date anybody else?" Pushing an old railroad tie flush up against the barn.

"I just told you I'm a hooker."

"I don't mean that. That's your business. I mean personally?"

Jinx has her hands out of her pockets, and turning around to sit against the barn.

"Where's my doober?"

"Right here," handing her one and lighting it.

"Maybe. Maybe there is someone."

"You love somebody else?"

"Love? You are really funny tonight. What'd you do to your toe?"

"You love someone else?" Erik's doing a doober.

"Look guy. I date who I want. End of story."

"Who?" Erik's having a toke, looking up at the stars.

"I'm dating a colonel in the army."

"You're what? Dating a fuckin' colonel in the army? Get serious. What base is he from . . . the Yellow Ribbon Little Niangua Fort in up-fucking Ozarks?" Erik's looking over at her.

"I'm serious," Jinx says, looking ahead.

"Well, I'll be damned. Jar Head deluxe. A fucking army officer. You've got to be kidding."

"I'm not."

"Well, then, you've got some serious fucking problem. You must be out of your mind."

"Why's that?"

"Where you from? Fucking nowheresville . . . a whore in the backwoods. A major stoner. You've got as much in common with an army officer as I've got with Laura fucking Bush."

"You'll be laughing out your ass when I marry him," Jinx's voice is languorous. Taking a final hit on her disappearing doober.

"No. I won't be laughing out my ass. I'll be pleased you scored a Jar Head. Then, I'll kill him, and we'll take the insurance money . . . . A fucking officer," shaking his head.

"You that hard-up for money?"

"No. I am not. I make more in a year than that fucking parasite makes in twenty. I could kill him to make a point."

"What point?"

"I'll tell you what the point is. He's . . . look Jinx. I know what I am. You don't get anybody else, better or worse. I'm the fucking man. Get it? I'm not going to share you . . . . Fuck . . . . I'm the one that loves you. You can engrave that on your little druggy heart. Forever . . . . I'm not going to talk about love or anymore touchy-feely stuff again. Not until we're together . . . . But, this is the point . . . . Until we're together, this thing with the army guy is about dowry. You can marry him, so I can kill him for the insurance money . . . . This money is your dowry . . . . You've got to be kidding about this guy?"

"I'm not kidding."

"Well, I'd like to know how the hell you think that could ever work. Look here . . . look at me."

She's getting stoned, but she floats her head to the right to see his face. He gets his face in hers.

"I know I'm right on this. You and I are peas in a pod. I'm your male counterpart. We're soul mates . . . . If it's true, you dating an officer, you should marry the ignorant dumbfuck and I'll kill him. I'm serious. I don't need the insurance money. That money would be your dowry. Payback from the government."

"I just saw a falling star," languidly.

"What's his name? This colonel's name?"

"I'm not telling you that!"

"You get married to a fuckin' Jar Head, you're good as in prison. You'll see. No more Sinsemilla . . . no more sport fucking . . ."

"I need some more dope."

"I brought some sweetheart. It's back in the truck."

She's trying to get up, "Let's go back. I'm cold."

He's getting up, pulling her up too. Puts his blanket over her shoulders. The two of them walking back towards their vehicles. Jinx is shivering and Erik is limping and shivering.

At the truck, Jinx is standing here, waiting for the baggy. Erik pulling back out of the cab and handing her the dope. She's trying to pull the blanket off.

"Keep the blanket. You can give it to me next time. By the way, that's all bud baby. One hit will last you three hours."

She pulls the blanket back up over her shoulders, with the dope in her hands underneath. "Unzip your jeans, Erik."

"Unbutton," he says. "Can you unbutton them?"

She's kneeling down in front of him, letting the dope baggy fall on the ground and the blanket open. She unbuttons his fly and reaches in and pulls out his penis. Puts him in her mouth. The whole thing is dreamscape, for both of them.

She's swallowing, and he's buttoning his jeans up, and she's picking up the baggy and pulling the blanket close around her.

"Can you drive," he's asking.

"I can drive."

"You going to give me your number?"

"Maybe . . . someday."

"Well, how about it? Just tell me; I can remember it."

"Not tonight. I'll call you, Erik," and she's pulling the blanket off.

Erik's got one foot on the ground and another one in the truck, looking over at her. "Yeah. You do that. Keep me posted on this officer."

She's handing him his blanket, and gliding back towards the Vette.

"Good night, Erik . . . maybe we are soul mates."

CHAPTER XXII

Catcher's jogging down this county rock road, watching the eastern sky change from pink to yellow as morning creeps into the Ozarks. It's his favorite time to run. Unlike running on military installations, his course here is over rock roads. There's very little traffic. This Monday morning, he got up in the dark, did fifty push-ups and leg raises, then headed out for the jog. He's counting on the run to facilitate clarity of thought. This Jinx thing, over the weekend, has opened-up a phantasmagorical world. So, he's jogging along, watching the pink sky graduate to yellow, smelling the ditch weeds and meadow mists, thinking about his future.

He wants Jinx. He can't remember feeling as exhilarated. Maybe a similar 'rush' after a particular combat mission in Central America. But, nothing else. Now, it's about a woman . . . . Steps in a dip and almost twists his ankle. Keeps on running and thinking . . . . The goal was to establish a cattle ranch, when he moved here. He's been dragging his feet on this. Like, maybe, he didn't want this kind of commitment. Cattle mean a daily expense in money and time. Not yet, he's thinking. Going to keep working on the land; cleaning it up; going to wait on the cattle. Wondering at his resolve. Remembering his sentimental troops as pussy-whipped . . . the guys who steered their careers to accommodate women or children. This had never been his way. He was known to 'massage' his superiors and the Department of the Army for 'hot spot' assignments. Operated with a one-track mind: put the women and children to bed and get into combat. A soldier is a warrior. Now, here he is, jogging down this misty gravel road twisting around overhanging oaks and hickory trees, rationalizing a delay in going forward with his civilian objective. Course, now, his mate is deceased, he's alone, and his situation is changed.

He's seeing the upper rim of the sun now, rising over the leafy ridgeline ahead. Thinking he earned the money to afford a leisurely approach to developing his property here in the Ozarks. There is no hurry on the cattle. Jinx is another matter. She seems to be a catalyst for his transformation from grieving, discharged military officer to emancipated civilian freebooter. He's thinking, if he's a Bedouin tribal chief, he's just encountered a maiden within a seized Sahara village. Victorian restraint be damned, go collect the girl!

Late morning, Catcher's in his cargo pants and black cotton t-shirt, driving the Ramcharger towards Warsaw. Traveling through this sunny, sultry, pollen laced day spread out over the jagged, timber cloaked ridges; dipping low on the paved road, crossing small open meadows and old bridges, then accelerating up steep inclines on the curve. The Tahiti charm is swinging on its chain off the rearview mirror . . . . Catcher is more than a little fascinated by this simple charm from the distant isle in the South Pacific.

In good time, he's in line at the Warsaw Bank drive-thru window. Hasn't got any business here at all. He's here to see Jinx, period.

She's seeing Catcher's Ram coming up, and Jinx is jolted with apprehension. Her hands are getting the willies.

"Good morning Catcher, long time no see," a cheerful projection belying an underlying insecurity.

"Can you go eat lunch," sitting here in the idling Ramcharger.

"Yes. Give me a few minutes," feigning calmness. Pointing over to a parking place, "Wait for me over there, Catcher."

Jinx has a substitute at the window now, but instead of going outside, she goes to the basement. The supply rooms and electrical terminals are down here. Going into the supply room, turning on the light and closing the door. There's a step stool down here, and she's pulling it over in front of the air return and sitting down. Getting her purse open and shaking half a Xanex out of the bottle. Swallowing this with no water, and pulling a used 'J' out of her purse. Lighting this and taking a long hit. Putting the joint out and back in her purse. Just sitting here, in her brown shirt and jacket and matching strapped shoes, hands on her knees. First time she's even been close to a meltdown since she started smoking Erik's Ozark Gold. Will never be without Sinsemilla again! Gets really scary when the darkling worm starts to surface. She can't deal with the darklings and do anything else . . . . Erik's supreme contribution—a panacea for her disabling memories and consequent panic—Ozark Gold. She has a Xanex and a toke every morning, including today. Wasn't enough. But, now she's regaining her composure.

Holding her hand out in front of herself. It's steady. She's up and going back upstairs. Out in the parking lot, heading to Catcher's truck.

Catcher's out of the truck, waiting for her. She's coming towards him, and he's checking her out. So unassuming and natural she seems, and without pretension. The thought flits through that she is vulnerable, like a little hummingbird.

"Hey, guy. I was hoping you'd come to see me," and she's going around to the passenger side.

"Couldn't get you out of my mind," closing her door.

Back behind the steering wheel, "Want to go eat?" he asks, looking over at her blue eyes going purple.

"Yes, but just a drive-thru or something," rubbing his forearm.

Backing up, "How about the Sonic Drive-in?"

"That'll be great," and she's cupping her hand around the Tahitian charm, studying this intensely. "What's this? It's beautiful. I love it."

"Take it off the mirror."

She's getting it off the mirror and holding it over next to her open window for light. "What is it?"

"It's a dolphin and a shark intertwined. Made out of silver, I think," watching the road ahead.

"Where'd you get this? I love it," holding it up between her face and the dirty windshield.

"Found it buried beside an old foundation on my place."

"You cleaned it up?"

"I did."

"What's the engraving on the fish?"

"It says TAHITI. Imagine that if you can."

"Tahiti. That's way out in the Pacific somewhere . . . . A tropical island with erotic natives. Free love, and all that, I think," she's got the charm in her lap, turning it around with her hand.

"You can have it," Catcher looking over smiling.

"Are you serious? I love it," slipping it over her head. "Tahiti. Sometime we'll go there," and she's looking over at him, holding the charm in her right fist.

"We're going to Tahiti?"

"Yes. I think someday. Far and away from our lives today. Together on a Pacific island," rubbing his arm again.

"You think you'll wear that much?" Catcher's smiling, looking over at her. "You never wear jewelry."

"I'll never take it off." She means it.
"I'm pretty sure it's silver."
"I'm sure it's silver . . . you cleaned it yourself . . . right?"
"Yes."
"When did you find it?"
"Yesterday. Sunday."
"After we made love."
"Yes."
"I'll never take it off." Jinx is looking way off past the windshield. "Tahiti."

They're at the Sonic, in the truck, eating burgers out of their wrappers and fries from the sack.
Catcher's smiling, "Not wearing any hose today?"
"Nope," between chewing her fries. "Shaved my legs and let it go at that."
"They're gorgeous. Your legs."
"You should know," she's returning his smile, trying to push an onion slice back into the bun.
"I'm coming after you, Jinx," trying to keep his burger from sliding out of the bun.
"You sure you want to," she's studying him, chewing the fries. "You don't know anything about me."
"I'm sure. Tell me again where you grew up."
"An unincorporated community over on the Sac River called Algiers." Still watching him.
Catcher's got a teleflash crossing the frontal lobe. Visualizes the loser sewer-plate with no shirt in Shittown, U.S.A. All the weeds and shacks. The café with Vaseline and Preparation H on the table, and Jerry Springer on the television.
"You grew up in Algiers," dumbfounded, looking over at her, trying to imagine this beautiful creature coming from this place.
"Yes. All the way through school. Bussed over to Osceola."
She's watching him closely, holding her burger below her chin.
"What's your dad do?"
She drops her burger, and is looking down, trying to put it back together on her napkin. "He was an alcoholic handyman . . . jack of all trades, master of none. My mom was rarely home."
"What's your last name?"

"Jenks. That's how I got my nickname."

"Jinx Jenks," Catcher is smiling at her.

"My name is Jo Ann Jenks. But as long as I can remember, I've gone by Jinx."

"Who started that?" Emphatically.

"My dad, I think," and Jinx isn't smiling anymore. She's feeling her right eyelid flutter.

"Cute nickname. Your dad and mom alive?"

"They are both dead," looking out her passenger window.

"You have any other family?" Catcher's putting the straw to his milkshake in his mouth.

Jinx looking back at Catcher, "I have a sister in Oklahoma. A twin sister. She's a teacher, married to the superintendent of schools. We don't communicate much."

"You don't have anyone," Catcher's saying empathetically.

"My cat . . . and one good friend lives in the area."

"Ever been married?" Catcher's head is down. But, has his eyes up to meet hers.

"No. And, no children." She's stuffing her scraps back into the brown paper bag. "Look. I grew up like a tomboy. Rode a bike, had tree houses, that sort of thing. I always made good grades. Dropped out of school my senior year . . ."

"Why?"

She's looking back at Catcher. "Family problems. I think they call it dysfunctional."

"What'd you do then?"

"I hightailed it for Warsaw. Hitchhiked. Stayed with a few kids I knew, switched around jobs till I got on at the bank. The bank gave me a test. They liked my scores, and hired me." Jinx starting to get this challenging look . . . almost combative.

"I'm sounding like a detective," Catcher says, putting his scraps into the paper bag.

"It's OK. You're coming after me, remember," and Jinx laughs, and holds the Tahiti charm a second.

"You believe in God?"

Jinx is looking out the dirt-crusted windshield. "We never went to church. I went to Sunday school a few times with friends. Maybe. Maybe I believe in God." Her eyes narrow, "Maybe not."

"Guess it'd be a stretch to say you were Christian?"

"Maybe. Maybe not. He was about love and forgiveness. Right? . . . . I remember the story about Absalom. He was a man that killed his brother for raping their sister . . . . I didn't have anyone." Staring past the dirty windshield, dead-like.

Catcher's stuffing the paper bags of trash into the console between their seats. "Where do you live, Jinx?" Pretending he didn't hear this; not wanting to hurt her.

"I'm buying a little seven acre place with a shack on the Little Niangua River. Over by Climax Springs," turning to face Catcher. Giving him a forced smile.

"I know where Climax Springs is."

"I'm south of there a few miles."

"You have a phone number?"

Jinx doesn't respond. She's holding the charm around her neck, and sitting sideways in her seat facing Catcher. She's got her lips pooched together and staring at Catcher. But, she's not saying a word.

"Hello. Earth to Jinx . . ."

"I'll give it to you," and Jinx gets a bank business card out of her purse and a pen, and writes her Climax Springs, unlisted, home phone number on the back of the card. Looking at the card as she gives it to Catcher.

"You don't have to give it to me, if you don't want me to have it," Catcher's saying, holding the card without looking at it.

"I want you to have it, Catcher," and she squeezes his leg.

"OK then. The hunt is on. I'm coming to get you," Catcher's saying while putting the card in his wallet.

While they're driving back to the bank, Jinx asks, "Why would an army colonel from high-up be interested in a girl from Algiers? I've only been out of Missouri once . . . to Kansas."

"What's that have to do with romance?" Catcher flashing serious. "I have a passion for you . . . . I want you . . . more than anything."

He's slowing down and getting over on the centerline, going past a hippy girl trying to thumb a ride. Musing about the courage to get outside your paradigm. Don't see many hippies in the Ozarks. Looking back in his rear view mirror . . . . She's going to hitch a ride and change her life, maybe.

"It could be a big mistake. I might not be what you want."

"I want you."

"And, what if I'm not . . . what you want?" Jinx is sure she's not.

"Jinx, I haven't any family or anyone in this world. Not even a cat. Tell me, what do I have to lose?"

CHAPTER XXIII

Going to lose his life fucking around with his soul mate, Erik's thinking. One Starbuck sipping, biscuit nibbling, Jar Head officer going once . . . going twice . . . gonno. Turn the card Vanna. Erik's the winner. Give the red haired Viking chap the money and girl please, Vanna. Jerks his steering wheel to go around a road kill.

Picked up the water pumps today. Got six of 'em. Six five-horsepower, gasoline utility pumps, each about the size of a small generator. Got four at different places in Springfield, and two more in Sedalia. An all day pump shopping spree, for the OMP. They'll be pumping in the morning, they'll be pumping in the evening, and they'll be pumping along about suppertime.

Jinx is his girl, end of story. He can sniff the thing between them. It smells pink and fresh and a little bloody today. Got an open body smell. Hand me my .44 MAGNUM please, Nurse Ratchet. I'm going to remove this officer prick from inside our patient. Then, we'll put in for the insurance money. That's how the 'She Lays'em—We Slay'em' surgical procedure is done, with regards, the venerable Dr. E-r-i-k S-t-a-r-r. An officer Jar Head faggot comes down here in the hills and pokes one of the girls; he'll find out about the Code of the Hillbilly . . . make the Hatfield-McCoy feud look like a playground squabble.

Erik's reaching up to change stations. Can't stand fuckin' 'tear in the beer' bullshit country music. Western rock has the juice. Got it up loud, cause his window is down and the air is whipping into the cab.

Erik, the mastermind, is doing the 'think tank' thing . . . . Got to give her lots of hard dick. Keep her 'sassy-fied'. Shower her with Ozark Gold. Lots of ganja for the lady with home folk habits. That's it. Hard sex and pure bud. Gotta treat her with kindness. Help her through the courtship with officer what's-his-fuck, get'em married, and then help Jar Head through his accident. Pickup the insurance money. Take a trip. Cleanup the OMP and set-up in style. Buy her a Cadillac or a Mercedes. Have Kid Starr to carry-on the gene pool. Fuck, smoke and travel. How do you like that Daddy-o, stuck outside Pontiac, Michigan, one ball bat ahead of nobody-o.

Erik's got his wrist laying over the top of his steering wheel, and he's opening and closing his fist, watching the sun lower west of 65 highway . . . . Needs to get Jinx seeing it his way, then, 'oops, sorry sir,' Erik just punched your ticket. The officer won't be killing kids again. Here's his purple heart. Play a little Pink Floyd at his funeral. Wonder how much insurance he'll carry? Whatever Jinx says, after she's been on his stuff. Get up on him Jinx. Give'm the million-dollar ride baby, and then I'll give him the forty-story push. Maybe help him drown in the river . . . between patches five and six. It's like this, he's thinking. He and Jinx are two of a kind, and this officer prick is in over his head. But, useful. Jar Head will provide his wife's dowry. Finally, the federal government's going to do something for Erik Starr . . . . Meanwhile, he's got to send a message to that nosy fuck with the boat. What's his name, Catcher Riley.

He's arriving in Preston, and instead of going east on U.S. 54, towards the OMP, he continues north on 65. Goes up to Cross Timbers, where he exits East. Going to scout Riley's layout . . . . Shortly, he's idling past the cedar trilevel, noting that Riley's driveway runs back past the house to a barn . . . . Gets turned around, and comes back by the place. He's knowing he'll be back. Fact is, you don't crowd a Starr and get away with it. Fuckin' A . . . . Then, Erik's gone. Back to the highway.

Coming up the lane to the OMP. The boats are gone and no one is around. Just the guineas and dogs. Going across the old porch, wondering how long the phone's been ringing.

"OMP."

"Erik, is that you?" She's no-nonsense today.

"Jinx baby. It is I."

"You didn't sound like yourself." She's relaxing a little.

"It's me," trying to catch his breath.

"I need a fix." Real plain.

"Smoke?"

"That too!." Just as plain, "I was thinking more of your big tinker toy."

"Let me look in my pants . . . yep, I've still got it. Thought you missed 'dessert' last time." He just started to swell.

"I'll meet you same place as last time," very matter-of-fact.
"What time?"
"How's eight-thirty?"
"I'll be there with bells on."
"You still crippled up," sounding warmer.
"The toe is fine," laughing.
"How's your middle toe?" She's sounding mischievous.
"The opposite of in-grown, baby doll."
"I'll check it out," she offers.
"I'll be there early."
"By-y-e." She's gone.

So, here he is, sitting behind the boarded up cabin, in silence, studying the stars. Cold up there in the Big Empty, he's thinking. Nothing but a few blackened planets and disconnected stars. Here he sits on the one green planet, waiting for a hot connection. Stolen moments in eternal blackness, ramming it home, in one pussy or another. He likes the one coming down the road.

Jinx has parked the Vette, and she's out looking up at the stars. Got a sweatshirt on with her Wranglers and boots. Erik's door slamming. They can hear crickets and grasshoppers. An occasional owl off one of the ridges and some coyotes barking.

She's lighting a doober.

"You're horny tonight." Erik's standing here watching her with his hands in his back pockets.

She's coughing, "The temperature is perfect tonight."

"Let's get in my truck and drive back to the barn. I'll leave my lights off."

They get back to the barn, and Erik shuts the engine off. "You going to smoke that whole thing?"

Jinx purrs, "You'll like it, Big Dick," and hands him the end of the J.

Erik finishes it. "You going to get in my jeans or not?" He's watching her darkened face watching him.

"Get your blanket, I think," as she's getting out of the truck.

He spreads this out, and she lays down on her back, looking up at the night sky.

He's standing over her.

"Take your pants off, Erik. Let me see you."

"I can't wait," and he's stripping off.

"Let me see you play with your Dolly," she slurs slightly.

Erik's standing here, and she's looking up at him and he's slowly milking his penis.

"You can do this, baby," he says.

"Take my clothes off."

He's got her undressed, and gets in a 'sixty-nine' position, licking her vagina and she him.

He's turning around, facing her, straddling one of her legs. "Let me see you masturbate."

"Like this," and she's fingering her clitoris and sticking it in, moaning. Got her one knee raised up so the front of her upper thigh is against the back of his testicles.

He's leaning over, kissing her neck and down to her breasts.

"What's this?" Erik's cupping the Tahiti charm in his free hand.

"Get your hands off it . . . now," Jinx doesn't sound so stoned.

"You never wear jewelry."

"Get loose of it," serious like.

"What if I don't sweet tits? What if I rip it off?" Erik's smiling in her face.

She gets still. "You do that and I'll rip your balls off." She's got one hand on her vagina, and the other one wrapped around his nuts.

"Just kidding, baby," letting go of the charm.

She's steering his hand, gently rubbing her clitoris with it.

He's stretching his body over hers, and arching so she can steer his cock in.

She's stretched out naked on the blanket and got her legs spread and knees up. He's slowly, methodically pumping her. But each time he takes her to the edge of orgasm, he stops. During these brief rest stops, he's hard up inside her. Pulsing inside her.

"Baby, it could be like this the rest of our lives." He can feel her body quaking.

"Give it to me, Erik . . . C'mon," and she's squeezing the blanket with clenched fists.

"It's good isn't it?" Pushing in a little.

"It's fine." Her chin's up, her head's back and she's closed her eyes.

"Fine? That's all," and Erik pulls back a millimeter. "When'd you have better, bitch?"

She's rolling a little, back and forth, from one buttock to the other, getting out of her head, doing avaricious groaning.

Erik pushes in, "When better, baby? When?"

"Nobody beats my daddy," she's moaning.

He stops. Leans back to see her contorted face. "Daddy? Who you calling Daddy?"

She's got her hands in the small of his back, pulling him.

Erik's serious, "Who's Daddy? Jar Head? The officer Fuck?"

She's bucking, "Give it to me, give it to me, give it to me . . ."

He fucks her hard. Really hard. Shoving far up inside her, until they climax.

They are laying here on the blanket. Jinx rolls Erik off, so she can breathe.

She's seeing the stars again. Next, she can hear the night sounds.

Erik's laying here with his mouth next to her cheek, below her ear. Breathing hard, "You are going to marry the officer . . . then, I'm going to kill him. Then we'll get married . . . . Barrels of cash. Hard sex. Sinsemilla. For life."

Jinx has caught her breath, "You bring a J with you?"

"Did you hear what I said Jinx?"

"You are talking about killing someone asshole. We just finished having sex!"

"I will kill him. You won't." Erik laying beside her, looking up at the sky with her. "You're just along for the ride . . . . Don't you get it? There's them, and there's us. When did anyone in the establishment ever help you . . . . You must fucking get it, this guy, if there is a guy, if he is an officer . . . he's never going to stay with you. Get serious gorgeous, those guys marry debutantes, not country whores."

It is what it is, Jinx is thinking, losing her syrupy buzz, figuring Erik's telling it like it is.

He's still laying beside her, studying the night sky. "I've got about a million five, you bring in another five in insurance payout, and this year I'll have another mil. That's over three million for us to start out . . . . I hate the pricks that run the system. He's one of 'em, and he's fucking outside his territory. I'm going to kill him."

"Men. Fucking men," she says. She's thinking society never helped her . . . she's been alone all her life and a half million dollars with an unending Sinsemilla supply . . . .

"I'm going to kill him. You get that?"

Holding her hand up in the air, flexing her wrist, "What happens, happens. I'm not going to be killing anybody." She loathes her life has sunk to this. Drugs to sex, sex for money, to murder for sex and money. Welcome to the damned, honey.

Erik laying beside her, looking up at the sky. "It's just you and me, Jinx. The rest are all Jar Heads."

"You have a joint?"

"I'll get it."

Getting one out of the truck, and coming back and laying down beside her. Firing up the doob, and the two of them smoke this while watching the sky.

"You didn't use a condom." She sounds emotionless.

"Sorry about that. You in a dangerous time of the month?" Erik could care less.

"I don't think so," more like she's talking to herself.

"Whatcha mean, 'nobody beats daddy.'"

"You're my daddy, Erik."

He's laying here looking skyward, sorting through the stars. Thinking. Needs to get Jinx back in the Vette. Then, he needs to go back to the OMP and get a few things. The thought of killing this army prick, whoever he is, who has been sharefucking Jinx; the Sinsemilla; and the evening's sexcapades; they've all combined to invigorate him. Figures this would be a good night to deal with the asshole with the boat, local yocal Catcher Riley.

"Jinx baby. We'd better get rolling. I've got things to do."

"Tonight?" Totally isolated.

"Yeah. Tonight."

CHAPTER XXIV

His truck is sitting out on the road around the corner of the driveway entrance. Out of sight from Riley's house. He left it with the engine idling and the lights off. This is where Erik parked, before walking down the driveway to this old barn. Walked right past Riley's house in the dim light of the early a.m. Dressed in black, face covered with grease paint and the BORN TO HUNT cap pulled down on his head. Pistol stuck in his waistband, pump shotgun in his right hand, and his sack of goodies in his left. The way he'd come down the drive, one would think it was Sunday afternoon. But, what-the-fuck, this asshole didn't even have a dog . . . . Listening to the distant owl, browsing around, noting the old Ramcharger, comfortable in the wee hour coolness.

He's in this fucked-up old barn, trying to make sense of things. Has his sack of tricks open, retrieved the flashlight and looking over the boat; some cheap ass little aluminum thing. Doesn't figure there's a chance in hell Riley what's his name is awake . . . and, he's right.

Has the can of purple spray paint out. Holding the flashlight beam on the boat while he spray paints. Finishing the graffiti, he proceeds to loop a long strand of duct tape over an overhead wire. Tapes the flashlight to the end of the dangling tape, so as to hold the flashlight in a horizontal position in front of the message he's sprayed on the boat. An imperceptible draft slowly twirls the flashlight round and round, filling the inside of the barn with shifting shadows, and casting intermittent blotches of light outside the barn opening.

He gets the roll of tape and spray can back in his sack, and this stuffed into a cargo pocket in his jacket. Then, Erik picks his shotgun up and steps up onto the trailer hitch. Grinning out of the grease paint, enjoying the eerie spectacle he's manufactured here, pumps a shell into the chamber and blows a hole in the bottom of the boat.

Running out of the barn, back out the driveway in front of the house. Figures he'll be out to the road before this bumpkin gets his lights on . . . doesn't even have a dog.

He's right about the dog, but he's wrong to think Catcher Riley would turn on a light.

Catcher Riley is a longstanding fan of Tecumseh, the eighteenth century Shawnee Native American leader. One of Tecumseh's tactics was to immediately charge when caught by surprise . . . charge through a line of ambushers immediately, in the dark or not, with a fierceness and suddenness that momentarily astonished his enemy . . . . At the sound of the shotgun blast, Catcher rolls out of his bed to the floor with his loaded COLT .45 in hand. This is his killing firearm . . . used before. In the here and now, he's lying on the floor in his underwear, scanning the bedroom doorway over the barrel.

He springs to his feet, crashes out of his bedroom and down the steps into the living room, pointing the .45 out in front. Gets to the backdoor and checks that it's locked. Pushes the inside of the front door. It's secure . . . . All this in less than sixty seconds. Conscious thought catching-up to his reflective response. His breathing shallow. Cracks the window covering, scanning out front. There's the old Ram . . . sees light winking from the barn . . . . Looking out the driveway, towards the road . . . . Nothing he can see.

Getting back from the window, finding fatigue pants and tennis shoes and jamming into these and grabbing his keys. Quietly letting himself out the backdoor, locking it behind. Keeping out away from the house, circling around to the back entrance to the old barn.

Dead silence inside, but the light is moving. Slipping into the barn, Catcher instantly sees the flashlight suspended by duct tape, slowly twirling around. Holding perfectly still till he's satisfied he's alone in the barn. On the ready, coming to the flashlight, grasping it and pointing the beam towards his boat. 'Mine Yer Own Biz' is what it says, spray painted along the side. Directing the light downward into the bottom of the boat, seeing the hole . . . . So, the morons on the river traced the registration number back. He switches the light off. Edging out towards the front of the barn, looking out the driveway . . . . He sees the shadowy figure now, standing out by the road. Too far to do anything about it. Barely twitches when the figure discharges the shotgun into the sky . . . . Seconds later, hears the vehicle crunching away.

Got the message. He's not going to report a thing. He doesn't know local law enforcement. He doesn't know who's who or what's what in this neck of the woods. But . . . this just took a more personal turn . . . . All in good time. All in good time.

CHAPTER XXV

Her modus operandi is compromised. Jinx made this deviation with Catcher Riley, and now it's bothering her. The phone number. She gave her phone number to him. She does not receive phone calls, except from the bank or Jake. Until now.

Her shanty asylum has been compromised. The phone is ringing more, and she's not answering. It's unnerving, not knowing who, and it's probably Catcher Riley, and she has to be 'on' to talk to this guy.

She has several reasons for not giving out her phone number. For one thing, she's a call girl working the trade assbackwards—she calls you, don't call her. When you are a call girl, where this is illegal, caution is essential. There's the creeps and the law. You get her phone number, there's a potential for an address trace. Find out the route number, and then the box number, and then you've got her shanty pinpointed. You get her phone number, you can call her according to your dictates, not hers. She loses control.

There's the issue 'large' of privacy. Her shanty is where she hides. In her aloneness is her rejuvenation. Going out of her shanty is a Major Domo. Anywhere: the bank; SHADOWS; R4; the store; the dentist; a date . . . . Every outing is an event. Jinx has to emotionally prepare for any outing. Has to brace up, do her drugs right, be groomed in her method.

This phone thing usurps her control. She doesn't know when the damn thing may ring. Maybe when she's contemplating suicide, or when she's got her music up a thousand decibels. Maybe, when she's doing 'Graceland'.

Doing Graceland—the chemical junkie drug drill. Let's see, she's smoking doob morning, noon and night. Got the Xanex in her purse and Valium too. There's the Prozac in the dresser. Skelaxin in the medicine cabinet. Naproxen in the pantry. Darvan and Demeral in the cupboard. Flexeril in the dressing table. The Klonopin and Percoset . . . not sure where.

Excedrin, aspirin and Codeine Tylenol. All in all, Graceland with the King. The last thing she needs is a phone call.

Maybe the phone rings when she's pleasuring herself. Masturbating. Or, when she's reading. Really reading. Tripping on the author's virtual reality; her version of astral projection. Or, when she's in the shower, window open to the Ozark backcountry.

Reach out and touch someone? What a chop to the trunk nerve. She's got a dappled nervous network, and loneness is her best recuperative. When they've got your phone number, you're not alone. She likes her nonexistence.

Tonight, she's more angry than usual. She knows Catcher Riley will call until he reaches her. Maybe come by the bank. Wants him and doesn't. Nice little girl's pick, but the nympho's problem male. That's Catcher Square Riley.

So, she's in the silver blue Vette headed for R4. Needs to talk to someone. Let me see, who'd that be? There's Jake, then there's Jake, or maybe she could talk to Jake. No party at R4 tonight. Just her and Jake, and the security guys . . . if they're there.

She crosses the low water bridge over the Little Niangua, got her radio on ROCK FM, smoking a J and creeping along the back roads in the low-flung Vette. Has the faded top down, hair flicking in the wind, watching the shadows pass and the starry sky.

Knocking and knocking at R4. Waiting. There's the El Dorado. He's here. Ozark river night sounds droning on and a few lights shining from out the octagon. C'mon Jake . . . . Answer the frigging door.

The darkened form of a huge man is coming towards her across the parking lot. Must've come out of the woods. Knocking harder on the door.

The giant's coming up the steps.

"Hold it right there. Stop!" She commands, pointing at the figure.

He stops, "It's OK, Jinx. I am Big Track." He has one hand on the railing, just standing here, one foot one step up.

"Jake's maintenance Indian?" Jinx, one hand on the octagon door knob, half-turned away from him, inward towards the door.

"I have a key," the Indian says.

She's noticing the gleaming eyes. "Can you unlock this?" standing back.

"I will. Jake's inside. He can't hear you," and Big Track's coming up the stairs, getting the keys out of his baggy jeans.

As he's unlocking the door, he turns to face a wary Jinx. She can see gleaming eyes shining forth from the big head looking down at her.

"The stars say to run. You should run away like a puma."

"Where's Jake? I want to see Jake now!"

"Jake's OK. See Jake. Then go far away." He's not opening the door; just standing here looking down on her.

"Get the door unlocked. You're giving me the creeps, guy," backing up, glancing behind.

"I know this Jinx," his eyes like two fires. "Three come together, then there is death."

"Where'd you get my name?" Jinx is in a demanding tone.

"You are a moon in the tides of two planets. Always pulled two ways. Riptides coming in. In the pull of separate forces. Must get away. I know this." The fires in his eyes seem to die. He's opening the door. She's bolting past, before the door is completely open.

"Jake! Where the hell are you, Jake?"

The door slams behind her. No Indian. Just the closed door. Gives her the willies. What's with all the moon gibberish?

"Jake," she's crossing the dimly lit, empty club.

"What?" And, Jake's coming out of a back room. Got some ragged jeans on, faded black t-shirt and tennis shoes with no socks. "Jinx! What are you doing here?" Glad to see her.

"Wanted to talk. That's all. Who's the big Indian outside?" she gestures towards the front door.

"Big Track? He lives in a shack next door. Was here before I got R4. I made him my maintenance man . . . I should say, he took the job. Hangs around and watches things, mows, trims, repairs windows," getting over where he can see Jinx better. "That sort of thing. Why?"

"He let me in. Gave me a start. Giving me some kind of séance thing on the deck." She's standing here in her Wranglers, sweat shirt and boots, relaxing now that she's with Jake.

"He's OK, Jinx. A complete loner. Must be seventy years old. Who knows how old. Claims he's an Osage Shaman. A medicine man. He may be," and Jake laughs. Puts his arm around Jinx, "He scare you?"

She pulls back, "Nobody scares me, Jake."

"Yeah, right. C'mon, we'll have a drink over here," and Jake's got her hand, leading her to a table over in the light.

Sitting here, across the table from each other, drinking beer from the can. "What's this visit all about, Jinx?"

"Feeling neurotic is what it's all about, as usual," sipping her beer.

"What's new," and Jake's patting her hand. "God, you are beautiful . . . what's with the necklace," studying the Tahiti charm outside her sweatshirt. "You don't wear jewelry."

"I wear this," cranking her head down to see the charm. "It's from Tahiti. All silver."

Jake's leaning over, holding it between his thumb and index finger, examining it. "Two fish?"

"A dolphin and a shark," her head still down, looking.

"The two of you," Jake laughing and letting it fall back onto her sweatshirt. "Well, what's up?"

"I've met a nice guy. He's a retired army officer. He likes me," back to looking at Jake.

The club is quiet. Just the sounds from the river and out of the woods.

"This is a good thing, Jinx."

"Maybe. Makes me nervous."

"Don't think you're good enough, huh?"

"I don't know what I think."

"You still at the SHADOWS?"

Sitting here, watching her hand turning the beer can.

"Guess that's a yes," he says. "You've got to quit that. Straighten up and fly-right. Cut back on the drugs and give this a chance Jinx . . . I mean it."

"Maybe," she's still turning her beer can . . . staring at it.

Jake leaning back, looking at her real serious like, "You aren't seeing Erik Starr. . . . When are you going to get it?"

"Leave Erik out of it," and she drains her beer. "You have another one of these?"

He gets her one. "What do you mean, leave Erik out of it? Look at me, Jinx." He's leaning over the table trying to get in her face. "You can't keep a good guy and be fucking someone else. Why? Why do you do it?"

She drinks about half the beer, and sets the can down. Resting her ganja/alcohol violet eyes on black haired Jake the rake. "I'll tell you why."

"It's about sex, Jinx."

"I'll tell you why." She belches, puts her hand over her mouth. "I'm a sexual person and I crave sensuality. I stick with my kind."

"Erik is that? Give me a break. He's a baby. He's a dangerous baby."

"Take it easy, Jake," she swallows more beer. "He rings my bell."

"Like I use to?" Jake wants to know . . . not really.

"I got sexualized early, Jake. You know how . . . you have another beer?"

Jake gets more beer.

Her eyes are getting glassy. "Some abuse vic . . ."

"Incest victims, Jinx. It's called INCEST!"

"Call it anything you want. It has the affect of turning you up . . . and on . . . wet pussy forever. I like it. What don't you understand Jake? You loved it . . . banging me everyway from . . ."

"You are a love starved nymphomaniac, Jinx. I'm not knocking it. I understand why, and I love you."

"You have another beer?" she drawls. "I don't understand it. He was fucking my sister, too. She's married, and she won't even do it with her husband."

Exasperated, "OK, Jinx. OK." Jake's bringing back another beer.

"Erik fucks me like my pop did."

"Yeah. And you like this?"

"Don't you get it, Jake," and Jinx is slurring. "I crave it, and I loathe it at the same time."

"Look, Jinx. Forget the sex thing. Erik could kill somebody. You, the officer . . . what's his name . . . the officer?"

"Catcher Riley."

"Catcher Riley! I'll remember that. What I was saying, Erik could kill you or Catcher Riley or both. He's got low impulse control and no sense of deferred gratification. He came by here trying to get your number, and I had to throw him out."

"Catcher Riley isn't going . . . I mean, Erik Starr . . ."

"So why you here, Jinx?" Jake getting frustrated. "To tell me you're fucking two guys. One good, one bad, and can't help yourself? What do you want from me?"

"Jake, sometimes you are an ass. Sometimes people just need to talk to someone who cares. Someone to listen." She's getting teary.

Jake coming around the table and squatting down beside her chair. Putting his arm around her, and getting close to her cheek. "I care, Jinx. Hell, I love you."

"I gotta go," and Jinx is up, pulling away. Wants Jake's touch, but doesn't need it, she's barely thinking. 'Not scared of anybody,' but frightened of everybody and everything.

Crossing to the front door, with Jake right behind her. "You going to be OK driving?"

Turning around in the open door, "Hell yes, I'll be OK driving. You know me; I'm always under some fucking influence . . . . Where's the fucking Indian?"

"I'll walk you to your car."

He's slamming the driver's door to the Vette behind her. "You call me when you get home."

Backing up, "I don't need to call anyone." Spinning her tires on gravel going out.

Crying behind the steering wheel, looking over towards the woods from whence came the big Indian. What'd he say? 'Three come together, then there is death?'

CHAPTER XXVI

He's out here by the barn, going through the motions. But, Catcher's heart isn't in it. Sticking the five foot long, steel digging bar through the open passenger window, back between the two bucket seats. Leaves the front end of the bar laying on top of the Ram's console. Throws his gloves in the passenger seat beside the thermoses, and sticks a sharpshooter spade in on top of the dig bar. Taking an offhand look around at this morning's sunny display. Always the turkey vultures circling in the sky. Dew's still on the land, and it's cool yet.

He's studying the aerial map of his ranch, looking for the trail going back to the lost forty. It's the northeast corner . . . needs a corner post before he can fence. He plans to drive back in, using the Ram 4x4, and dig the hole for the corner post. In the Ozarks, this is a project. The stony soil makes a shovel useless, except for cleaning the edges off the hole. The way Catcher digs a hole, is with a steel dig bar. He's thinking about the forthcoming effort. Got to hoist the steel bar vertically, both hands gripping the bar, pointed end down, then drive it into the dirt. Gouge out about a fifteen-inch diameter circle in the dirt with the bar. Then, the job is to repeat the exercise till there's enough loose dirt and rock to scoop out with the hands. Repeat the exercise, going deeper, and then scooping more dirt out with the hands. So on and on, until there is a cylindrical hole about four feet deep. In the Ozarks, one man, in good shape, taking minimal breaks, might get this hole dug in a day. Towards the end, this one man, none other than Catcher Riley, will need to be on his stomach beside the hole, stretching his arm down in the hole to scoop out the loose dirt. No wonder Catcher's in no hurry. It's a backbreaking, muscle-stretching job ahead. And, his head isn't really into it.

For days, he's been trying to call Jinx. In the evenings. She doesn't answer her phone. Catcher's gone over the Sonic luncheon in his mind, wondering if he gave her some offense. Maybe her reference to rape . . . when she was talking about Absalom? Can't see how . . . thought about going to the bank, or calling her there, but decided he wouldn't do this . . . . Still figuring a course of action against the pot growing hillbillies that blew a hole in his boat.

Now, he pulls the aerial map off the hood, folds it, and walks around and tosses it into the passenger side on top the gloves and thermoses. Takes another look around and walks back to the driver's side. Gets 'Old Trusty' started, sitting here letting it warm-up, when he's hearing a horn honking behind, up by the house. Looking in the rearview mirror, he sees Marco's Suzuki and Hattie's old pickup truck. Smiling, turning the Ramcharger off.

Catcher's out of the truck, going up the dew grass towards the house. Marco's out of the Suzuki, in his bib overalls, yelling, "Good morning Colonel, reinforcements have arrived."

"Good morning, Marco," Catcher comes up, shaking his hand. Looking over at Hattie. "Good morning, Hattie. What are you doing out this fine day?"

Hattie's remaining in her old pickup. "Hi, Catcher. Marco waved me in."

"Sure did," Marco's saying. "Thought we'd come in for coffee."

"Good idea," Catcher's saying. "Get out and come in, Hattie."

Hattie's getting out of the truck; in jeans, scuffed boots and a white linen blouse, black hair spread over her shoulders.

The three of them going into the house, Marco talking all the while.

"You gotta see the house, Hattie. The way the better half lives. If I had this, I'd have a Ham radio to talk to my international contacts . . . keeping up on developments . . ."

Hattie's looking around. Catcher's heating a kettle of water. "Hope instant coffee'll get the job done folks."

"Make mine regular," Hattie's saying.

Marco, "Can I show her the house, Colonel?"

"Go ahead, Marco," Catcher answering. "Don't look at the mess Hattie."

Hattie gets the tour, Marco Tours Commentaries ad hoc. She is noncommittal, absorbing details silently . . . . Then, they're all sitting around the table drinking instant regular. Hattie's cigarette smoke swirling overhead.

"You gotta a nice place here Catcher," she's saying, taking a last draw off her Camel cigarette.

"Thank you, Hattie. I like it," Catcher draining his cup.

"What're we doing today, Colonel?" Marco wants to know.

"I was going to load a corner post out of the barn, take it back to the northeast corner and set it. I didn't know you were coming Marco."

"I'm out of money, Colonel. Could use some work . . ."

"You bet. You're on." Looking at Hattie, "Ladies do fencing down here, too?"

"I followed Marco in. Check'n on my neighbor who misses church. Thought I might file a miss'n persons report."

Catcher's laughing, "Nope. I'm not missing yet."

"She could haul the corner post back with the pickup," Marco's got his monstrous frame rocking back in the kitchen chair. Busting the glue seams in the chair, Catcher figures.

"How 'bout it Hattie? Going back there with us?" Catcher grinning at her.

"Sure thing," getting up, taking her cup to the sink.

So, they're all outside, down by the barn, loading the eight foot long, eight inch by eight inch, treated corner post into her pickup. Catcher's up in the truck bed, guiding it in, while Hattie and Marco push.

"Your blouse is getting dirty," Catcher a little breathless.

"She doesn't care, Colonel," Marco's saying.

"It's no matter, Catcher," Hattie's going around to get in the pickup.

Catcher and Marco lead out in the Ramcharger, and Hattie follows in the pickup. Back across the wet weather (now dry) creek beds, across meadows, past the monstrous hay barn, down 'tunnel' trails winding through thick woods. Sun's higher and it's getting hotter. They squish a copperhead crossing the trail, and scare a sleeping doe. And, as usual, the turkey vultures are floating overhead . . . .

Unloading the corner post, and Hattie's helping do this.

"Gosh Hattie, you don't need to do this," Catcher says chivalrous like.

"I know, Catcher. I'm enjoying myself. I'm OK. Right?"

"You bet. Stay as long as you like. Help yourself to the water," Catcher's getting the dig bar ready to mark the beginning of the hole.

The three of them, out here in a shaggy meadow, next to a dry waterway, between two timbered ridges, digging this hole with the bar, under a hot sun. Marco and Catcher take turns raising and jamming the pole down, breaking rock and dirt open. Shortly, it's mostly Catcher doing this. Marco standing by, scooping the dirt out of the hole whenever Catcher stops to rest. Hattie's got the truck tailgate down, and sitting on this, simply enjoying being.

A little over an hour glides by, with Catcher breathing hard and the clanking of steel point against rock. Almost eighteen inches down.

"Better take a break, Colonel."

Marco's going at it. Slowly, and huffing and puffing. Catcher sitting next to Hattie, drinking from the thermos.

Catcher's back on the bar, and Marco is laying on his back in the grass.

"You'll get ticks, Marco," Hattie cautions.

Marco moves over, props himself up against her rear tire. "If we knew the secrets of the ancients, we could displace this dirt here electro magnetically, like the great stones of the pyramids were put into place."

Catcher's breathing hard, slowly jack hammering the dig bar up and down.

"Marco, the stuff you come up with," Hattie shaking some heat out of her hair.

"No, Hattie. It's true . . . there's whole other realities our culture will not recognize as valid, so we have to do it the hard way . . . like this post hole," he answers, still breathless.

"Whatcha you think, Catcher? Are there other 'realities' than the one we're in?" Hattie's watching Catcher.

Catcher's leaning on the dig-bar, catching his breath, looking at the two of them. Rolling sweat.

"Yeah, Colonel. How about it? Do you recognize other groups operating out of the lime light, successfully, according to other concepts of reality?" Marco is leaning up off the tire, looking past Hattie's dangling boots towards Catcher.

Catcher's got the hole down over two feet and past humorous retorts.

"Here's what I think, girls," pitching the bar down. He walks over to the Ramcharger and gets the aerial map out. Lays it face down on the flattened, dirt-specked grass in front of Hattie. Pulls a pencil out of his cargo pants. Sketches a series of pyramids in an even line. Still catching his breath. Marco's crawling over where he can see, on his hands and knees.

Catcher pencils in dots around the bases of the pyramids. "These are the great unwashed majority," Catcher grunts. "These dots. They're the people." Then, pointing the pencil at the pyramids, "These are the corporate entities, institutions and organizations in place that give the people law, order and meaning to their insecure existence," taking a deep breath, "and offering routes to financial and emotional security. You might call these pyramids the American estates." Pointing at one pyramid, "the church," pointing at another pyramid, "the military," pointing at another pyramid, "the government," pointing at another pyramid, "the media," sweeping the pencil across the other pyramids, "so on and so forth." He writes 'Pope' on the point of one pyramid, 'Generals' at the point of another, 'CNN' on the point of another, and 'President' on another. Then, he's leaving the pyramids and returning his pencil point to the dots.

"These dots," scribbling around on the dots, "these are the people on the 'outside' of big organizational entities . . . outside the pyramids. Many of these people," holding the pencil point on the hodge-podge of dots, "choose to do their own thing. Small businesses, criminal enterprises, cults, maverick-psycho philosophical units, crazies, dysfunctional malcontents, artists, writers, poets, disassociated geniuses," breathing more normal, "like you Marco . . . . It's rough, down here in the dots. The easiest route is to pick a pyramid, and work your way up . . . taking the perks, benefits, insurance and inclusion this offers . . . . Those groups espousing alternate realities, Marco, are part of the dots. Little guys with unproven, unestablished ideas. Little groups of the excluded, outside the pyramids of establishment power. Maverick religions, terrorist groups, new age followers, and what all only God knows."

Marco's still on his hands and knees, looking down at the sketch. "You are here, Colonel," and he points to the military pyramid.

"I was, Marco," and Catcher gets up on the tailgate beside Hattie. "Not anymore. Existence in a pyramid means programmed living. I'm not there anymore." Pointing his boot toe at the lower dots, "I'm here now." Laughing. "A nomad outside the social engineering and beyond inhibitions."

Hattie looking over at Catcher, "I'll bet. You just think you are."

"Nope. I'm out of the pyramid. An independent wanderer, punching out my own little mini-reality. A post hole today."

"No way," Hattie says. "You're dream'n, Catcher. You couldn't shake your family upbringing if you wanted," chuckling. "You still get a check from the pyramid."

"Colonel, it's time you joined the Astral Projection Society," Marco is watching Catcher.

"The realities, Marco, are the ones we make. The underground press and late night talk radio shows are just entertainment."

Marco is lumbering up, "No way! There are great discoveries among the dots, yet to be accepted by the power elites in the pyramids, Sir." Pulling up his pants leg, looking for ticks.

Hattie's watching Catcher. "Well mister, if you've really joined the dots, you'd better be careful. These dot people play by different rules than the people within your military pyramid . . . ." Looking off at a ridge. "I know, cause I'm a dot person. An independent Ozark cattle rancher . . . off the pyramids. A dot person operating with the dots gots to be alert." Smiling.

"Yeah," Marco's saying, "could get messed up by the OMP. This would be a local dot organization."

"The OMP?" Catcher and Hattie ask together.

"What's that?" Hattie's swinging her legs hanging off the end of the tailgate.

"The Ozark Mafia Posse. The marijuana growing outfit west of here." Marco's got his bandana out, wiping the sweat off his forehead. "But, there's good dots too," he's saying. "Like me . . . and like Jinx."

Hattie's studying Marco. "The Jenks girl? Drives the Vette?"

Catcher's listening, taking another drink from a thermos.

"That's her, Hattie," Marco says. "Prettiest girl in the Ozarks."

"She's one of the Jenks twins from over by Osceola," Hattie's recalling. "She's got a bank job in Warsaw, Marco. That's a corporate entity pyramid," looking over at Catcher. "Right, Catcher?"

"At the base," Catcher's grinning back. "She's at the base of the pyramid."

"The girl came from a rough outfit over by Osceola. The Jenks family. Mom couldn't stay home. Always had her tail up. The dad was home with the girls mostly . . . he was worse than none." Hattie's taking the thermos from Catcher.

"How'd the girls turnout?" Catcher, frozen in place, awaiting her answer . . . .

"The girls were twins. One moved away, got a college degree and married. The one called 'Jinx' never got away. But, I guess she's been at the bank several years." Hattie stops talking for a drink of water. "The girl's got grit."

"Good looking too," Marco adds.

Catcher's getting off the tailgate, looking around for the dig bar. "What do you know about the OMP, Marco?"

Marco's getting the bar for Catcher. "Got a big ranch west of here called October Mount Pontiac. A rough bunch. Came down here from Pontiac, Michigan. Named their place October Mount Pontiac. We call them the OMP.

Some folks say this stands for Ozark Mafia Posse cause they grow marijuana and traffic it up north. I dunno though. Try to stay away from trouble."

Catcher's got the bar, and getting his legs spread over the post hole. "They surely don't grow the stuff on their place . . . could they plant it along the rivers?"

"Some folks say so." Marco's shifting his weight from one foot to the other.

Catcher's got the bar resting in the hole, turning around towards Marco. "Who's the owner of the OMP. The boss?"

"A young guy named Erik Starr, I think." Marco's patting his neck with the bandana. "Getting hot out here, Colonel."

"Do you know where this OMP ranch is?" Still giving the bar a rest.

"Yes I do," patting himself with the bandana.

"Could you draw me a map to their place? Do it on the back of my aerial photo, next to the dots and pyramids . . . I could get the location at the courthouse."

"I'll do it, but don't you ever tell I did," Marco picking the pencil off the tailgate, getting down on the ground to sketch the map. "I don't want'em after me."

Catcher's moved over beside Marco, looking down at his map.

"You understand this?" Marco tracing the pencil along his sketched roads and highways. "The place is west, over here," pointing with the pencil. "It'll have a sign up at the entrance. Says, Ozark Mount Pontiac."

"I got it," Catcher picking up the map, going around to throw it in the Ram.

Hattie's lighting another unfiltered Camel.

"You oughta quit smoking, Hattie," Marco says. "It's dangerous for your health."

"There's lots of things dangerous to your health, Marco." Hattie's got her head back, studying a nearby circling red headed turkey vulture. Takes another draw on the cigarette. "Living is dangerous to your health."

The three of them get the posthole dug four feet down and the corner post in. Get the small rock and dirt tamped in around it. They're hungry and the water is gone, but the corner post is in. Even Hattie worked the dig bar a few times. They're headed back to the house as the sun nears the western ridge.

Catcher has no real food at home. So, the trio is in Cross Timbers eating steak dinners, compliments Catcher Riley. It's a good time for all. They're wolfing down the meat, smelling like the outdoors, with dirt smudged faces, and unbridled vitality, butted up against the oil, checker table cloth. Passing the salt and pepper back and forth. Marco's doing a run-down on the Earth's ongoing relationship with the Annanaki from Nibaru. Hattie and Catcher exchanging amused looks, raising eyebrows and laughing out loud.

Standing around in the gravel parking lot, talking under the streetlight. Hattie's laughing at Marco's interpretation of Revelations as a thinly disguised forewarning of a final alien invasion.

Catcher's paying Marco in cash. "Don't spend all this in one place."

Hattie's getting in her truck, while Catcher's coming towards her with money in hand. "Don't even think about it, Catcher," slamming her door. "You'll insult me. I'm your neighbor."

"Thank you then, Hattie."

"You're welcome, neighbor."

Marco's pulling out in the Suzuki; gotta get to his bus at White Cloud. Catcher pulls out behind Hattie. Follows her to her lane, hits his brights a couple times, and goes on to his place. He's decided. Sooner or later, he'll visit this OMP. Meet this Erik Starr . . . . Meanwhile, he wishes Jinx would answer her phone.

CHAPTER XXVII

Jinx's got the THC (tetrahydrocannabinol) and Xanex transfer in progress . . . doing the narco cruise . . . through the Barren Straights towards the Anesthesia Sea. Sitting on the floor of the front porch, leaned up against the outside wall, dead doober aside. Listening to the wind chimes and night sounds, looking for an opening between the stars. She's hearing the phone and decides to answer. Gets up and through the screen door.

"Hello."

"Jinx? This is Catcher Riley."

"Hi, Catcher."

"I'd like to see you. Is this a possible?"

"Catcher, can I call you back in a minute?"

"You have my number?"

"Yes."

"OK. I'll wait for your call."

"Thanks, Catcher."

"Bye-bye."

Jinx hangs up.

She's standing here in this dimly lit living room, barefooted, in ragged, faded wranglers and black sweatshirt, light blonde hair disheveled and eyes glassy. She's looking around the place. Trying to get an idea of what she wants . . . what she is . . . by attitude of her home. Her gut instinct is, she talks with Catcher, and he's going to come here someday. He may come to know her.

She goes back to the front porch. Fires up a dead doober for a hit. Squeezes it out and goes back in her shanty. Starts a turtle's pace examination of the interior of her shanty. She knows it's messy, but it's clean.

The living room: old couch against the white plaster wall; solid oak coffee table, extra large; oak end tables, covered with books, like the coffee table; TV and stereo on homemade bridge plank shelving over concrete blocks; beige painted pine floor; ornate unpainted pine trim; framed pictures of wild horses, a big poster of Janis Joplin, a small framed black and white photo of herself in a dreary dress alongside a weedy road about eleven years of age. She's meandering into her bedroom. Quilt blanket rumpled up in her sheets and pillows on a saggy mattress atop steel springs in front of an antique spindle headboard . . . peeling paint. A garage sale dresser and a flea market dressing table covered with books. And there's the mechanical clock. Books over the floors mixed in with wadded jeans and tops. A spare pair of cowgirl boots laying under the edge of the bed. She slides the drawer open on the bedside table, checking the .32 revolver there. The lamp here has a yellowing shade wee wad on the lamp. Leaves the bedroom and looks into the bathroom. Goes in. Claw foot tub with homemade shower. Curved rod above the tub with a flowered shower curtain attached. Window is open over the tub, darkness beyond, with the katydids' strident song coming through.

Opens a small trap door into the wall housing the plumbing. Opens the safe herein, counts the separate stacks of thousands. Thirty-five thousand plus dollars. Stripper and paid-for-sex monies. Small change up against, say five hundred thousand dollars. Closing this up, listening to the katydids outside. Wondering how she put aside this money. Truth is, it's easier for her to hoard the money, than it is to spend it. Easier to save than spend. The decisions required to spend money are nonviable for her. Hasn't got the nervous system for shopping, and there's nothing she wants bad enough to suffer the anxiety. She's got what she wants: the eighty-seven Vette, shanty on the river, and her music, books and drugs. And money. Real cash money. Just in case.

She's looking in the second bedroom. Plaster coming off the laths in here. Uses the room for storage. Stacks of clothes, magazines, scattered shoes and boots, and taped up boxes.

She roams back to the living room. Has a very old Donna Summer's tape. Puts this in the stereo and punches it on. Going back onto the uneven front porch, listening to the disco tunes merge with nature's concert. Figures, she continues with the Catcher Riley connection, he's a man that will want to see her place . . . . Maybe she'd like this too, for a change, with this man. She's out here on the porch a while. Chasing through the mind's chemical mists, searching for resolution. Standing outside the screen door, looking over her pink painted fingers and toenails. Looking back at her Vette. Going inside.

Turning off Donna Summers, and picking up the phone.
"Catcher Riley," he answers.
"It's me, Catcher."
"Hi, Jinx. Is it OK I called you tonight?"
"Yes. It's a good thing."
"I've tried before."
"I know. I've been too scared to pickup."
"Scared? Of me?"
"No. Not you. Scared about us."
"Whoa. It just happens a day at a time. Nothing to be overcome by."
"That's how you feel, Catcher?"
"Yes. . . . I guess that's not entirely true . . . . Actually, I am overcome. But, I'm not afraid of it."
"You come from a different place than I do. Yeah, that's it. Come to think of it, why would you be afraid of anything?"
"Jinx . . . could I come over?"
"Tonight?"
"Yes."
. . . . "OK, Catcher."
"How do I get there?"
She gives him the short cut from Cross Timbers. "Catcher, I'm not cleaning anything up. What you see is how things are."
"Good. I'll see you in a bit."

When Catcher comes rolling-in, Jinx is sitting out here on the porch, listening to an old Bee Gee's tape.

This is what Catcher sees. Jinx, barefooted, sitting on a shanty porch, ringed round by this strand of dim yellow lights. Hearing the Bee Gees disco tunes and Katydids and a lonesome whippoorwill.

Jinx gets up to meet him at the edge of the porch. She's surprising herself, returning his hug.
"You want to sit out here, or inside?"
"Why don't you show me your place."
She does. Standing back, at each room, letting Catcher soak it up.
"The banker's a hippy me thinks," he's saying. "I like it."
"Honest Injun?"
"Honest Injun. I like it. A real Ozark bohemian pad."

Going back to the porch, "You want something to drink?"

Catcher's smiling at her, "I can't believe you!"

"What'd ya mean?"

"Living out here by yourself in this cozy cabin . . . it's not like I figured . . . . You are a host of contradictions," embracing her around the waist.

"How so," looking up sideways at him.

"You're driving a Vette and live on nearly a 4x4 trail. Work at a bank, and live like a hippy. Got disco on, and it's 2001 in country music land. I don't know. You are full of surprises . . . . You must read a lot . . . . You've got a ton of books."

"Yes. Is it OK?"

"I love it. Your bathroom is great. Open window to the outdoors and claw foot tub. Give me more of this."

"I'm glad you like it. It's me."

"And, all the books. You read them?"

"Yes. I read. You want a beer?"

"Yep."

She's gone a minute, and comes back with two. Beckons him to sit down beside her on the porch.

"Nice feet," he says.

She wiggles her toes, "You like them, huh?"

"You bet I do."

. . . . Drinking their beers, listening to the sounds.

"Where are we going, Catcher?"

"Wherever you want I think."

"It would be serious with you. That's the kind of man you are, and the only thing left for me."

"I am not afraid," pinching her knee.

"Sure?"

"Yes . . . I told you before. I have nothing to lose. I have no one."

"You have your health, prestige and money."

"You have a contagious disease, Jinx?"

"No. Who knows for sure? But, there's no reason for me to think so. Why?"

"Well, you're not going to destroy my health. I'd say the contrary with all these endorphins jumping around," and Catcher takes another sip. "How are you going to hurt my prestige? You couldn't embarrass me, I don't know anyone. A retired Colonel away from the base is a fish out of water. He's a nobody."

"You could lose your money."

"How's that pray tell?"

"We go along. We get married. We get divorced. I take some of your money."

"I have enough money for a split. I'm too much of a romantic to do a pre-nuptial agreement. Besides, I might take half your riverfront property here," chuckling.

"You're older than me. Odds are you'd die before me. I'd get your money."

"So? Who am I going to leave money to? I have no one. Better you would have it than the Knights of Columbus or whatever."

Jinx is sitting here beside Catcher. Got one hand on his thigh and another around a beer. "I smoke pot. How do you feel about that?"

"I don't smoke it," he says. "But, I may. I kissed the square life goodbye a few days ago. Left Narrowsville on Yuppie Road. It's a whole new ball game now . . . . How much pot you smoke?"

"Like most smokers, now and then," uneasy with this lie. Truth is, she'd kill for a lifetime supply of Sinsemilla.

"It's illegal, where do you get it?"

"From friends."

"You lonely out here?"

"I don't think so."

"Maybe that's why you smoke pot."

"I smoke pot for the same reason you drink beer," she lies again. She smokes dope to keep from having a nervous breakdown. It's a 'must.'

"I don't think pot would bother me. It's foreign to me," Catcher offers.

"I'll get us a couple more beers," Jinx says as she gets up. "No reason to jump ahead of ourselves."

She's back with the beer.

"What happens if we are good together, Catcher?"

"We get married and I take care of you. The Christian-American way."

"And me you . . . ." The Christian American way is a vast hostile territory to her.

 . . . . Drinking. Thinking about what they've said.

"Catcher, you're the first man I've ever had on my place . . . except for Jake."

"Who's Jake?"

"An old, old friend from kindergarten on. In fact, you're the only person, except for Jake, ever on my place."

"No one ever stayed over or just come to visit?"

"No sir. No one!"

. . . .

"What time you have to be at the bank in the morning?"

"Six A.M. I get up at four-thirty."

"Whoa." Catcher takes a big drink of his beer, "I'd better get out of here."

"You can stay if you want." Jinx tilts her head up sideways towards him.

"That wouldn't bother you?"

"I don't think so, or I wouldn't ask . . . . I trust you."

"I'll stay." Catcher's heart is speeding.

"C'mon," and Jinx is getting-up, waiting for Catcher to follow her into her shanty castle.

She's given him the bathroom first. He's in the claw foot tub, showering, peering at the night through the open window, wondering at his changed circumstances. Thinking of her bed, and the open bedroom windows. Very natural.

He's brought his rolled up clothes into the bedroom and gotten into the bed naked. Hears Jinx taking a shower. Listening to an owl out in the woods somewhere. Off in the distance, makes out the bellow of bullfrogs.

The sheets are fresh. Wondering where the washer and dryer are. Must be on the back porch. He didn't see this. Pulling up the sheet and quilt against the damp, cool night air. Like camping out, except he's on this cushy mattress in Jinx's bedroom. Everything seems clean. Messy, but clean.

She's shutting the shower off, coming out in a towel, hair wet, turning the bathroom light off. In the light of the bedroom lamp, she's taken the towel off to dry her hair. Standing at the foot of the bed, smiling at Catcher. Puts her arm down at her side, holding the towel.

"You like?"

Catcher's got his head propped up by a pillow leaned against the spindles, "I'm mesmerized."

Jinx goes back to drying her hair. Then, she hangs the towel on the closest doorknob, winds the alarm clock, turns off the lamp, and gets in under the sheets with Catcher.

Something strange happens on the way to love tonight. Maybe it's because Jinx skipped her last J of the day; maybe it's because she's never had a man in her bed before; maybe it's because Catcher's loving her instead of fucking her. And, fucking is the only loving she knows. Nonetheless, it's strange. She's sandpaper agitated. Got the creepy crawlies or something. Where's the greed? Where's the humiliation? Hoping Catcher cannot sense this. He's caressing her instead of fingering her. And, she's slowly getting wet.

Catcher says something about a corner post and back breaking work. More murmuring than talking. She's feeling embarrassed to do him the way she does a man. There's a modesty issue she hasn't felt. And, when it's over and he's asleep, she's inking the whole thing down to bad karma. Angry. Somehow, he's made her feel this way. There is twisted anti-logic at play. *Fucking is love, love is not fucking*? Finally, her misshapen sexuality slackens so her body can rest in an uneven sleep.

When the alarm goes off, Catcher wants to get up with her.

"It's still dark, Catcher. Go back to sleep. You needn't lock up when you leave."

He's sitting on the edge of the bed, rubbing his back. "Sore," he mutters.

She kisses him, and pushes him back under the blankets. Gets her suit and pumps out of the plaster closet and turns the lamp off.

When Catcher reawakens, it's daylight. As it happens, something strange happened on the way to love last night . . . to Catcher. He fell in. So, he's laying here in the cool of her room, absorbing the Jinx experience. Leaf splattered sunlight and shadows, leaves clicking in the breeze outside. Very cool, and very cozy under the quilt.

Showering in the claw foot tub, watching the trees waving in the breeze outside. And he's dressed and made the bed and gone out. Before getting in the Ramcharger, he takes a good look around at Jinx's shanty castle. It's sitting here in a little patch of meadow, up against the Little Niangua river. Distant rough-cut ridges off to the sides. The color green is everywhere—in the wood lined ridges, in the fescue meadow, in the yard oaks and in the weeds lining the perimeters. Blue sky plopped down on top of this. Cotton candy clouds floating overhead and the ever-present circling turkey vultures. Then, there's Jinx's shanty itself. Metal roof, Cajun style habitat. Can tell somebody cares, but wastes nothing on frills maintenance. Looks like a lover's hideaway.

Catcher's shifting into reverse. Thinking he'd rather live here with Jinx than at his place. Far and away from the American estates, in the vacuity among dots . . . the excluded. Course, Catcher hasn't a notion as to dot asymmetry. In other words, he hasn't seen anything yet. Sometimes, a dot is not just a dot. Each is his or her own sovereign, unbounded atom . . . i.e. Jinks the Jenks the Jinx.

Catcher is visualizing Jinx and himself, out here in this imaginary utopia . . . far from the blacktop. You might say, Catcher's out of his mind . . . . May be . . . . His next item of business is to meet Erik Starr.

CHAPTER XXVIII

Erik's got a problem. This is the median intelligence level of the OMP gang. It's a hair low for the job at hand. Erik also has the solution. His 'jury' says Bugs is the low end of the intelligence curve. His 'judge' rules the death penalty. And, Erik's 'executioner' says he'll kill him . . . . Erik is going to kill Bugs!

Erik is angry. Jinx doesn't call him like she should. What kind of bullshit is this? He doesn't know her phone number and doesn't know where she works. The bitch needs to get with the program. She's his woman, and he fucking well ought to get laid when he wants it.

Erik is very angry. Thinks about his father driving them off with a ball bat. Couldn't do a thing to satisfy the prick or the brownnoser his dad married. That is, his mother. Must have some hardy genes, cause he couldn't remember his mother ever taking him to a doctor. He'd show 'em just how hardy his fucking genes were.

That Riley fuck over at Cross Timbers? Something funny about that. The guy never turned a light on . . . . Went around and came in the back of the barn. Switched the light off in there . . . . That fucker likes the dark. Bet he lives alone . . . . Never yelled or anything. Fucking weird. Shot a hole in his boat, and he never turned a light on or made a sound.

He's got this Bugs roaming around, all over the place, and he knows all about the OMP operation, and he's so fucking weak, he'd start blabbing if a cop asked him for directions.

Erik's sitting here on the front porch of the shabby two-story house, in the hazy morning sunlight, watching the boys get ready to leave. The guineas are cackling, and the dogs are after a rabbit. Smoking a J with his coffee. Watching the guys gas up the boats and loading the coolers. The place is starting to look like some fucking guerrilla camp. Snipers dressed in full camo with their faces blackened and toting high-powered rifles with scopes. Damn fucking good thing they've got hidden dirt ramps to launch the boats.... Amused at the idea of launching the boats from Truman Lake public access areas.... Excuse me Catcher something-or-other and family, while we back our boats down the ramp and off load the commandos.... No, we're not going to blow up the dam, we're just guarding our marijuana fields, thank you very much.... Hell, it would be hard to explain if they got stopped by the County Mounties. But, Erik knows the guys would handle it, if this happened, and they wouldn't get nervous and spill the beans. That is, all of 'em except Bugs.

Pretty soon, they'd be culling the male plants out. The female plants putting out the THC rich resin, and no male pollen to fertilize it. That's the goal. Send Bugs out there, he'll be pulling the females right along with the scragglier males. Fact is, Erik's not even sure if Bugs could distinguish between Cannabis Sativa and thistle weed. One dumb fuck for sure.

Looks like Boomer and Swede are driving today. Judging by the camo, it appears Mark, Trace and Swede are pulling sniper duty. Some of the others are in camo and with rifles. Risky business, this crew pulling boats on the public highway system of Missouri.... Sarge coming towards Erik...

"We're out of here, Erik..."

"Leave Bugs today, Sarge," Erik putting his coffee cup down on the porch floor.

"You got it boss," Sarge going back to find Bugs. "I'll get him."

Erik's watching Jack and Steve get in the trucks, but he's not seeing Bugs... low end of the median curve for sure. Then, Sarge is bringing him up from the barn, Bugs looking sleepy and bewildered. Dumbfuck probably been dozing in the barn while the rest are loading. Sarge leaving off before getting to the porch, but Bugs coming on up.

"What's the deal, Erik?" Bugs is nervous and shifty eyed, avoiding direct contact with Erik's eyes.

"Hold it here a minute, Bugs," and Erik's sliding off the porch, standing up past Bugs, hands on his hips, watching the trucks, trailers and boats pulling out. Then, it's quiet, except for the guineas and the shrill cry of a distant hawk.

Erik turning around to face Bugs, thinking about the chipped wooden ball bats in a corner crib of the barn. Putting his arm over Bugs' shoulders, looking over in Bugs' face.

"Let's take a walk, Bugs," moving him towards the barn.

"What for, Erik? What're we doing?" Trying not to face Erik. Seen the murder-behind-the-eyes look in Erik's expression.

"We're going to have a talk, Bugs, in the barn, Starr family style," pulling Bugs along towards the barn. Bugs seeing the butt of the .357 revolver stuck out of Erik's jeans. Really scared now.

"What'd I do, Erik? I didn't do anything," whining through thin quivering lips.

"Anybody care you were born, Bugs?" Erik holding Bugs up close to him, walking him towards the barn.

"What'ya, what'ya m . . . m . . . mean, Erik?"

"Like, who cares what happens to you?"

"I du . . . dunno, Erik," and Bugs starts shaking.

They're going past the horses, through the big opening now, into the barn. Erik walking them to the center. There's straw and old manure smell, and some startled vultures fly out overhead. Erik's letting loose of Bugs, looking around the barn for some wire.

"Wha . . . wha . . . whata'ya going to do, Erik?"

"Just stand here Bugs, I'm looking for some visual aids. I want you to get the picture here."

Erik's pulling a strand of barbed wire, about seven foot long, off a nail. Goes over to the corner crib and picks up the old ball bats from out of the straw and fuzzy spider webs.

Gets back in front of Bugs. Drops the bats and is straightening this strand of old barb wire.

"What'd I d . . . do, Erik?" Bugs almost crying.

"You were born, Bugs. That's all. You didn't ask. You just got born," and Erik's holding Bugs wrist up, wrapping a loop of barbed wire around it . . . tight.

"That's cutting me, Erik," and Bugs is pulling his hand back, thinking about making a grab for Erik's pistol. Terrified!

"Would you hold still, Bugs? In some ways, I'm more fair than father Starr." Erik's wrapping the other end of the wire around his own wrist, twisting the end around, so it's fast.

Both men are wired together, about six or seven feet apart, bleeding around the barbed wire fastened around their wrists.

Erik pulls Bugs over a little, while he picks up a ball bat. Giving Bugs this, putting it in his free hand, wrapping Bugs' fingers around it. "Hold it, damn it Bugs. Hold it."

Erik pulls the revolver out of his jeans and tosses it over on a pile of straw. Picks up his bat. Now, the two men are standing here facing each other, wired together, each holding a wooden ball bat. Erik aggressive and powerful; and Bugs, a shivering, pathetic, narrow little man with a stark stubble on his ashen face.

Erik's kind of smiling. Still got the murder-behind-the-eyes look. Bug's perplexed and frightened out of his mind.

"Wha . . . wha . . . what we doing, Erik?"

"I'm going to give you a Starr family lesson, Bugs," just standing here watching Bugs. "Here's how it works. You can take the first whack at me . . . we didn't get that from Pops. Then, I'm going to beat you to death Bugs. How do you like that?" Erik's smirking at him.

"Wh . . . why, Erik? What'd I do," crying more than saying this.

"You're the weak link Bugs. A chain's no stronger than it's weakest link. I'm going to make you the missing link." Erik isn't smiling anymore. "C'mon. Take your swing." Erik's standing with his arms down at his sides, pulling the wire tight, the bat dangling from his free hand.

"I . . . I . . . can't hit you, Erik," and Bugs wants off the wire and a hole to crawl into.

"Make your first blow count. You get lucky, you could kill me and save your life." Erik is commanding him.

. . . . Nothing. Nothing happens. Bugs just shaking, in the grip of terror.

"Get with it, Bugs. In a minute, I'm going to kill you."

Through the paralyzing fear, Bugs knows this is his last chance. Gotta hit Erik with the bat. He's crying, but the survival instinct is calculating his best blow. He's got the bat back, and he tightens his grip. Bugs' survival gnome is readying a swing at the red haired predator . . . even through the molasses fear. Crying.

He does it. He swings, enfeebled by fear. Erik deflects it with the wire on his wrist.

Erik hunches over. Got the wire in his hand, so he can jerk Bugs where he wants him. Then, he begins in earnest to beat Bugs to death. It's grisly, and will get more so.

Bugs drops his bat, and is fallen in a heap on the floor, trying to hold his hands up over his head. But, Erik's full bulk is slamming the bat down on him, blow after blow. There's blood all over, and Bugs' crying has stopped. Then, Bugs is a limp pile, and the wire is loose between them. Erik pulls back, so he can deliver a crushing blow to Bugs' skull. The horses making a racket out in the corral.

He's loosening the wire between them, throwing it aside, towards his bat. Breathing hard, and got the pinpoint pupils. Looking down at Bugs, "You fucking, whining baby." Hears the horses outside, banging into the sides of the corral and letting out shrill, high pitched shrieks.

Erik goes back to look out the barn opening. Scans the grounds for anything out of the ordinary. No noise from the guinea quarter and no dogs. Good thing, Erik's thinking. Nothing should mess with him right now. He's feeling extra powerful at the moment. And, very much in control. Eerily, even the horses have become still.

Goes back and stands over what's left of Bugs. Stupid morphodite son-of-a-bitch. Just a pulverized heap of blood, bones, tissue and hair. Looks like a dead calf wrapped in rags. Now, what is it he tells the men to do with the bodies?

He's going out of the barn and up to the house. Coming back with a handful of Hefty, Cinch Sack, and plastic trash bags. Goes over to the tools leaned up against an inside wall. Reaches through the shovel and rake handles to the double-headed axe. Brings this back and lays it down beside Bugs' pile. Looking around. Spies part of a woodpile left over from last winter. Pulls half a bolt from the pile. Takes this back near the body, and lays it down on the flat side. He reaches down, and pulls Bugs' arm out and lays the wrist over the bolt. Stands back and raises the axe. Brings it down with a hard chop, severing Bugs' hand. Then, he repeats the process with Bugs' other hand. Takes the two hands, stuffs them down in a trash bag and throws it off to the side.

He's pulling Bugs' head out, dragging the body by the broken head until he's got the head over the bloody bolt of wood. Arranges this so Bugs' neck is arched over the bolt. Stands back and raises the axe. Brings it down with a driving force, severing the head from the body. Takes the head by it's hair and drops this in an open trash bag.

Erik walks over and uses a bloody hand to pick up his revolver. Stuffs it back in his belt.

Now, he's carrying the trash bags, with the head and hands, out the rear end of the barn. Going into the woods behind . . . . About an hour later, he's back. Brings the two empty bloody trash bags into the barn and throws them down on the dirt powder floor. It's getting hot in the barn, and the flies are gathering over the bloody heap that was Bugs.

Erik takes off his bloody shirt and throws it aside. Gets what's left of Bugs' body up and over his shoulders, holding an ankle and forearm in front. Heads out the rear end of the barn, and into the woods.

It is afternoon when Erik comes back. He scares the dogs away from the fly covered blood. Kicks them out of the barn. Throws the bloody bolt of wood over with the bloody trash bags, and gets a shovel. Shovels dirt around till most the blood is covered. Picks up the bolt of wood and trash bags, and carries these to the smoldering trash barrel. Gets this fire going again, so that the wood and bags will burn. Goes back and gets the axe and his bat. Carries these over to an outside, freeze-proof water faucet, and washes them off. Puts the cleaned bat, along with Bugs' bat, back in the crib, and places the axe back with the tools.

Finally, Erik is stripping, washing off at the outside spicket. Rinsing off his t-shirt, shorts, jeans and boots. Shutting the faucet off and carrying his clothes, boots and revolver up to the house. Walking funny across the barnyard and lawn, naked and barefooted. Doing the rocky beach, barefoot gawky walk.

Lays the .357 revolver on the edge of the porch floor. Gets his clothes going in the wash machine and takes a shower. It's late afternoon before he's back on the front edge of the porch, next to his .357, smoking a J and drinking beer . . . . That fucking Jinx is going to get some stiff pipe; lots of it. And, he's going to improve their commo procedures too. But, first, he's going to lay some pipe.

Watching the turkey vultures circling on the thermals overhead. That's when he sees the old brown Ramcharger coming up the lane . . . . Looks like the one he saw at Riley's place. Can't be sure. It was dark, and he wasn't paying attention to the vehicles . . . . Just looking for the boat.

CHAPTER XXIX

Maybe it's love, the Jinx spell, but Catcher's feeling bulletproof. Going to drive right into the OMP, meet Erik Starr, and ask if he's had any vandalism . . . if anybody's shot holes in his boats. A bit reckless, uncharacteristic you might say, but, hell, this isn't a special ops mission. It's the Midwest, not Central America. Still, he's wearing the loaded .45, in plain view, in a shoulder holster over his sweatshirt.

Driving under the October Mount Pontiac sign, past the No Trespassing signs, and easing along the lane, dodging anorexic cows and cow pies. Dust stretching out behind and the heat of day coming in the open windows. Crossing the little stream traversing the lane. Then, he's coming over the last little rise, in full view of the ramshackled improvements up ahead.

Sees the man sitting on the edge of the porch, and drives right up here, past the guineas and mangy dogs. Shuts the engine off and dismounts the Ram. Approaching Erik, figuring this one's a hard case for sure.

"Can't you read. The signs say no trespassing," Erik squashing the J on the porch floor, glaring out glassy eyes at this dumbfuck, come in here like the cavalry or something.

"Call the sheriff. I need him too," Catcher giving him a phony grin. Coming across the dirt lawn, up closer, spying the .357 on the porch beside Erik.

Erik's just sitting here, on the front edge of the porch, glowering through glazed eyes. "I don't need the sheriff," feeling around on the porch for the revolver.

"My name's Catcher Riley," unsnapping the .45 shoulder holster, gripping the COLT therein, casual like, like holding a strap on your bib overalls. Exaggerating his fake smile, "I wouldn't touch that."

Catcher's boldness shocks Erik into a moment of clarity. He's pulling his hand back, up in front, "Hold it, mister. Just hold it right there." Even after the ganja and booze, his hand trembles. After all, he's murdered and butchered a man today. He doesn't need this shit.

"Be careful," Catcher's eyes drilling through Erik, still with the phony, exaggerated grin plastered on his face.

"What do you want, old man," Erik resting both hands to his side now. "You don't know much, come bustin' in here past those signs," shaking his head, but eyes straight ahead to Catcher's, looking mean as a snake. Erik's thinking about Bugs, out there in pieces, in the woods. The blood.

"You been having trouble with vandalism?" Talking out that very phony grin. "In the middle of the night, shooting things up?"

"That's totally not happen'n here," the hint of a smug grin forming on the criminal's face. Sweat beads heavy in the making.

Catcher *knows* this guy is the one. He's *knowing* that the stories about the OMP are true, and this is the bunch that pointed the rifle at him. *This is the one* that came onto his property with the shotgun . . . . "Well, you aren't much help, are you?" Big phony grin, staring with his head cocked to the side, treating Erik like a stupid child.

At gut level, Erik's jolted by a sense of caution. This is new for him. "Get off my place, asshole," gripping the front edge of the porch floor on both sides, leaning forward, like 'What you going to do about it.' "You're trespassing. This is my place."

"Nice to know what you look like, Erik," Catcher dropping the affected grin, leaning in towards Erik, real serious like. "That is your name, right. Erik Starr. Owner of the infamous OMP. Cash crop king of the neighborhood."

"Fuck you," without a trace of humanity in his voice or on his face. Hands holding-on to the edge of the porch either side, into an unblinking icy stare. Gets a flash of Bugs' body coming apart.

"You better grow an eye in the back of your head, Slick," Catcher using some psy-ops on him, before backing up.

He walks backward, keeping his hand on the .45 in the holster. He keeps it this way until he's in the Ram. And then, he unholsters the .45 and lays it on the passenger seat. Backing the Ram up, past the guineas, even farther, until he backs into the pasture and swings around, driving forward now, towards the OMP exit.

He's going to continue his education on the OMP . . . . But, for now, his thoughts drift back to Jinx.

CHAPTER XXX

Endorphin (en dor' fin), n. Any group of peptides, resembling opiates, that are released in the body in response to stress or trauma and that react with the brain's opiate receptors to reduce sensation of pain. (1970-75: end (ogenous) (m)orphine, with—ine resp. as-in')—Webster's, Copyright 1991

The word is not in WEBSTER'S DICTIONARY, Copyright 1947. The word is not listed in the Index of Tortora's and Anagnostakos' *Principles of Anatomy & Physiology*, Copyright 1978.

By year 2001, the word is in the dictionary and endorphins are known to be released in the body during sex. You might say, love flies on it's own wings.

Catcher is not on morphine. It must be the endorphins. His critical thinking has evolved into opportunity thinking . . . as regards the ranch and Jinx.

He's got this idea to skip the cattle all together, and instead, develop a hay farm. His thinking is not to get rich, but to make the ranch a paying proposition.

He already has the huge metal hay barn for storage. Figures he's got about five hundred acres of grass. On a ten-year average, he calculates he can get about three bales, the five by sixes, for about eleven hundred and fifty pounds to the acre. In an average year, he can get two cuttings, but the second cutting will yield only sixty-five per cent of the first cutting. That means a total of five bales per acre per season . . . times five hundred acres, is a total of two thousand and five hundred bales. Selling bales at twenty dollars per (fescue and clover), he should gross about fifty thousand dollars. He's already got the monster hay barn back in the middle of the ranch. He'll store the bales in this, and improve access to the barn, so buyers can get their trucks and trailers in and out. Figures he needs a rake, bale spikes and trailers. For field hands, he's got Marco. Marco always needs the money.

The love opiate is particularly observable in his attitude towards Jinx. Little does he know, it's more his endorphins than hers. Not to take anything from her. She's beautiful all right. And, younger. And, got an hour glass midsection with lean arms and legs, and painted nails on proportionate toes and fingers, and a medium neck and intelligent face framed in lightened blonde hair. And a stimulating ambivalence vis-à-vis the male gender. Walks and moves in a considered manner, it would seem. She's got the breath of ripe melons and smells like the Gobi Desert. Catcher's got some ideas about her.

Today, he's in Springfield, shopping used farm equipment dealers. Not buying, but shopping. Towards day's end, he's in a jewelry store. Not shopping, but buying.

Coming back through Cross Timbers in the humidity. Dust and pollen and micro moisture droplets in the Ozark troposphere. He's coming home to his no-cattle-and-not-much-going-on ranch. Gets in just before dark.

Cleaned-up and sitting on the settee in the living room, considering the phone. A small luminous banner floats through his cerebral fluid: 'There's no fool like an old fool.' Catcher's analyzing this idea. Far as he can see, you're only a fool if you've misread reality. He doesn't think he has . . . misread reality. Of course, this is why there's the saying.

'No guts, no glory' is more along Catcher's style of thinking. 'Nothing ventured, nothing gained.' Then, there's his oversimplified and erroneous presumption that he hasn't anything to lose. He dials Jinx.

Jinx is out here on the Ozarks' rough cut, enjoying her personal cocoon spun from Ozark Gold. Took an extra Xanex to insure this silky cover. Recovering from an anxious day caused by a conflicted night. The brainteaser is still there. *Fucking is love, love is not fucking* . . . . The first part, she started to learn about seven, from her pa.

She's trying to read Steinbeck's *East of Eden*, an interesting choice given her circumstances. Now, her phone is ringing, and she's figuring it's Catcher Riley. Even in the golden Xanex cocoon, she's got some very mixed-up feelings on this. She doesn't answer. Knows he'll call again, so she's having another doober.

His lovemaking was deeply disturbing, precisely because it was . . . love making. Her sub-zero self-esteem is intimidated here. She understands and responds best to hard sex.

Still, she's got an unexplained affinity for Catcher. Boils down to: Jinx West goes for Catcher and Jinx East does not. Maybe she belongs on the other side of the river. She's taking another hit, concluding she'll answer the phone. After all, Jinx West needs all the encouragement she can get.

"Hello," sounding dreamy.

"Jinx?" Catcher checking to make sure.

"Yes."

"Thanks for last night."

"Thank you," she says, "for coming over."

"I like your place."

"What for? It isn't much."

"It's got a lot of features mine doesn't. First, there's you."

"Thank you, Catcher," and Jinx sounds vague.

"How was your day?"

"Seemed long. I wanted to come home all day. What have you been up to?"

"Trying to map out a way to get my land on a paying basis . . . where you're concerned, trying to decide between a HAHO or a HALO."

"Wanna run that by me again," Jinx sounding more alert.

"Trying to decide between a High Altitude / High Opening or a High Altitude / Low Opening. The intel's a little sketchy."

"You're losing me, Catcher," and Jinx getting interested.

"My fencing is good on the ranch, but I don't know a damn thing about cattle, so I've been figuring how to turn a dollar out here. Bout decided to make this place a hay farm."

"This part I understand Catcher. I'm not understanding about HAHOs and HALOs. The part about me."

"I know what you meant," Catcher laughing. "HAHO and HALO are parachuting terms. On a High Altitude High Opening you jump out of the plane at a high altitude, maybe twenty thousand feet, open up your chute right away, do a twenty-mile parasail, more or less, to target. Tricky getting where you want to go, but very exhilarating. A HALO, the High Altitude Low Opening, is where you jump at a high altitude and free fall to a low opening, say under two thousand feet."

"You did that?" Jinx leaning forward.

"I was a special ops army officer, Jinx. I did it in ice, above oxygen, at night . . ."

"What for?" Jinx asks before thinking.

"Taking out tangos, my dear," Catcher's laughing again. "It's more about coming in on target, where you're concerned."

"How many times you do that, jump out of a plane," Jinx wondering out loud.

"Let me see . . ." Catcher is playing daffy, "one week, fifty times," laughing. "No joke."

"That is dangerous," she comments. "You could bust your head open."

"They've got titanium plates for that," cavalier like.

"You have one of those?" Jinx laughs.

"No. But I've got a few souvenirs."

"Like what?" She wants to know. "I've had a pretty good look at you. I didn't see anything." She's smiling through the phone.

"Nothing you would notice. What's important is the kind of jump I'm going to do on you," laughing again.

"You going to open high or low?" Jinx is laughing.

"I am thinking a HALO . . . open just before I hit the tarmac . . . that means, I'm coming on fast to target. That's you."

Jinx is laughing. Can't tell she's been to Dooberville. "How you going to do that, sir?"

"How about I explain it over dinner?"

"When?"

"Whenever you like."

"About any night but Friday."

"What's going on Friday night?" Catcher's hearing the night sounds through Jinx's phone.

. . . . "I do my shopping Friday nights," flatly.

"Well, how bout I take you to dinner Saturday night?"

. . . . "OK."

"I'll pick you up at five."

"That's pretty early."

"I think we'll eat in Kansas City."

"It takes two hours to get to Kansas City, you know."

"I'm up for it, if you are."

"What should I wear?"

"A dress and heels, if you'd like."

. . . . "I can do that." Jinx is thinking she'll take her Xanex.

"Five o'clock then. Saturday?"

"Yes, Catcher. I'll be ready."

"Anybody else you'd rather go with?" Catcher asks administratively.
"Pardon?"
"Is there anybody else you'd rather have a date with this Saturday?"
"No, there is not," conclusively.
"Good. I'll be there at five."
"Goodnight, Catcher."
"Goodnight, Jinx."

Catcher is emptying his pockets before undressing to take a shower. Putting his pocketknife, loose change and dollars, keys and checkbook on his bedroom dresser. Stops before laying the wallet down and opens it. Pulls out the scrap of paper he picked up on the brushy bank of the Sac River. The one that has a phone number written on it next to the notation, 'R4'. He's thinking about the OMP and the head creep, Erik Starr. Goes down to the living room and dials the 'R4' number.

Getting no answer. Then, an answering machine kicks on, 'This is Jake Boss. You've reached R4 nightclub on the Little Niangua. Please leave a . . .' Hears a phone receiver pickup, "Hello, hello," the answering machine echoing in the background. "Hold on a second . . . ." Hears a beep, and his connection clears.

"This is Jake Boss. Sorry about the answering machine. Can I help you?" Jake is short of breath.

"I've got this phone number and don't know what it's for," Catcher somewhat abruptly.

"You've reached R4," Jake's recovering his wind. "A private, membership only, nightclub in Camden County."

"How do I get a membership," Catcher sounding a little testy.

"You can come by here or I can mail you our package," Jake's breathing more normal. "Who am I speaking to?"

"This is Catcher Riley. Where are you located?"

. . . . Jake's taken back. Catcher Riley is the name of Jinx's new friend. The one she mentioned. "Got a pencil and paper?"

"Got it."

Jake gives the location of R4, and the directions thereto.

"I'll come by and see you, Jake. Thanks for the info."

"No sweat, Catcher. I'm closed tonight. Was working on my air conditioning."

"What kinds of folks belong to your club?"

"You name an occupation, it's probably represented here. Lots of country folk and professionals from town, too. Mostly all single or getting that way."

"Music, drinking and dancing?"

"Live music. It's a B.Y.O. club. Bring your own bottle. We have a large dance floor . . . nice setting. We're right on the Little Niangua. I think of it as a country-country club. Our brochure has all the details."

"I'll come by, Jake. Thanks again."

"Have a good one."

CHAPTER XXXI

The guineas are quiet. The dogs have run off and the men are taciturn. They've got an idea of what happened to Bugs, and they're scared shitless . . . . Erik still hasn't heard from Jinx . . . . The Bugs dismemberment . . . . Had that disturbing visit from the old geezer, Riley whatever. Came driving in here like he owned the place . . . . All things considered, he's having a junior fucking high day. A bad fucking hair day.

He's sitting here by himself in the living room at the OMP, studying some aerial maps under a lamp, when the phone rings. Trace comes running down the stairs, but when he sees Erik, he goes back up.

"OMP."

"Erik," she says.

"Who the hell you think it is?"

"Oohh, nice mood, must be missing your lovey dovey."

"Where are you?"

"I'm on my cell," and she is. Driving out her lane in the '87 Vette.

"Where can I meet you?"

"Same place as last time. I'm leaving now." She sounds cool enough. Truth is, she's got butterflies . . . another one of those days. Feeling the scrape across the chalkboard.

"See you there," and Erik sets the receiver back in it's cradle, scowling.

Yelling upstairs, "I'll be back in the morning." Out in the pickup, spinning the tires down the lane.

Jinx is parked behind the boarded up cabin. Smokin' her last doober. Top is down on the Vette and she's resting her head back on the top of her seat, watching the crescent shaped moon in the east, floating her eyes upward to the celestial sparkles. 'How many stars are there,' taking another toke.

'Where are you God? Out there somewhere, on your own paradise planet? Why am I so angry God?'

Erik swings in with his lights off.

"About fucking time," he's ranting as he exits the truck. Comes over and lifts Jinx's arm to get her out of the Vette. "Come over here, I wanna show you something prissy pants."

Erik is leading her over to the truck. She still has the doober going. Taking a final hit as Erik is opening the passenger door to his truck.

"See that tackle box on the floor your majesty," he's letting go of her and pulling the bright yellow fishing tackle box out, setting it on the ground. Opening it up in the light from the truck interior. Removing the tray with fishing lures, and pointing to the tightly packed quarter pound baggies of bud. "See that, bitch?"

Out of the blue, she reaches out and scratches him across the neck. "Who's a bitch, you punk."

Erik grabbing her wrist. "You do that again and you'll be looking for your head across the road." He's down in her face, and she can see the crazies in his eyes . . . like he's got some rabid bacteria wildly multiplying in there.

"Let go of my wrist, Erik."

He drops her arm.

They're standing here staring each other down, next to the knocked over fishing tackle box.

"You call me a bitch again Erik, you'd better say it nice and sweet . . . while you're giving me eight inches." Givin' it to him straight and level.

Erik's got his hand up on his neck, checking the blood there.

"Look at the fucking box, Jinx. That's just a drop in the bucket, saved back from last year. I can get seven or eight hundred dollars tomorrow for each bag. You want some or not?"

Stepping back, "Give me one, Erik."

"No way. I'll give you part of one when we are done."

She's not answering.

He steps up close, kneels down and roughly unbuttons her Wranglers, yanking the zipper down, pushing her around against the truck fender. Can't get his tongue in where he wants it, so he's jerking her boots off. She holds up one foot, then the other, for him to pull her jeans off. This is her last voluntary act in the matter.

He's shoving her legs apart for rough cunnilingus. Yanking her off the truck fender to the tall grasses and forcing his penis into her while her head is reeling. Ripping the tank top off and licking, sucking and biting her breasts.

And, when she feels him finish, he repeats this rough sex. And, again, while she's laying flat, semi-conscious, he assaults her again, stopping to roll her over. He's pulling her hips up to do it doggy style, and gripping the nape of her neck, forcing her to the edge of unconsciousness. Finalizing the attack with a thrust that drives her cheek hard into the ground. Through all this, her only sound is to groan or grunt. She offers no resistance. And, when it's over, Erik rolls back on the grass, breathing like a wounded rhino. All he has on is his t-shirt.

Getting up and padding over to the pickup. Fumbling inside for a doober, and bringing this back. Straddling Jinx and squatting over her with his buttocks on her pelvis and his privates over her bottom ribs. Firing up the J.

She's laying here in mild shock, with her eyes closed. Her vagina is burning, and she's got a hard hurt in her uterus.

"Here Jinx, take a hit," and Erik is giving her pure bud.

Without opening her eyes, she's dragging on this potent ganja stick. Feels the pain thawing, and beginning to hear the night sounds. Hearing the katydids and occasional whippoorwill. Then, some coyotes running. She's opening her eyes, looking straight up at the moon. Watching the stars spreading out from the lunar crescent . . . and, Erik's overhanging shadow. Taking another toke, looking for stoner heaven.

Erik reaches over and grabs his jeans. Pulls his wallet out, and withdraws a card with a number combination on it. "21-57-48," he yells. "That's the combination to my safe baby. I've got over one million, five hundred thousand dollars in cash. It's for us."

He puts the card back in his wallet and the wallet back in his jeans. He rises up and goes back to the pickup. Comes back and straddles Jinx again. He's gripping a .357 MAGNUM in his hand, and he rests this on her breast, pointing upward at the bottom of her jaw.

"And I've got the bullets to keep what I want." He uses the barrel of the .357 to raise the Tahiti charm. "What is this Mojo bullshit?" Letting the charm slide off the end of the barrel. "You better not forget what class of people you come from baby doll."

He gets up and takes the pistol back to the truck. Coming back and picking his jeans up. Starting to put these on, "You baby, are out of your class with a Jar Head officer. So, here's what you're going to do," slamming one leg, then the other into his jeans. "You're going to go right ahead with this farce. Have sushi and frappacinos on the high towers in the My-Shit-Don't-Stink-Beverly-Fucking-Hills Country Club. You're going to marry this Fed asshole, the one I don't have a name for. Then, I'm going to kill him on your honey-fucking-moon. You're going to collect the insurance, and we're putting it with my money, and we're going to go somewhere and make a baby . . . . You are mine forever, sweet cheeks."

"Give me my purse, out of my car," Jinx is barely audible. Flat on her back in the grass. Her voice is strangely apart.

Erik's looking over at her, buttoning his jeans. Sees a trickle of blood coming out of her nostril. "Yeah, baby, I'll get it."

Coming back holding her purse, getting between the moon and her. "You're going to plan a honeymoon floating some river or doing a yuppie back-fucking-pack trip. I'm going to do him out there in the woods . . . so it, it will look like an accident. Then, you'll collect your dowry. You got it?"

. . . . No answer.

"You got it, baby? You gotta choose. It's either the dweeb or it's me. We all make choices, baby."

Jinx groans, has her eyes open.

"We're two of a kind, Jinx. Two black sheep left to the wolves . . . just say yes."

"Yes . . . . Give me my Xanex, Erik," her voice strangely separate.

He's pulling a prescription bottle out, holding it in the moonlight.

"It says AL-PRO-SO-LAM, or something like that."

"That's it. Give me two." Feebly reaching up.

"No, baby. This isn't Xanex."

"It's the generic. Give me two," timorous. She's propping herself up on her two arms behind, the torn tank top hanging off her shoulder. Screams like a crazy person, "GIVE ME THE XANEX!"

He's shaking two out. Gives 'em to her.

She pops them in her mouth, using saliva to swallow them whole.

Laying back down and curling up on her side in the fetal position. Crying softly, then louder and louder.

Erik's standing here watching. He's never seen this before. She sounds like a little girl now. Crying like a little girl.

Her mind is slipping out of the present, making room for the darkling.

'Lick it good Jinx. Lick Daddy's Dolly clean . . . now put it back in my pants, and zipper me up.' She's pulling her pa's zipper up, and he's got his hands behind her ears, pulling her delicate face into his stained trousers. She's holding still here, just watching her fishing pole laying in the grass at the edge of the water.

"Jinx, what the hell you doing. Cut it out," Erik's snarling down at her.

'Don't tell your mommy about our little game Jinx. Don't tell her about Dolly. If you tell her, she'll shoot herself. She will be mad about our little secret.' Her daddy's unshaven face down in hers now, smiling at her, then pulling the bill on his cap down, and staggering away . . . she's getting her fishing pole up and letting the hook back into the river.

"Jinx, get the fuck up," and Erik's pulling her up. The Xanex is kicking in and she's coming into the present. Standing here, nearly naked, looking around, getting her bearings.

"What are you fucking doing girl? You're acting nuts," Erik handing up her jeans. "You need a doober," going over to the pickup.

Coming back with the J, while she's trying to pull her boots on. She hurts . . . up on the inside.

Stumbles toward the Vette. Gets her door open and falls in behind the steering wheel. Erik's putting her purse in. Closing the door.

He lights the doober and hands it down to her. She takes it and leans back for a hit.

"You understand what we're doing with Jar Head or not?"

Holding the joint in her left hand, out the side of the Vette, putting the ignition key in. Erik reaches in and pulls her keys out.

"You and I together, baby. What's your choice?" Erik's standing back, looking down into the Vette, watching her take another hit. She's got the doober, resting her free hand in her lap. Leaning her head back on her seat.

"I'm going to marry this colonel," she pauses, to take a hit. "Then, we're going to kill him . . . on my honeymoon. You have my dope?"

"Yeah baby. I've got some dope." He goes to the pickup to get her a baggy. Bringing it back and handing it over . . . a token amount. "What's your hubby's name?"

"Don't ev-er ask me that again. I'm warning you . . ."

"I need your phone number," he says pissed.

"I'll give you my cell. Don't call me unless it's an emergency," very calm sounding.

She gives him the cell number.

"Make sure he's got a minimum of half-a-million insurance!" Throws her the keys. "How big is this guy?"

She's got her keys back and starting-up the Vette. Looking distracted. "He's a few inches taller than you. About a hundred and eighty pounds."

"We won't be seeing a lot of each other till we kill him," Erik setting her straight. "By the way, I'm about ten feet tall, standing on my money."

"Give me more weed."

Erik's laughing, going back to recover his tackle box. "We'll see each other enough for that . . . ." Back over his shoulder, "Just don't let the old fart know."

Putting the tackle box back in the truck, he's thinking about how Bugs' head popped off . . . rolling heads arouse him. Maybe he'd decapitate Sir Missionary Position, Shit-for-Brains . . . . No-o-o, gotta make it look like an accident . . . . Maybe it's best he doesn't know Jar Head's identity. Then, it's not like she's fucking a real person.

CHAPTER XXXII

The arrow is loosed from the bow. Catcher's got a one track mind; get done with the errands and call Jinx. After leaving the surveyor's, he pulls over at a pay phone edging Highway 54.

"Hello." She sounds like a prepubescent teenager.

"Jinx, this is Catcher."

"Hi, Catcher. We still have a date?"

"You bet. Right now I'm in Camdenton."

"What are you doing over there?"

"I got a front-end alignment and visited with a surveyor. I'll probably survey the ranch this summer. What are you doing?"

"Hey, on the Saturdays I don't go to the bank, I rest. I've been reading and waiting for you to call," sounding more energetic than usual.

"Since I'm in Camdenton, maybe I could come by there and pick you up . . . if you could be ready. Maybe about forty-five minutes." Catcher's looking out the telephone booth at the traffic.

"Whoa. I dunno about forty-five minutes. You can't be ready?"

"Nope. I'd pick you up on my way home. Take you by there, and I'd get ready. Then, we'd go. Leave from my house." Catcher's playing with the change in his pocket and holding the phone booth door closed with the toe of his boot so he can hear. The booth is in the sun, and he's getting hot.

"Could you give me an hour?"

"Sure. I'll nose around in the lumber yard, then head over." Holding his head down, keeping the sun out of his eyes.

"Is a black dress appropriate?"

"Perfect."

"OK. See you in about an hour," and Jinx is getting off her couch, laying her book aside.

"OK. See you then."
"Bye."
"Bye-bye."

Stripping for her shower. Thinking she'll take an overnight bag, in case, and seriously thinking about her drug combinations. Doesn't want to be smoking much doobage while she's with Catcher. She's scheduling Valium and Skelaxin. Take some doobers in an empty ALTOIDS tin. Maybe get some cigarettes . . . . Right now, she has to keep moving. When Catcher arrives, she intends to be ready to go . . . ready or not.

She is ready when Catcher arrives. Black sleeveless dress, above the knee, and black pumps and no jewelry save the Tahiti charm. Got her backpack with the clothes, toiletries, and drugs of choice. Catcher notices the bruise on her cheekbone, but his mind clicks onto her violet-blue eyes before commenting.

"We going in this truck, or whatever it is, all the way to Kansas City?" She's incredulous.

"I'm thinking about it." Catcher's smiling, looking ahead through the sunlight filtering through the dusty windshield. "I'm kind of 'fraid to park it up there. Somebody might steal it."

Jinx hasn't much to say on the ride to Catcher's . . . thinking the ride to Kansas City is going to be damned uncomfortable.

Then, she's sitting on the settee in Catcher's living room, with iced tea, thumbing through a magazine, listening to Catcher shower upstairs. Lifting her glass, the coaster sticks, then falls off the bottom of the glass. Jinx is holding the tea in one hand, and down on the other, to retrieve the coaster from underneath the settee. This is when she makes an intriguing discovery.

She gets the coaster, and puts it back on the coffee table and sets the glass on it. Then, secures this book from underneath the settee.

She's back upright on the settee, examining the old, obviously much used, army manual. It's about six by nine inches, and maybe a half-inch thick. Faded denim blue, with duct tape down the binding. It's water spotted and the embossed gold colored lettering is thinning almost to none. This reads: THE ARMED FORCES OFFICER, Department of Defense, Department of the Army P-T-N . . . this last part, she can't make out.

The bibliophile in her is getting wired. Jinx opens the book. The pages are yellowing and almost fuzzy on the edges. The front page is heavyweight paper. At the top is handwritten—Captain Catcher Riley. Below his name, handwritten, in varying colors of ink, are the death dates of five personnel.

> *Sergeant 'Froggy' Maxin—KIA 14 Nov. 1989*
> *Private 'Tarzan' Cool—MIA 14 Nov. 1989*
> *Lieutenant 'GungHo' Joslin—KIA 3 June 1990*
> *Sergeant 'Bullet' McCahn—KIA 5 June 1990*
> *Specialist 'Doggy' Coats—died 11 March 1991*

Jinx is turning to the second page. Reads UNITED STATES GOVERNMENT PRINTING OFFICE WASHINGTON: 1950. She's turning pages, on through the CONTENTS . . .

"You OK down there?" Catcher's yelling from the bathroom.

"I'm doing fine," without taking her eyes off the worn pages. Thumbing through the book, two hundred and sixty-seven pages.

She sees where Catcher has underlined in blue, red and black ink, some of it beginning to fade. She figures different pens at different readings. He has put stars and checks in the margins opposite certain paragraphs. Many of these margin notations are faded, and some are more recent.

"I'm going to shave," Catcher's yelling again.

"Go ahead," and Jinx turns back to Chapter One—THE MEANING OF YOUR COMMISSION. She starts to read this:

> *'Upon being commissioned in the Armed Services of the United States, a man incurs a lasting obligation to cherish and protect . . . This is the meaning of his commission. It is not modified by any reason of assignment while in the service, nor is the obligation lessened on the day an officer puts the uniform aside and returns to civil life . . .*

Catcher's coming out of the bathroom in a towel, going into the bedroom, "Hope I've got something to wear besides my camos," curious about what he'll wear.

Jinx looks up, "Or, come as you are." Turning back to the book. Reading:

> *The character of the corps is in a most direct sense a final safeguard of the character of the Nation . . .*

"I had to unpack a box to find my slacks," Catcher's yelling. "I'm almost there."

Without looking up, still has her eyes in this fascinating book, "I'm in no hurry, Catcher." Takes a sip of tea, and carefully turns a page.

> *'The military officer is considered a gentleman . . . officers need to be gentleman . . . qualities are the epitome of strength, not of softness. They mark the man who is capable of pursuing a great purpose consistently in spite of temptations . . .*

Jinx hears Catcher turn the fan off, and she's holding this ideological novelty in her hands. Standing up and turning to face him. Got a sense they're two continents separated by an ocean, her in the third world, him in the first. "May I bring this book?" Holding it up.

"Yes, sure . . . I wish I had a window in my bathroom like yours," he's saying. "These newer houses gave up some qualities I like, i.e. front porches and windows in the bathroom. You ready to go?"

Jinx is coming around the settee, picking up her backpack, "I think so." She's got the book with her.

Catcher is turning on the outside light, "I'll leave this on. Ready?" Jinx is coming out the door.

She starts for the Ram 4x4, but Catcher is steering her towards the lower end of the house. He opens this garage door, goes in, and drives out in his black Mark VII . . . . Surprised that Catcher has a luxury car, Jinx mimics slapping her forehead, in an exaggerated gesture.

"May I read this to you, while you drive?" Sliding into the passenger seat.

"If you want to. Reading in the car won't make you sick?"

"No way. You just drive. I'll do the reading . . . ."

> *Moral and emotional stability are expected of an American officer . . . maturity of character which expresses itself in the ability to make decisions in detachment of spirit from that which is pleasant or unpleasant to him personally . . .*

"I'd say you are very stable, Catcher. Don't you think?"

"Yes, I'd say so," watching the road ahead.

> *... They develop courage in their following mainly as a reflection of the courage which they show in their own action ...*

"Hey, it's getting dark, you'd better quit," Catcher's rubbing her leg. "Just a little more."

> '... *What is the main test of human character? Probably it is this: that a man will know how to be patient in the midst of hard circumstance ... His ability to remain whole, and to bound back from any depression of the spirit, depends ...*

"It's getting too dark. I can't see it anymore," and she's closing the book.

"What do you think?"

"About the book?" Looking out the passenger window.

"Yesss . . ."

"It's a magic carpet ride."

"Going where?"

"Going up higher."

The date. They are sitting at a table for two at a sidewalk café on the Plaza. The empty plates are gone and they're having coffee, enjoying the night's cooling air, watching the passing pedestrians.

"Good, wasn't it?" Catcher's commenting, leaning over the cupped candle and dinnerware towards Jinx, loosening the top button on his shirt.

"Delicious," from somewhere between the Valium and Skelaxin, missing her Ozark Gold. Got her legs bent under her chair, leaning back with her hands in her lap. Thinking to get back on Percodan.

"You want to catch a late movie or walk around the Plaza?" He asks.

"I like sitting here . . . does it look kooky, having the back pack instead of a purse?"

"It matches your dress and it's got a world traveler trendiness to it I think," smiles Catcher, watching her eyes.

"I need to hit the girls room," looking back for this door.

"I'll walk you . . ."

"No sir-ee, Catcher. Sit there and enjoy your coffee. I'll be back," lifting her backpack up over her shoulder.

"Promise?" Catcher's leaning back now, with his legs stretched out straight, hands slid into his pockets.

"I promise," smiling, over her shoulder.

Jinx finds the girl's room, and she's in a stall taking a hit from the J out of the ALTOID tin . . . got a three hour ride ahead on a ten second toke.

Back at the mirrors, she's washing her hands, then extricating a Valium out of the backpack. Swallowing this, and taking a studied look at herself.

This middle-aged woman comes in. She sees Jinx. Clicking and rustling in her one-time wear, all about the label, skirt and blouse, over to Jinx's side.

"You're the blonde sitting next to the sidewalk, aren't you honey? With Captain Marvelous I think."

This material cusp of fermented womanhood, up beside her, admiring Jinx in the mirror. She points at Jinx in the mirror, out of her swirl of bracelets, "I want your life."

"You can have it." Jinx pushes past for the door, rallying herself for nightlife in the city with Captain Marvel . . . ous.

"I'm looking for Mr. Right Now," the customized woman yells after Jinx.

Catcher slides her chair out, and Jinx sits down. "Whew, some crazy lady about talked my arm off," Jinx is communicating a message from the outer rim planet she's gotten to . . . hello from the skin goddess with no hose or panties to Captain Marvel . . . .

He's talking to her over the candle and table clutter, "You spending the night with me, Jinx?"

"If I do, you're not going to get any sleep," Jinx the lynx coquettishly.

"That's something I want to talk about, Jinx."

"Me too," mischievously.

"I was on a black op once. We had neutralized a terrorist in this hostile republic. We're doing some escape and evasion, waiting for orders to hijack this riverboat docked below us. I had a gut feeling the boat was getting ready to leave. I was the commanding officer and led my shooters down early . . . without orders. We took the boat just as it was pulling out. Another five minutes, and we'd have missed the boat."

"Sounds dangerous to me." Expression is 'where are you going with this.'

"Point is, there are 'he who hesitates is lost' situations."

"There are 'haste makes waste' situations also," Jinx adds. "Maybe you just got lucky that day."

"Night, Jinx. We went in about 0200."

"Myself, I'm not a very patient person," Jinx offers, taxiing along on Valium and Ozark Gold.

"You believe in love at first sight, Jinx?" Catcher's got his elbows on the table, staring into her violets.

Jinx has her chin up on her two crossed hands now, elbows on the table, the candlelight flitting around her face. Meditative, "Yes Catcher . . . I think I do. Why do you ask?"

"I believe I'm in love with you." Catcher still resting his elbows on the table. "I want you in my bed every night, all night," he says softly. "Could you do that?"

"You mean, live with you Catcher?" and Jinx leans back, putting her hands in her lap, watching his face.

"Yes. That's what I mean," and Catcher's sitting back, crossing his hands on the tabletop.

"Yes. I think I could," plainly said, without any body language.

"Do you have anyone else?"

"No. Just my cat."

"Do you want anyone else?"

"No."

"Have you got your listening ears on?" Catcher smiles at her.

"Yes . . . I have my listening ears on." Like hel-lo.

"Would you marry me," and Catcher tilts his head to the side, like a dog listening to a high pitch sound.

Jinx just sits here. Still has her hands in her lap. Feels her emotions slap up against the Valium sea wall. Can't move or say anything. Stunned that this man has asked her to marry him. Stunned by the simplicity of it. That, she is worth this?

Catcher isn't helping her. He's taking a drink of coffee, then holding the cup between his two hands, waiting her reply.

"Would I marry you?" she wants to know.

"Would you marry me?" he wants to know.

"Yes." She's got a hundred reasons for saying yes, and a thousand reasons for saying no. But, she's never been asked before, and yes is a celebration, and no is a refutation. Her mouth is suddenly very dry, yet she's unable to reach for water.

"I don't want to start sleeping over at each other's house unless we're planning something larger," Catcher says. "And, I like being with you." Still sitting here with his hands around the coffee cup, watching her.

"It would be more appropriate if we planned to live together," she says between parched lips.

"You think it would be more gooder?" Catcher's smiling at his pun.

"Of course it would," a quicker reply than she expected of herself.

"We are agreed to marry one another then?"

"Yes . . . when?" Now she's reaching for her water glass.

"When makes no difference to me. Listen to me Jinx," Catcher's leaning forward a little . . .

"I've got my listening ears on," she smiles.

"You could quit the bank job. You will never have to worry about security again. I've got a retirement, the ranch is paid for . . . . I'm older than you, but if something happened to me, you'd still get part of my retirement and a half-million in life insurance."

Jinx leans forward, placing her hands on his wrists. Has this 'float trip' going into his eyes, "Wouldn't you want to think this over . . . all you've worked for and won, just placing this at my feet?"

"It isn't all I've won. The big things I've won can't be counted. They are not material. Regarding the money, Jinx, who else do I have? I have no one . . . . Hell, once I'm set to go, it's all the way."

"You're no more bold than me. Far as I'm concerned, we could sell your place and live in mine."

"I'd rather. I love the window over the tub . . . and the old house and how it sets in there." Catcher's face isn't far from hers. He strains forward to kiss her. And, her him.

They lean back. Catcher pulls his hand free of her grip and gets in his pocket. Withdraws the ring he bought in Springfield. It doesn't have a one-carat diamond, or an emerald cut, or a round brilliant. It's a white gold band with a small inlaid radiant diamond. "There's a wedding band I'll give you on that day." He puts the ring on her finger.

"How'd you know what size, Catcher?" Never looking away from the ring.

"I have my ways."

She's got one hand on the edge of the table and the other out flat. So she can admire the ring.

"First my Tahiti charm, and now this ring. You really are Prince Charming . . . where do we go from here?"

"Let's walk around a little. Then, we'll go home."

It's like this. Sometimes we get what we ask for. And, then we pay for it.

CHAPTER XXXIII

Erik's got the stiletto eyes now; two blue bulges of hypertension courtesy his own deficiencies. Like, he's got the heart of a pimp and the conscience of a killer, and wheels of details making demands on a dime size brain. Trying to stay on top of a major covert guerrilla farming operation, and manage Jinx the mink.

It's the middle of June, official summer approaching, hot and dry already, and the boats are coming and going with water pumps and sniper teams, night and day. And, no matter what he's doing, he's got the Jinx worm seed somewhere back there in his grainy cerebral cortex. Now that she's living with Jar Head, he's lucky to catch her on the cell phone, much less fuck her. Doesn't even know where she lives. Or, this fucker's name.

Hypertension not withstanding, Erik has the X-out plan. He's done the recon and crafted a scheme for killing Jar Head, whoever he is. All that's left is to key Jinx into the formula. Better not be playing fucking possum.

He calls her cell again. She answers. And, a daytime meet is set. Going to meet at the same boarded up cabin on blacktop M.

Arriving late, she leaves the Vette behind the cabin and rides in Erik's truck to the barn in the valley behind. He parks behind the barn. Both windows are down, and it's warm enough to draw perspiration. There's the sound of an occasional grasshopper, and Jinx can hear them moving in the grass. Figures they'll be bad this year. The shrill of a chicken hawk floats into the cab, and some tin on the barn is scraping. They're both sitting here, looking out the windshield across the meadow backed-up by green ridges and blue sky dotted with little white clouds.

"You better have the dope," the hint of desperation in her voice.

"He let you smoke it?"

. . . . Jinx giving Erik the silent treatment.

Erik snorts, "Guess he doesn't know you smoke it."

"Let me have a doober, Erik."

He's getting one out of his t-shirt pocket, lighting it and passing it to Jinx. "You're going through the doobers, aren't you Jinx?"

"So what," leaning back resting her head on the headrest. "A white truck would be better in the sun."

"I'll back-up in the shade for the Queen-Bitch," as Erik reverses the truck. Gets it back and turns it off.

"You bring a baggy for me, Erik?" She's anxious.

"Let me see your ring," Erik's picking up her hand to take a look-see. She lets him.

"I don't think this is very fucking much. I'll be getting you a diamond the size of a bucket," as he lets her hand go.

"Yeah. You'll probably steal it," taking a final hit on the J.

"Like, what's the difference," twisting to lean against the driver's door. "You need to get married right away. I got the plan."

"We'll be getting married right away. I'm two weeks late on my period." She's pinching the doober out.

"What? That's probably my baby," Erik's raising up.

She's studying this hunk of testosterone protoplasm with the red hair and freckles and the blue dots called eyes.

"Yeah. It's your baby, Erik."

"Tell Jar Head you wanna get married the fourth of July. You understand?"

"Sure, Erik. I understand," head back on the headrest.

"You really preggers?"

"I'm regular as clockwork. I'm pregnant alright."

"Isn't this something," leaning back against his door. "Tell your army officer you want to get married on Independence Day . . ."

Jinx interrupts, "Fuck, Erik. The courthouse won't be open on the fourth of July. We'll probably . . ."

Erik interrupts, "Get married on Tuesday, the three of July. You're going to marry at the courthouse?"

"Just drive down and get the license. That's it . . . . He wants to take me on a cruise."

"No way, honey bumps. I got a plan for your honeymoon. You gotta sell him on it . . . you listening?"

"I'm listening." Looking tentative. Knowing this man beside her is 'her kind of people.' What she is goes with what Erik is. And, he's got the Sinsemilla. And, she's not going to kill anybody. He is.

"Tell him you want to camp out the night of your marriage, under the stars and all that shit. Maybe while you're hot tubbing and drinking Chivas Regal . . ."

"Fuck you, Erik. We don't own a hot tub and . . ."

"We? Now, it's we. There's only one 'we' baby, and that's us . . . . Lean over here and unbutton my pants . . . . C'mon, do it."

Jinx raises up and turns so she can unbutton his 501s. He's hard as a gun barrel, and she's got it out, massaging the tip with her hand. "You like this, Erik? You'd better have my dope jerk off."

"Suck it," he says. "Lean over and suck it. I want you to swallow it."

So, she's giving him this blowjob in the cab of the pickup truck, and he's reaching out so to unzip her Wranglers. She's getting up, one knee on the seat and one foot on the floor, so he can stick his big finger into her.

"Stop a minute baby, and look at me," while he's fingering her. "You're going to take your husband on a back-fucking-pack trip after you get married. Go the same day you marry, so you can make love under the stars." He's pushing his finger in and out of her wetness, and her bottom lip is quivering. "The trip will be down the gravel bars of the Little Niangua River. You'll get on the river where it runs underneath Highway 54, in Hickory County . . . . How's this feeling, your pussy is good'n wet."

"Good . . . Erik . . . good," breathlessly, with the back of her head pressed against the headliner, looking down at his handy work, discombobulated.

"You'll hike down the river to County Line Cave. You know where that is?" He's jigging her with his finger, and then stops. "You know where the cave is?"

"I know the cave." Her face screwed up. *She knows all about the County Line Cave area . . . better than anybody in the world. It was her childhood 'Absalom.' Her name for it. Her secret refuge. Years ago.*

He's got her down in the seat, and he puts his penis in her.

When they're finished, she's totally spent. Just laying here, him pushing her around while he gets buttoned up and back behind the steering wheel. Sweating like in a sauna. Her too. He gets the doors open so there's a draft.

"Jinx, get up. You'll be late for His Highness. I said, get the fuck up!"

"OK. OK. Don't push me." She's getting upright. Trying to get her Wranglers up. *The final twist to her pathetic life. Going to kill Catcher at Absalom.*

"You understand what I said about the cave?"

"Damn it, Erik. You think I'm retarded?" She's fastening her Wranglers, soaked in sweat . . . . *By what perverted twist of fate did this guy find Absalom? This particular spot on the river? Of all the secret places along the river?*

"I want you to camp on the gravel bar below the cave. Get your fire and food going, eat, whatever. Then, you've got to motivate Jar Head to check the cave out."

"In the middle of the night?" Jinx is looking over at him with an anguished expression.

"Before you go to bed. Give him a flashlight. There's a thin trail up the face of the bluff. When he gets to the mouth, he'll fall." Erik's smiling. "You'll see him fall."

"It must be twenty-five feet there . . . or more," Jinx guesstimating out loud.

"It'll probably kill him. But, if it doesn't, I'll come down and make sure he's dead. I'll drown him."

"Drown him?"

"The river's up against the bluff . . ."

"I know the land there, better than you."

"He'll fall in the water. I'll come down and hold him under. Then, I'll let him go and I'll leave. You'll try your cell phone, it's a no service area. Then, you'll walk out for help. Probably best if you go down to the first low water bridge, then follow the road to a house. Or, if your phone gets in a service area, call information for the sheriff. Tell him about the accident . . . your husband falling from the cave . . . Don't call me, and I won't call you for a while. You'll get the insurance money. You'll be insured, right? A half-million minimum?"

Jinx's been watching Erik while he gives her the blueprint for murdering her husband. It's like her mind is this extremely calm bay on a deserted island. And, Erik's idea comes in like a dingy, purring over the surface, and the noise of the idea is the only sound. An idea out there by itself, making a noise and making ripples. An idea . . . not a plan. *Thinking about fucking, having more money than she ever dreamed of, and an infinite supply of Sinsemilla.*

"He's already got a half-million life insurance," absentmindedly. "When we get married, I'll become the beneficiary." *More sex and money than Daddy ever thought about.*

"Make sure. You're going to get married on Tuesday, the third of July. And that night is when he'll have his accident." Erik's watching to see she gets this. "Make sure you are the beneficiary before this date."

"You have a J?" She's looking out the windshield at the meadow and white puffy clouds. Slipping downward on the sixty degree midnight slope she divines as life. Feels herself slipping . . . . *She's not killing anybody . . . he is.*

Erik lights one up and gives it to her. "Why don't you call me? I'm always calling you, Jinx, ever since you moved in with that motherfucker. And, where the hell is that? And, what's Jar Head's name? You keep secrets baby."

"What if they look over my phone bills after the accident, Einstein?" She's taking a long hit . . . Murder! Spilt from the same dark melon as the twisted seed beside her. A murderess! Cracked loose from the brittle molasses of humanity.

"You were calling me before."

"Yeah. So, we saw each other a few times before I married. Then, I quit seeing you." She's getting sick. "The 'Jar Heads' don't expect you to be talking to an old beau after you get married, pervert."

Erik takes the J from Jinx. He has a hit.

"You really pregnant?"

"What I tell you, Erik?" Just sitting here, leaning back against her seat, looking at Erik. Has black rings under her eyes.

"I'll bet it's a boy."

"It could be an innocent little girl," tired sounding.

"The timing isn't right for it to be the Jar Head's. Was he fucking you five to six weeks back? I figured he'd be a gentleman and all that. Maybe just be getting around to it . . . was he fucking you back then?" Looking at her hard.

"No," and Jinx is looking out the windshield at the meadow grass, watching a hawk swoop down low.

"It'd better be mine, fucking A."

"Better the devil's than mortal man's, right Erik?" still looking ahead.

"Speaking of the devil, bitch, let's hear the honeymoon plan again. You tell me . . . make sure you've got it."

Jinx looking over at him, bold faced and unsmiling . . . . She's studying his face, then squaring off at his eyes.

"Get on with it," he says.

"I'm going to get my marriage license at the courthouse in Hermitage, Missouri early on July the third, two thousand and one. I will already have done the paperwork making me his beneficiary."

Erik interrupts, "How do you feel about that, girl?"

"What do you care?" Cold as an icicle.

"Could affect how you tell your story later, that's what!"

"I can tell any story I want, to anyone, if I want, dealer man."

"Yeah. I bet you can and have." Erik's smirking.

"We'll have planned a hike and overnight campout down the Little Niangua, following the marriage. We'll park off Highway 54, probably near the cemetery, and drop off in the riverbed there. The river will be about half dry cause of the dry spell. And, if it's raining, we're going anyway."

"Yeah, no matter what."

"We'll pitch camp at County Line Cave. After we eat and drink, he's going to explore the cave. He falls about twenty-five to thirty feet. It's dark, he's been drinking and he slips. If the fall doesn't kill him, he'll drown in the river. I'm hysterical. In actuality, I'm stoned cause I'm a known pothead. I can't get out on my cell phone. I pull him over to the bank, but I can't save him. I get down the river fast, looking for help. The authorities get into the picture. Probably just before daylight. They go up and find his body. He's got a blood alcohol content. They look around in the cave and in the mud, but they find no evidence of another person or foul play." Jinx is staring hard at Erik.

"And there won't be," he offers.

"I need to go to the hospital. They discover I use marijuana. I tell them I always have . . . that, I grow my own . . . . Was thinking about quitting since I got married. I'm discharged. I am the grieving widow. No one seriously suspects foul play because I had it so good . . . I mean, 'how could she.' I get a check from the insurance company for half a million dollars, or twice that if there's a double indemnity. Plus, I get his other assets under Missouri law." Completing her abstract summation.

"Yeah, that's probably right."

"Pretty soon, I start dating an old beau . . . that's you, Erik. I put my half million or million with yours, we have this kid, and go off to Happyland where we get-off and smoke Ozark Gold everyday."

"Fucking our brains out in a bed, Jinx," and Erik's got the giggles. "You got it baby, you got it."

"Erik, lean over here a minute." Jinx is twisted toward him, leaning over slightly.

"Like this, sweet thing," and Erik leans forward, like he's going for a kiss.

Jinx claws him across the face really good, leaving about three bleeding scratches.

Jerking his head back, Erik busts his head on the driver door window frame, bringing his hand up to his face. "What the fuck . . . you fucking . . ."

"Don't say it, Erik. Don't say it," and Jinx is leaning forward in his face. "Don't ever call me a bitch unless it sounds like love talk . . . next time I'll slice half your nose off."

"You fucking cunt," and Erik's got his hand out in front, where he can see the blood on it. "Fuck you," and he's folding his hand into a fist . . .

"Don't do it, Erik. I swear you'll be sorry."

He's soaking in his own sweat. Lowering his fist. Got his strained 'blues' on her very violet eyes.

"We'll name our ranch the House of the Rising Sun, peckerhead. And, you'll mind your manners or die. No one gets away from the House of the Rising Sun . . . alive . . . . The House of the Living Dead. Forever. Together . . . ."

Erik's glaring at her.

"Remember, you'll have to call me on my cell. I'll keep it off unless I'm available. Don't leave any messages, or say a word to anyone but me . . . And, I want a bag of Sinsemilla now . . . right now," holding her hand out palm up. Sweat beads on her face and neck, and her blonde hair is wet and clingy.

He gives her about an ounce. "You'd better answer your cell."

She's leaning back in her seat, clutching the zip-lock in her lap. "You freak. You may not talk to me again before County Line Cave. I can't turn the phone on when he's around . . . mid-morning is probably the best time."

Erik's sweating like a banshee. "You have to give up dancing and hooking don't you, baby?"

"Yeah, Erik. For you," a hint of anger. "I gotta get going. Let's go."

They're back at the boarded up cabin, and Jinx is in the Vette. Erik standing over her, face marked with scratches. "This is gonna be good, baby. Real good."

"You are the devil, Erik," and Jinx isn't smiling.

"Only if there's a God, Jinx . . . You believe in God, don'tcha Jinx?"

CHAPTER XXXIV

"Jinx, a one ton megaton nuclear device just exploded in Warsaw."

"Jinx, your biopsy came back, and I am sorry to inform you . . ."

"Jinx, you are dead." . . .

There isn't anything one could say to rattle her. She's taking between four and six Valium a day, capped off with a one-hit ganja bud whenever, and popping Skelaxin in between. So, it takes her days to have the 'talk' with Catcher.

It's not like they don't talk. They do. All the time and about anything and everything—except about her being pregnant and wanting to get married the third of July. Like, for real? Talk to Catcher about this pregnancy? About getting married? The third of July? Honeymooning at her Absalom?

Frankly, she can't believe Catcher hasn't asked her if anything's wrong. Can't believe she can live in this drug inspired dreamland she creates daily, without him noticing . . . . Maybe he does notice . . . . Waiting for the right time to say somethin' . . . .

She forgets that Catcher is on the endorphins gratis Jinx the Lynx. She doesn't know her breath is like melons and her skin smells like the Gobi and that her age and conformity stupefy this man from Honor Heights . . . . The surface of her body, her sound and smell and touch is ecstasy par none to Catcher Riley.

She's been waiting for the 'right' timing. She was going to tell him in bed, but his passion for her precludes this. Out in the yard a few times, before he headed to the back of the ranch, maybe there was a window of opportunity, but he seemed focused on the fencing job.

She's grilling these T-bones on the back patio, in the afternoon sun. He's coming out with a beer, and sitting beside her in a lawn chair.

Got to tell him now, then cut back on the drugs . . . don't want to hurt the baby.

"Catcher Riley . . . how's the fence job?" She's sitting here holding a long fork.

"Slowly. There's an art to the simplest activities, and I'm no artist. You go over to your place today?" Catcher's watching the steaks smoldering on the grill.

"No. Not today. Cleaned the kitchen and bathroom . . . . There's something I want to talk to you about."

He pats her leg, "What?" turning to face her.

"Help me out here, Catcher. Can you trace our slow flight from safe sex?" She's sitting here with the fork, watching him watch her.

"We're not talking V.D. are we?" Serious like.

"No, Catcher. And we call them STDs . . . Sexually Transmitted Diseases."

"But we're not talking STDs are we?" Just sitting, looking at her, holding his beer.

"Absolutely not," and Jinx reaches down and uses the fork to flip the steaks. "I just want to know our evolution into unprotected sex."

"We used a condom that first time. Remember?"

"Yes."

"Then we didn't. We've been hitting it just before and after your period . . . Catholic style." Catcher sits up, leaning toward her. "And they have large families." Catcher takes a gulp of beer. "Is this about family?" smiling at her with a big question mark.

"Could be," and she puts her hand on top of his . . . partly to steady herself. The Ozark Gold-Valium euphoria flat-lines for a millisecond.

"You're pregnant," and Catcher's standing up. Puts his hand on her shoulder, "Are you pregnant?"

"Maybe. I'm almost three weeks late on my period." She's coming across like she's bewildered. "I'm never late."

"Hot damn, this is great," and Catcher's holding his arms up in the air like a touchdown. Spilling some beer. "Going to have a baby . . . what you know about that. Twenty-five years I've waited for this." Sits back down next to Jinx, pulling his chair up closer. "We've gotta get married . . . soon . . . . You've got to quit smoking dope honey, now . . . . Hot damn, a boy or girl, doesn't make a difference."

"I don't smoke much marijuana, Catcher." She's watching the steaks; her train of thought going into a tunnel.

A lot more than you want me to know," he answers. Standing up again and pacing around. "Hot damn, a baby . . . ." Turns around facing her, "It's no big deal honey, you can't smoke it while you're pregnant. I'll help you. It'll be easy, you'll see," leaning over and kissing her.

She's turning the steaks . . . they'll be doing 'well done' tonight.

"I know what I'd like to do on the marrying matter, Catcher."

He's standing up, facing her from beside the grill, "What's that, sweetheart?"

"Let's don't make it a big deal. I've looked at the calendar," her train of thought is deep in the tunnel, "and I'd like to get married the day before the fourth of July." Got the devil's grip around her heart and sick at the knowing of it . . . a murderess . . . of Catcher Riley and . . . finally, at last, herself. Thinks she may vomit.

"Hell, let's get married the fourth of July," Catcher has the saddle-up-and-ride look.

"Listen, Catcher. I don't want a wedding. I don't know anybody I'd invite . . . ." Self-loathing coming hither to the brink.

"Neither do I," he says.

"I was thinking we'd go to the courthouse and get our license on the third of July." Ancient hate and anger, couched in drugs, driving Jinx driving the devil's plan.

"That's fine with me," Catcher volunteers.

Her train of thought is running right along in this subterranean tunnel, fueled by the THC and Valium compound. "I know you said we'd take a cruise for our honeymoon, but I'd like to wait a few weeks. I'll book it, if you want, for later. What I really want is to camp out, under the stars, on the Little Niangua, with you." The last straw. *Murder her husband at Absalom. Her childhood refuge. Final severance . . . . You've come a long way, baby . . . . Keep those drugs com'in.*

"That's great, Jinx. You've never said anything about camping out, or we'd have already done it."

The train of thought is barreling through the tunnel now, "I'd like to drive down and get the license in Hermitage, have our gear with us, then backpack down the river to this beautiful spot I know." *Absalom. The Sunday school teacher said he was the most handsome man in all Israel—without blemish.*

"This is great, honey. I couldn't do better. We'll do the cruise later," Catcher's sitting in his chair.

"I know I'll get too big to camp, then we'll have the baby . . . I want to sleep out by the fire, under the stars, at least once . . . I think our marriage night." She's putting the steaks on a plate, her train of thought coming out of the tunnel. This man is right and she is wrong . . . bad girl. The swarminess oozing in.

"Catcher and Jinx Riley," Catcher's saying, "and a little Riley on the way," following her into the house. "This is a red letter day for sure."

They're getting their plates out of the cabinet, when they hear a car coming in the drive.

"Who's that?" The hint of alarm in Jinx's voice.

"I don't know," pulling a piece of meat off, putting it in his mouth. "I'll go see," heading towards the front door.

"Marco, what are you doing out here?" Catcher is yelling.

Marco's clamoring out of the Suzuki, walking by the '87 Vette on his way to the front porch.

"That's whose car I think it is, Colonel?" Putting his hands in under his bib, standing here below the porch, looking over at the Vette.

"I don't know, Marco. Whose do you think it is?" Chewing his steak niblet, holding the front door.

"Got good tires on it . . . I'd say it belongs to the queen of the Ozarks, Jinx," looking up at Catcher. "Right."

Jinx has come to the door.

"C'mon out here, Jinx. There's somebody I'd like you to meet," Catcher's standing outside, letting her come out.

"Jinx, this is Marco. Marco, this is Jinx."

Marco, pulling his hands out from under the bib. "Gee whiz," extending his hand towards her, "It's nice to meet you."

She's shaking his hand. "Nice to meet you, Marco." Has her cutoffs on and a halter-top and lots of tan . . . sweaty palms. Nauseated.

Catcher's got his hands in his pockets, looking at Jinx, "Marco was telling me about your beauty before we ever met. Seems he saw you on the road in the Vette." Looking over at Marco, "That right, Marco?"

"Yes sir, Colonel." Looking back to Jinx, "You're even prettier up close." Saying to Catcher, "How come Jinx is here, Colonel?"

"She lives here now."

"We're getting married, Marco," Jinx squeezing Catcher's arm, blushing internally.

"Getting married? The two of you? How come I didn't know anything about it?"

"You haven't been around, Marco," Catcher's grinning. "And, the announcement wasn't on late night talk radio."

"I've been working on a shelter, getting ready for the big one." Addressing Jinx, "I live in a bus over at White Cloud. I'd be wiped out in the event of a catastrophe.

"All kinds of 'em coming down the pike," got his hands in his side pockets now, rocking on his feet. "You get this world tilting on it's axis, and this'll cause storms more serious than a nuclear blast." Marco pausing, givin' Jinx the old evil-eye-going-over look. "You aren't one of those yuppies that believes the pabulum served up by CBS, NBC, ABC, or PBS . . . are you, Jinx?"

"No-o-o. I don't think so." No-o-o, I'm a murderess of things good and kind. Going to take Catcher Riley out next . . . my husband.

"Good thing. It'll be the death of you. No one wants us to know. Not about the upcoming weather changes or the aliens . . . ."

"I hadn't given it any thought, Marco. What's going on with the aliens?" Jinx hanging in there, pained face and all. Trying to keep up her 'front.'

Marco is leaning his head forward, adapting a conspiratorial tone of voice. "The Annanaki from Nibaru, Jinx. They are getting in position to save us. I don't know if there's enough time though. That's why I'm building my shelter."

"How are you building your shelter, Marco?" she's asking, still holding on to Catcher's arm. Depending on it. Nauseated.

"I'm going to build it out of concrete. There's a big sinkhole behind my bus. I'm chipping this out, building up around it with concrete blocks. Then, I'm going to put a thick concrete lid over this. The sinkhole is huge, probably ten by ten feet."

"You aren't serious, Marco. You aren't really spending time or money on this . . . you don't even own the land, do you?" Catcher with this incredulous look.

"Colonel, it doesn't make any difference who owns the land. I'm doing it for survival, not investment," Marco's fooling with his bandanna headband. "You guys really getting married?"

"Yes we are . . . on the third of July, I think on a Tuesday," Catcher nonchalantly.

"Going to be a wedding?" Putting his headband back on.

"No, Marco," Catcher's standing here with his hands in his pockets and Jinx on his arm. "Think we'll go down to the courthouse and get a license." The first sounds of the tree locusts and frogs are reaching them.

"How did you all meet?" Marco asking, like it's a trick question.

"At the bank in Warsaw," Jinx answers. "Catcher came through on business . . . and here we are." Good guy and bad girl. I'm going to kill him.

"Can I still work for you, Catcher?"

"You bet, Marco, anytime." Shadows are getting longer.

"Guess I'd better go," Marco's saying. "Nice to meet you, Jinx. I gotta get back and start getting ready for late night talk radio."

"It isn't even dark yet, Marco," Catcher says.

Marco's turning to leave. "I know. But, I gotta pop my corn, get my couch made up, and make some tea and all that. Have to bring my journals up . . ."

"Your journals?" Catcher rearing back, like 'what else is there.'

"Yeah. Someone's gotta keep a chronological record of the countdown. I'm writing all the important stuff down, off the show. I like to go over the notes of the last show or two before each new show." He stops at his Suzuki door. "They'll find it clutched in my hand in my sink hole, and the new ones will know what happened . . . . I'll be back Colonel, when I need some money," getting in the car.

"OK, Marco. That works."

Back in the kitchen, Catcher and Jinx finish their cold potatoes and steak standing up, talking about Marco.

Marco . . . Marco Polo . . . traveler extraordinaire. Spirit of the Little Niangua River basin. Captain of the Suzuki 4x4 Land Cruiser. Carrying news from afar. Of a royal wedding. Between the Emperor and the Hun's daughter. Always on the cutting edge . . . the first to know . . . .

The meal is finished and the dishes are done. In the living room with their books. Jinx reading through the taped-up, Department of Defense, THE ARMED FORCES OFFICER. "We really going to get married, Catcher?"

Catcher looking up from the novel he's reading, "Yes, Jinx. We surely are. It will be the best day of my life." They go on reading. "You're the prize of my life, Jinx."

In bed, one bedside lamp on, "You can quit the dope, honey," with his arm around her back, hand on her hip . . . her head on his shoulder. "You'll be so fine."

"It's no big deal," she whispers. "I will."

"You going to call the courthouse about the license?"

"I'll take care of it all," she answers.

"While you're at it, call the insurance company and get the right papers here, so I can sign them." He's switching off the lamp. "I don't think we are in a very good school district."

"Don't worry about it. That's five years away." Kissing his neck. "A lot can happen in that time."

He's got her scent. Rolls her over on her back and straddles her and kisses her nipples.

Jinx has the ghost train running again. She's hearing it running the subways, her train of thought, going *clickety-clack, clickety-clack, clack, clack, clack*, tripping the rails of her brittle mind, deep in the tunnel of limbo.

"I love you, Jinx."

"I love you, Catcher." Not that she knows, she does.

"You don't know how much, Jinx . . . but, I do. I'm going to find the original Jo Ann Jenks . . . the virgin."

"You think that little girl is alive?" Saying to the ceiling, her vision disrupted by dark blotches of 'floaters'. Nearly delusional, sensing her pupils as becoming vertical ellipses.

"Uh, huh. We're going to lose the drugs. You will learn to trust," Catcher's yawning. "Then, there's faith . . ."

CHAPTER XXXV

"Saxony, is that you?"

Jinx is coming out of the grocery store in Warsaw, pretending she doesn't hear him.

"Saxony, Ross Keets. You remember me?"

She's trying to get past him, before Catcher notices . . .

How could Catcher miss this? He's sitting here in the sun-baked parking lot, waiting for her.

"You've got me confused with someone else," trying to get by Ross.

But, Ross keeps pressing. "From the SHADOWS, Ross Keets. You were going to call me?"

Jinx, grocery sack in front, abruptly stops and turns to face him. Ross damn near runs her over.

"Oops. Almost ran you over. I got excited seeing you again. You remember me right, Saxony? Ross Keets from the SHA . . ."

"Mister. I don't know who Saxony is . . . You've got me confused with someone else." Feels the nerves and blood pressure do the geyser, and then the Valium bringing it down.

"No. I haven't got you confus . . ."

"My husband," she lies, "is waiting for me," turning to leave. Back over her shoulder, "Good luck finding Saxony."

Getting into the Ram, while Catcher's watching Keets go into the grocery. "What was that about?" Has a fleck in his eye she hasn't seen before.

"I don't know. He thought I looked like someone he knew," putting the sack behind the console.

"Pretty persistent."

"Yes he was. I thought I was going to have to lead him back inside by the hand," she's thinking about another Valium.

Pulling out of the parking lot, "What's he call you? Saxony?"

"Something like that," and she's making a thing out of getting situated in her seat. "My jeans are getting tight. I think I'm getting bigger."

Catcher's thinking about Fletcher Christian standing on the Bounty following the mutiny against Captain Bligh, severed from everything he's considered elemental to his life . . . unloading groceries. "Sweetheart, I've got an errand to run. Why don't you take these in the house. I'll be back shortly."

Standing here with the grocery sack, celery stalk sticking out, "Where're you going?"

"Going to see a man about the river rats that aimed a rifle at me, . . ."

"Why don't you forget it, Catcher?"

"Cause that's how general conditions go from bad to worse! This is the United States, not some podunk banana republic." Catcher's waving at Jinx, pulling away in the Ramcharger.

Jinx, waving back, calculating the seconds to her next hit on a J.

Traveling over the route Jake described, Catcher's having a hard time believing a nightclub could be this far back in the boonies, wondering what R4 stood for. Coming down this narrow gravel lane under the tree limbs. Got the definite feeling he's going back in towards the river. Then, the lane enters this huge gravel parking area, with this octagon-shaped building on the far side. Big oaks around the edge and a few in the lot. He can see where the lawn falls off to the river. There's an El Dorado Cadillac and an old pickup pulled up to the octagon. He parks beside these.

The door is locked to R4. Catcher's knocking and waiting. Knocking again. And waiting, listening to some birds down the river.

Jake's on the telephone. Figures whoever's at the front door will have to wait. Jake is waiting for someone to pickup at the OMP.

"Hello," with an attitude.

"This is Jake Boss calling for Erik Starr." Jake's short.

"He ain't here."

"Give him a message for me . . . OK?"

"What is it," can't be bothered.

"R4's got a live band, eight to midnight, on three July. Tell Erik I called, and he's invited."

"He won't be there." 'Gotcha' is the tone.

"Why's that?" Jake, looking out to the front door.

"Cause, he said he's going fishing on Tuesday night . . . on the Little Niangerr," like 'fuck-you buddy.'

"Tell him Jake Boss invited him anyway."

"Yeah, yeah."

Hang up.

Getting to the front door. Getting it unlocked and open. This is the kind of hub-bub Jake's sick of. It's the broken shoelace that gives you a nervous breakdown.

Catcher's going back to the Ram, when he hears Jake yelling.

Ushering Catcher into the dimly lit club, Jake in jeans and boots, Catcher in cargo pants and boots.

"Hi, I'm Jake Boss. What can I do for you?"

Adjusting to the dark interior, "I'm Catcher Riley. I called you on the phone awhile back."

Jake shaking hands with Catcher, "I remember . . . for several reasons actually."

"How's that," Catcher's taking a hard look at this guy. Thinks he likes him.

"A friend of mine told me she had met someone nice. She mentioned your name." Jake's standing in front of Catcher, looking him in the eye.

"What friend?" Catcher asks.

"Jinx." Jake watching Catcher's face.

"You're a friend of Jinx?"

"Since kindergarten. Went all the way through school together. She was the smartest kid in school. And, the best looking."

"Small world," Catcher's got the hint of a smile and puzzlement combined. Thinking, Jinx and Jake could couple and not be a couple.

"We check in on each other now and then, and get caught-up," Jake's motioning to Catcher to move into the interior. "Pick a table, Colonel. I'll get us a beer. Beer be alright?"

Catcher's sitting down near the empty bandstand, taking in the décor of the peculiarly rustic nightclub. "Beer is fine . . ." raising his voice to reach Jake. "She's the one that told you, that's how you knew my rank?"

"Yes sir, she did," yells back Jake. "Said you were retired." He's coming back with the beers. "Said you were a good man."

"She tell you we were getting married?"

Jake, pulling up a chair. "No, she didn't. I'm glad to hear it though. She's a sweet person that never had much of a chance . . . . When you getting married?"

"Tuesday morning.... What do you mean, she never had much of a chance?" Catcher raising the sweaty can of beer.

"She came from a ne'er-do-well family, like mine. They never had enough money or anything else." Jake's thinking Catcher is the best thing that's ever happened to Jinx. "I can't believe she didn't send me an invitation."

Catcher laughing. "It's not like that. We're not having a wedding. Just going to the courthouse and get our license. Our honeymoon night, we'll spend camping on the Little Niangua. Go on a cruise or something later." Catcher's studying Jake, who's sitting here in a Polo shirt with his black hair all stuck out. Thinking Jake looks like a young buck, a generation behind himself... same age as Jinx, to put things in perspective.

Jake leaning over, resting his arms on the table. "You're going camping on the Little Niangua for your honeymoon? Jeez, the mosquitoes will eat you alive."

"It won't be so bad."

"When she was a teenager, she'd truck over to that area, then hike into County Line Cave. She calls that area Absalom." Jake's smiling a little, watching Catcher. "What brought you here today? I remember you called, and we talked about an R4 membership. I'm betting that's not it!"

Thinking about Jinx's connection to County Line Cave. Absalom.... "I had an odd thing happen early this spring." Figuring Jake's not a criminal. "Some guys on the Sac River aimed a rifle at me, when I got close to'em. They had boats pulled up in the weeds, and looked like they were planting..."

"Marijuana," and Jake laughs.

"I'm looking for information." Catcher's looking straight at Jake. "I went back to the site later, and there wasn't any marijuana planted. I think I scared them off. But, I did find a piece of paper with the R4 phone number on it." Looking at Jake impassively.

"I don't have anything to do with marijuana cultivation," Jake sitting back in his chair. "Fact is, hard as it is to believe, me being a nightclub owner, I don't do anything... anything... illegal. I don't know why the number was out there.... I couldn't tell you." Erik Starr is crossing Jake's mind. "Best thing, Colonel, is to treat it like a poisonous snake. You crossed its path, neither one of you got hurt, and that's that."

Catcher believes Jake... that he isn't involved. "I don't need the counseling, Jake. I want information."

Jake's still sitting back, "I try to live and let live."

"Good for you, Jake." Catcher's getting up.

"Probably the bartender in me," and Jake's getting up also. "I think it's interesting that Jinx wants her honeymoon at County Line Cave."

"How's that?"

"Like I told you. She used to go there as a teenager to get away. I don't think anybody knew except me. I've never been there, but I know that it was her secret place . . . she must think a lot of you." He's leading Catcher back towards the front door. "Absalom was her secret."

"Thanks for your candor, Jake," shaking his hand.

"Don't mind at all, Catcher. I'm glad to meet you. You're probably the best thing that ever happened to Jinx. Best wishes . . . and, I mean it. This makes me a friend of yours, whether you like it or not."

"Nice meeting you, Jake. I'd appreciate a call if you hear anything about marijuana growers. I live east of Cross Timbers."

"I've got your number on my caller I.D. log . . . . Whew, it's hot out here." They're out on the deck, and Catcher's looking around.

"How do you like running a nightclub, Jake?"

"In this country, if you can make a living, you're lucky. I make a good living. That's how I feel about it." What the fuck is Erik Starr doing on the Little Niangua the same night as Catcher and Jinx? Trying to remember when Jinx quit seeing Erik. If she did?

Meanwhile, back at the ranch, the head stoner is getting whacked. Not so that Catcher will be able to tell, but enough to banish the ghost train traveling the wispy subways of her brain. The frigging train of thought, getting so it's going all the time. And fast, too. Like a whoosh, whoosh, whoosh. Boxcar thoughts, whizzing by her narrowed window of consciousness. Can't focus on any one boxcar till it's gone, and the next one's going by. Enough to drive her crazy . . .

CHAPTER XXXVI

Hey, Jinx does better at five a.m. than one would think. Yesterday's narcotics are still cruising, and she's placid enough to forget about her next hit or Valium infusion. So, this Tuesday morning, three July, in the year two thousand and one, she's good company for Catcher. They've got their coffee and the radio's on. They are tightening-up their packs; packs with their ground cloths, sleeping bags, extra clothes, food, water, Catcher's beer, matches, hatchet, knives, grill, tin dishes, eating utensils, tick spray, toilet paper, and flashlight. Jinx has the citronella bucket and Catcher is shoving the COLT .45 into his pack, beside the instant coffee.

"Sweetheart, did you get the legal papers done?" Catcher's thinking of insurance. "I drop dead or something, I want you covered."

"I mailed them days ago." An icy shiver rippling down her spine. Thinking where to hide her pills and the ALTOIDS tin with the joints. Taking some painkillers on this trip. Darvon and codeine.

"You sure you scheduled us at the courthouse at eight a.m.?"

"Yes. Usually you can't. But, this judge starts early, and we're first." This isn't really happening? He isn't going to marry me. Surely not. In her heart of hearts, she never felt that he would.

"Sure we don't need witnesses?" Catcher's wondering about this.

"Honey, they said we could grab someone there as a witness." How long's he going to keep this sham up? . . . He's not really going to marry me.

"Sounds like a Vegas deal."

"No. This is an Ozark deal, civil marriage." This is his exit?

Catcher's saying, "The nice thing about the pack frame is you distribute the weight between the shoulders and the small of the back. It's much easier to backpack with these. You'll see."

"This is very romantic," saying from the bathroom, and tossing the Valium in the wastebasket. Not going to do drugs . . . yet. "I've never done anything like this, Catcher." By God, I'll not take another drug . . . ever . . . . What if Erik really is out there?

"I'm taking the packs out to the Ram." Catcher's gathered them at the front door; carrying them out to the Ramcharger. Placing them behind the rear seat.

Jinx comes up to make sure they're in. "What about a tent?" Trying to seem in normal homeostasis.

"You said you wanted to camp under the stars. That's what you're going to get. No tent, sweetheart. The sky is our roof," slamming shut the tailgate.

Jinx heading back to the house, "Let's eat." Have to eat.

They're in the kitchen, in a low light, eating fried eggs and bacon on toast. Drinking coffee . . . . It is unnaturally quiet, this time of day.

"I never figured on getting married." Realization that this man means to marry her suddenly jolting the psyche.

"I never figured on getting remarried. Then, I met you."

Yesterday's Valium still knocking around her liver and kidneys, but to the naked eye, she's in tiptop form. She's got a tan. In the Wranglers, with the purple sweatshirt and hiking boots, she's looking like a den mother. Except for the 'camel toe' in her crotch.

Catcher, he's wearing cargo pants, a black t-shirt and boots. "Never figured I'd get married looking like this."

"I never figured I'd get married at all." She means it. Thinking about the approaching reality. All of it!

Then, they're rinsing the dishes, turning off the lamp, turning one on in the living room, and shutting the door. The high ridges are blotted out in the blackness around them, but morning's light is beginning to thinly streak the sky . . . .

There's this bench on the south side of the courthouse in Hermitage. This is where Catcher and Jinx sit, drinking coffee from the thermos, watching daylight uncoil over the county seat of Hickory County.

A dog goes past, nose to the ground, snorting and running as fast as he can get the scent. There's some red birds in the middle limbs of the oaks, and a farmer parking his pickup across the street.

"You bring a camera?"

"I got it Catcher, and the film." Trying to control the monumental tour de force wrenching her anima . . . this man means to marry her. He's for real. What if Erik is out there?

"I can't believe a civilian judge is going to marry anyone at eight a.m. in the morning."

"I scheduled it." She's sipping on a refill. Trembling.

"Wonder how my coffee buddies are doing?" Catcher's thinking about the café around the corner, across the street, on the west side of the square. "Pretty soon, Mary will be topping off their cups."

"Who's Mary?" Feeling her pneuma rearrange itself. A seismic shift in the offing.

"The waitress at the café across the street to the west. She's got her regulars. Let me see. There's Lester. He's got a daughter in college. And there's Cutter, Lefty, and Covington."

"These are friends of yours?" As calmly as possible.

"Uhm . . . coffee buddies. They're all good folk . . . Mary included."

"You don't know 'em well enough to say," warming her hands around the plastic cup in her lap . . . just like she belongs here.

"I think I do. I'd say they're good people. What you see is what you get. Like most Missourians," Catcher's adamant.

"And you're from Illinois?" Looking over at him. Like she's seeing him for the first time.

"I'm from Missouri now. The Show-Me State . . . . And I'm getting ready to marry a girl who's hardly been out of the state. We ought to have someone take our picture when we come out."

"I've got the camera with me," Jinx says. "You nervous?"

"Not very. Happy would be the better word. I can't believe I have you. You make me happy."

"You could still be nervous." She's moving over on the bench, so that her head is in tree shade. Something happening to her personality anatomy. Deep down. At the core.

"Nervous? What'd I call nervous? The last time I was nervous, was followed by a classified Silver Star. That was years ago, Jinx. I'm happy. Period."

The pickups and cars are appearing, and a lady has unlocked the courthouse. Catcher and Jinx can hear talking and car doors slamming around the square, and it's starting to warm up.

"How are we going to work the car thing? I mean, the Ram will be at the cemetery off Highway 54, and we'll be headed away from the truck."

"We can go north to the cave, and hike back to the truck tomorrow . . . same way we go in."

"Yeah. We don't need to hike further north after the campout." Jinx has her first ganja craving. Yesterday's Valium 'thinning out.' Gets a split second view in her mind's eye of Erik peering from out of the cave.

"Going down the riverbed will be interesting. I hope it's down enough so we can hike the gravel bars." Catcher's picturing the procedure to skirt the areas where the river is full (climbing out of the riverbed and hiking around through the undergrowth and brush . . . and ticks).

"My boots are waterproof. Are yours?" Back into denial.

"Yep."

"It's time, Catcher," putting the top back on the thermos. The two of them go in.

"I'm happy about the baby, Jinx."

At eight o'clock a.m., the two of them are filling out the license. When they are done, a couple of women from the Assessor's Office sign as witnesses, and agree to witness the marriage. A younger couple is arriving to get married after Catcher and Jinx. The boy is in jeans and too skinny and the girl is unkempt and about seven months pregnant.

Catcher and Jinx are before the judge, in this side chamber, with their witnesses from the Assessor's Office. The judge has the morning paper laying off to the side. The room is on the east, and sunlight is streaming through. The whole thing takes about five minutes and the civil marriage ends with the judge saying, "I pronounce you man and wife." Right here, Catcher pulls a wedding band, matching the engagement ring, out of his pocket and slides it on Jinx's finger. He turns her to him and kisses her, and the witnesses clap. The judge is smiling; then, back to leafing through his paper.

Jinx is mostly blacked-out from the time they enter the courthouse, until they exit. Not that anyone could tell. It's like when too many people are yelling at you at once, and pretty soon you're unconscious to what anyone is saying. Jinx gets this 'channel overload' during times of stress. Today, she's going through a substratal change of psyche, detoxing, getting married, and conspiring to kill her husband. Have a nice day!

"Hallelujah Jo Ann Riley, wife of Catcher Riley and mother of Catcher or Jo Riley." Catcher's got her by the hand, stationing her beside the sidewalk in the tree shade. "Where's the camera, Jinx?"

Giving it to him. Strangely bewildered.

"Sir," Catcher is approaching a farmer in bib overalls. "Would you mind to snap a few pictures of us? We just got married."

"Okey-doke," the farmer grinning.

Catcher walks this through, gets the camera back, and thanks the farmer. Thinking about the two of them outside the courthouse in t-shirt/camos and Wranglers/sweatshirt and boots on their wedding day. "You OK, Jinx?"

"Yes. In shock. That's all. Can't believe we really did it. I didn't think it would happen." Eyes watering.

"It's the way it's supposed to work, Jinx. Man and woman fall in love, man and woman get married, and man and woman have children . . . you love me?"

"Yes."

"Well, let's go camping," and they're circling the square in the Ram. Then, out of town, headed east on Highway 54.

Parking at the Niangua Cemetery, when a black pickup pulls out from across the highway. Erik's got a wild, lunatic look on his face, and he's got a 'BORN TO HUNT' cap with his red hair sticking out. Can't get a look at Catcher . . . . Jinx is seeing Erik. Just before he accelerates off to the east, he waves at her.

"Come and get your pack, Jinx," Catcher's letting the tailgate down. "Get ready for the honeymoon, honey," laughing. "It's a great day in the morning." Walking away, toward the backside of the little cemetery. "I'm going to take a pee," yelling back over his shoulder. Cutting through the old headstones.

She is laid out naked on her back with her legs dangling over the edge. Daddy's got his cap on backwards, and he's down on his knees licking her cookie, very slowly and very softly. She's looking around at his tools and out of the dimness through the smeared window.

Jinx is groping into her pack. Got the ALTOIDS tin out. Hands got the big tremors. Gripping the tin. Like she's got seizures or the rabies. Imagining she's got convulsions coming on.

Daddy's doing this very lightly, and moaning. She's feeling a strange radiation from out her cookie. A soft, tingling warmth spreading outward with no place to go . . .

Jinx is fumbling with the ALTOIDS tin . . . . Stops, and shoves the tin back into her pack. She can feel this electrical charge roaming her body, and she can't ground it . . . Not going to do the drugs.

Roaming her body and the little girl can't ground it. This heightened sensuality and doesn't know where from or where to go with it. Daddy's playing with his Dolly...

Watching Catcher through the Ramcharger windows. He's coming back, stopping to look at the headstones.

It's all about her cookie. Her little cookie is the center...

"Look at this," Catcher's yelling at her. "Here's a headstone dating back to the early eighteen hundreds."

Trying to get a grip, thinking about Erik, with his red hair flaming around the edges of the 'BORN TO HUNT' cap. Looking through the Ramcharger at Catcher roaming around the cemetery.... Hell is right next door to Heaven... separated by this Little Niangua River that courses through her life like a crooked zipper. Hoisting her pack up, heading down towards the river. "Let's go," she's barely yelling. No more drugs, no more drugs, no more drugs... have to walk. Walk the river.

She's way ahead on the riverbed, when Catcher slides down the bank onto a gravel bar. He's stopping to adjust his pack, looking ahead at the bobbing backpack supported on Jinx's diminutive frame. Can see her blonde hair glistening in the sunlight over the top of her pack.

He catches up to her, as she's coming back towards him.

"Gotta go around," she's saying. "The water is too deep ahead."

Pulling themselves up a mud bank, clinging to roots. Getting up on top of the bank. Following this deer trail down the side of the river. They surprise a heron that lifts up out of the water and flies ahead. Sweating, picking their way through a tangle of underbrush, going back down into the riverbed. Jinx walking over to a stream pouring across the low end of the gravel bar and dropping her pack. Splashing water on her face and arms. Catcher setting his pack down and doing likewise. There's a bunch of water bugs in a stagnant pool off to the side, and Catcher's looking at the deer tracks.

Jinx pushes her pack over sideways and lays down on the river rock, propped up against the pack. Laying here watching the turkey vultures circling in the azure above. Catcher's kicking rocks over, looking for arrowheads. Sees a water snake whipping away in an eddy off to the side.

Soon, they've got their packs on again and hiking down the bars together. Whenever they come to a stream cutting across the bar, they cross on the dry-topped stones sticking up, or wade across in their boots. Neither one wants to climb out of the riverbed again unless there is no other way to proceed. The river is low enough, so they mostly traverse the gravel bars.

"You OK, Mrs. Riley?" Figuring her pinched features for exertion.

"I'm fine, Catcher." Nothing could be farther from the truth. A very bad abstract IDEA and the ACT of premeditated murder are two very different things, even to a disturbed drug addict.

"Good for you, huh?"

"Yes, very . . . . This river is special to me," kicking a rock, crunching over the gravel. Right now, the river is her only link to sanity.

"How's that?" Catcher's watching where he steps, to avoid a sprained ankle.

"There's a lot you don't know about me, Catcher." Adjusting the straps on her shoulders. "When I was a kid, I didn't have it so easy. Growing up in Algiers was like coming up in a cesspool." She's rationalizing, Erik will never make it to the cave . . . . He's only harassing her . . . .

"Yes?"

The two of them walking along side by side, down this long stretch of white gravel, along the edge of a narrow river channel.

"When it got too much for me, I'd jump in this old pickup and drive over here . . . so I could come down here on the river. I was doing this as early as thirteen years of age."

"You wouldn't even have had a driver's license." Catcher's wiping the sweat off his face.

"Who cared? My dad wasn't going to get on me . . . . He was so abusive, he was afraid I might tell someone."

"What about your mother?"

"Are you kidding? She was never home. Just daddy. And, he was mostly drinking." She's got her hands up on the pack straps beside her breasts. "When it got too much for me, I'd drive over here. Must be over forty miles from Algiers to here. I'd drive here, park, and hike in to the river. The first time I took off in the truck, I was hysterical, and just happened to end up here. I had parked the truck, and tore off through the timber, and by accident, stumbled onto the river. It is so beautiful and the water is so pure . . . it was like being reborn. This first time, I found the cave. My private name for the area was Absalom." Adjusting her pack. "Quite a coincidence, running away from home, stumble through the woods hysterical, and come out on the river right where the cave is."

"You're talking about this County Line Cave we're going to?"

"County Line Cave . . . Absalom . . . that area. I liked the spot so well, I came back again and again. If there's a geographical location that defines us, this was mine." She said 'was.' It's true . . . she was bad then . . . now, she's morally destroyed.

Catcher and Jinx are going through a spot where huge sycamores are hanging out over the river. There are scads of little yellow butterflies all over the rocks. As they hike, the butterflies are lifting off the stones, and it's like walking through a billion, wispy specks of gold, up and down the riverbed, as far as they can see either way.

"I was coming here until I ran away from home. It was my hideout . . . That's why I bought my place. It's on this river you know." Her face is sprinkled with sweat, and the ends of her hair sticking to her skin. "This river is my continental divide."

"Separating what from what," asks Catcher, looking ahead through the floating yellow butterflies.

"The good and evil in me."

"Evil? There's no evil in you, Jinx," looking over at her.

Hiking straight on, looking pained. "You don't come out of Algiers without being bent."

"So, you smoke dope."

"It's a coping mechanism."

"But, you've got the baby now, sweetheart. This is a good thing. You've got to quit the dope for little Riley's sake. Huh?"

"I quit today, Catcher." Shaky.

"You've got the baby now. This is a good thing to replace a bad thing."

"Yes . . . ."

Catcher tries to put his arm around her, forgetting about her pack. Reaches down and grabs her hand. So, they are hiking along through the yellow butterflies, hand in hand.

"You're going to make it, sweetheart," squeezing her hand.

Jinx doesn't answer.

"Everything is going to be all right. It begins with trust. You'll see . . . ." Letting go of her hand and adjusting the weight of his pack.

"I've got a lot of ghosts."

Catcher's thinking about the guy at the grocery . . . he called her Saxony! And, he's thinking about his conversation with Jake. He's looking over at his wife. He can't tell for sure, with all the perspiration on her face, but he'd swear she was crying.

Jinx is crying. Faulkner was right, 'the past is never past.'

CHAPTER XXXVII

Jake's made it a point to mind his own business. Running a nightclub, you gotta cut people slack. You get used to looking the other way. He has seen the worst in a lot of good people. And, forgotten it. Live and let live is the simple axiom around which he has built his livelihood—with a few notable exceptions.

1.) God. Jake won't tolerate an overt insult to his maker. He personally does not use the name of God when cussing. And, R4 is never open on Sunday.
2.) Himself. Jake does not cut himself any slack as regards achieving the minimal expectations he has for himself. And, he won't tolerate someone else messing with him.
3.) R4. If there's an issue that affects R4, Jake makes it his business. Don't mess with R4.
4.) Jinx. Jake has always been involved here. He's made her his business ever since kindergarten. When you grow up in a place like Algiers, with parents like he and Jinx had, you better have a good friend; to survive. He is Jinx's friend, and he takes this as a personal commitment. The role of a best friend, the way he sees it, is to 'be there' when needed. Be willing to protect your friend from others . . . and from themselves, if necessary.

On this day, Tuesday, July the third, two thousand and one, Jake's suspecting a trespass on all four aforementioned sanctums. Like, what the fuck is Erik doing on the Little Niangua at the same time as Jinx and Catcher? It doesn't smell right. There's a fly in the ointment somewhere.

He's watching the Tuesday night band unload their van, out here in the afternoon sun. Looking for his head of security.

"Hey, Tom!"

"Yes sir, Boss," running up.

"Can you handle this shindig tonight?"

"Yeah sure, Boss." Tom's face like he's surprised Jake had to ask.

"That's it then." Jake puts his hand on Tom's muscular shoulder, "You are in charge. As of now. I'll be back in the morning."

"You got it, Boss."

Jake's cutting across the parking lot towards the mower sound. Going to find Big Track. Not sure why he's wearing cowboy boots today. They are as uncomfortable as hell. Big Track sees him coming and shuts off the mower.

"Tracker, I need your help." Out of breath and starting to perspire.

"What you want me to do," Big Track bending his head to the left, then to the right.

"Go get the pickup. We're going to look for a friend."

Big Track is reading between the lines, and Jake's demeanor suggests a sense of urgency. He sees the vertical furrows between Jake's eyes, and the pain percolating in his iris.

"Got it, Boss," and the giant Indian is striding off across the lawn, removing the gloves. Jake following. Headed for the truck.

Jake and Big Track in the old pickup speeding down the highway.

"We're going to criss-cross every low water bridge crossing the river till we find Starr's truck or Catcher Riley's Ram," Jake is telling Big Track.

"North or South of here?" Big Track turning the truck onto the county road. The truck is banging and clanking and Big Track has to turn the steering wheel two revolutions around the solar system to negotiate turns.

"Go south. In fact, go down to Highway 54. We'll cross the river, then work our way back in this direction."

There's no air-conditioning, the noise is deafening, front-end needs alignment and the windshield is dirty and fly specked with a crack running through it. Still, the old truck makes it down to Highway 54, and back to the bridge going over the Little Niangua. Jake sees the Ramcharger parked up by the cemetery.

"Pull over, pull over Tracker."

"Got it, Boss," Big Track spinning the steering wheel to turn.

They go bouncing into the cemetery, too fast, hitting potholes and flying up out of their ragtag seats. Get the truck stopped next to Catcher's Ram. Big Track shuts the motor off. They get out fast. Jake goes to look in the Ram, but Big Track is already following the trail to the river.

"They go this way, Boss," as he studies the ground. Jake's right behind him.

"They'll be going north from here, Tracker." Jake's following the big Indian. For the first time, he notices what Big Track is wearing; moccasins, khaki pants, and an oversized, long sleeve checked shirt . . . hanging out. He's got his ponytail braided down his back and a sweatband on.

He's saying, "The killer smell is on the river, Boss."

"Hurry. Keep going, Tracker." Jake is right behind the Indian.

It is getting dark.

CHAPTER XXXVIII

Erik's sitting up here in this cave, relishing the idea of killing an officer. Killing an officer should be worth bonus points. Like, you've got these fucking Jar Head pinheads, trumped up by the federal government, paid for with monies stolen from the people, and protected by a bunch of over-armed, numbskull soldier zombies, and Erik Starr is going to take a colonel out. A 'bird' colonel. The feeling is like when he's real horny and waiting for his date to show up. Like he could cum in his pants.

He's hidden the truck a few miles east, in the woods off a county road. He's sure no one saw him hiking in. Checked the 'fall' sight below the cave. Perfect. Shallow water dotted with boulders and a couple of decaying logs.

It's starting to get dark, and he's stepping back a little to light his doober. Doesn't want to take a chance on Catcher spotting the match. Getting pissed. Had the doober in his t-shirt pocket and lost some doobage climbing up.

Everything is different. She almost hiked by it. This is it. Absalom. This is the spot. Here's the gravel bar. There's the big sycamores hanging over the water, and, in the shadows, the dirt trail going back and up to the cave. There's the boulder she would sit on . . . the sinkhole she rinsed in . . . . Temporarily removed from the gruesome reality by this nostalgia . . . . Taking a hard look at her abandoned refuge. It's so different. The trees are larger and hang over the riverbed further. The river is smaller and the gravel bar is narrower and there are sprigs of cocklebur and sticktight growing up through the gravel. It's more bushy. And, it's more humid and sticky and buggy . . . . She is relieved. This is nothing like the place she remembers. *There is no Absalom. No Shangrila and no paradise.*

Spying on Catcher and Jinx through the treetops. Smirking at their 'domestic' camping. Sleeping bags rolled out, stone fire ring, bright yellow yuppie packs, etc., etc., etc . . . . Erik's idea of camping is leaning against a tree, close to a patch of fifteen-foot Sinsemilla, with his .357 MAGNUM. Speaking of which, he has poked in the back of his 501s. Doesn't plan on using it, since he's going to make this look like an accident.

He hears'em. The two fucking lovebirds chirping around on the gravel, below and off to the side. Getting the scent of their fire . . . . Listening . . . watching the cinders blow up into the dark.

Catcher, "I'm going to take a peek at the cave."
Jinx, "No-o-o. I want to eat." Got the shivers and her muscles are aching. On a collision course with the truth. Keeping Catcher here a little longer.
Eating.
Catcher, "That was good . . . almost too dark to see the cave . . . you have the flashlight."
Jinx, "Finish your beer first. I need some help rinsing the dishes," and she's moving away from the fire, down towards the river. Hoping Catcher will follow, away from the cave.
He's not following her.
Catcher, "I'm going to see that cave tonight. How steep is the trail?"
Jinx, "Not too. When I was a kid, I sailed right up . . . . You can't go up there tonight." Going back to sit by the fire . . . . Waiting. "You can't go."

She's sounding like a fucking priss-priss . . . . What the hell is the cunt trying to do . . . ? Where's Jar Head? Now, Erik is on full alert.
A bitch like Jinx, you gotta giv'em lots of wood. They'll do anything for dick and dope. She's forgetting her daddy. He's going to give her some D & D . . . she was trying to stop that prick. Trying to save Riley? Trying to stop Riley from coming up here . . . . A surge of hate boiling up.
He's leaning out a little, trying to see in the dark, down the ledge trail. Too dark. Can't see it. Not going to be able to fucking see Riley.
He's backing up. The starlight delineates the cave entrance. Takes his 'BORN TO HUNT' cap off, runs his hand through his hair, and pulls the cap back down on his head. Gets this wood club in his hand. 'C'mon motherfucker, come to papa,' moving close to the side of the cave accessible to the ledge trail.

He squats here in the dark, feeling himself breathe, watching the etched opening and the stars beyond.

Dimly, hearing Jinx yell. "Come back down."

"I'm almost up," Catcher's voice startles him. Riley's outside the entrance. Erik can hear water dripping somewhere behind. Seeing the flashlight beam bouncing around the edge of the corner. Then, Jar Head's silhouette.

Stepping forward, "Fuck you, Colonel," slamming down hard with the club. Whoomp!

Dropping the flashlight, "What . . ." teetering.

Erik slams him again, and Catcher disappears.

Leaning over, peering down to the base of the bluff. Erik can't see a fucking thing. Throws the club outward and starts his descent. Thinking about Jinx, by the fire below . . . . He'll deal with her, you can bet on that.

She's down here alright. Frozen. A day late and a dollar short. Can't get out of deadlock. Thinks she heard. Thinks she heard Catcher fall. Has a 'distant' perception of Erik running across the rock and into the river. Falling into a trance . . .

Relief rinsing over her . . . she's become a wolf. In the animal drive. Into the freedom of bestial amorality. Her mate is the alpha wolf, and he's hunted down the challenger . . . making the kill in the river.

CHAPTER XXXIX

There's an owl here, on a bone white limb sticking out toward the river. A dark orb to witness the first act in Jo Ann Jenks' coming out.

The psychic crank grinding to its definitive latch. The tumblers into lock. Never so centered as now. Emerging from the trance.

She is her own sovereign!

Up and outward, a strand of diamonds hang over this river from its up and down; a billion blazing stars from before and after.

Timber tops and overhanging limbs, back behind and ahead on the river. The flickering light of the campfire reflecting irregularly off the current's ripples.

Thin horizontal sheets of mist hanging here and there.

A bulbous yellow moon coming up in the east, casting a softening sheen over the day's hard edges. The frogs, katydids, and tree locusts in their strange timeless chorus. There's a whippoorwill, even this hour, so past sundown. Some barking coyotes way off, above the river.

And, there's the river's continuous rushing sound.

People in extreme situations can perceive things in distracted, almost surreal ways. It's happened to Jinx throughout her life. But suddenly, in this moment, she's seeing this scene in all it's harsh reality. Keenly aware. Of the stars. And the moon. And murder.

A cooling breeze is coming up, blowing her hair around her face. There's a dampness struggling against the dryness of the fire. She's smelling the verdant woods along the river. *Got the scent of blood . . . .*

. . . and, a taste too. But, the wolf is leaving her.

Focusing on the killing . . . . Erik has made his descent and is holding 'Jar Head' underwater.

She's getting a long distance call from outside the cosmos. You might say, from outside the grid. Anger blasting out of her heart wells, blowing the locks and steel doors caging an ancient rage. A killer rage. "No-o-o," she shrieks.

She grabs the hand axe and is running towards Erik. Into the river, she's swinging the axe into Erik's upper back, chipping his shoulder blade and blunt chopping the muscle.

Erik letting go of 'Jar Head,' coming around in agony, freezing Jinx into focus. "You fucking bitch!" Swinging his body forward, slashing through the shallow current towards her.

She swings at him again, bouncing off his raised hand and landing the axe into his mouth.

He's got her by the throat and seems she's going backwards.

Letting the axe slide down to the head, just above her fist, then jams this into his balls.

"Fuck! You fuckin' cunt," screaming as he lets go of her throat and goes down on his knees.

She hits him again, on the side of his head.

Getting her wrist now, and tearing the axe away. Banging her with a slammer. "You fucking bitch!" He clobbers her again with the other fist. She falls down at the edge of the river, and he falls onto her like a mad-dog. "I'm gonna kill you, you fucking bitch," his bloody, contorted face coming over her.

She's got a rock out of the water and hits him alongside the head.

He's trying to get a grip around her neck.

She's flat on her back, face barely above the surface of the waters. Getting a handful of chatty dirt, which she shoves into the middle of his face.

He's trying to hold her with one hand, while he's splashing water on his face.

She's biting down into the meat of his forearm and holding this like a pit bull.

Pulling her out of the water as he backs up, dragging her out by her teeth. He pounds her with the bottom of his other forearm, and she's loose, falling face up on the river's edge. He grabs her by the throat with his left hand, blowing blood over her face, trying to rip her stomach out with his right hand. This hand slides off her stomach, catches in the top of her Wranglers, and he's ripping the zipper out of these.

She's pushing with her heels. Pushing away from the water.

He's on his knees, trying to choke her with his left hand, and breaking her ribs with his right fist.

Jinx letting out a blood chilling scream, and jamming her thumb into Erik's eye; using the momentary release to break his choke hold, running slumped over towards the fire.

He tackles her.

She goes down hard beside the fire, grabs a burning bough and writhes around. Jabbing Erik in the neck with this. He's falling, and she rolls him on over. The firelight flickering across her rage-wracked energy; going for redemption now.

Her pack is an arms-length away. She is able to unsnap the front pocket and withdraw the sharpened down screwdriver—an ice pick in reality. She comes around swinging the pick in Erik's direction and sinks it into his thigh, to the handle. Jinx lets go of the pick. She's a quarter century old fury served up out of the cellar, and she jumps on top of him. She's beating his face.

Erik slamming his fists through her slighter arms. Knocking her off.

Jinx pounces back on him, locking her legs behind his thighs and her arms behind his nape, biting into his neck.

The katydids and frogs are going full chorus. There's the chilly hoot of the owl. The river's steady pulse, coursing along its way. The night is chilling and mists rising all around. The sky is riddled with stars and a huge yellow moon is up overhead . . . . Indifferent to this deadly clash of wills.

Carrying Jinx, Erik staggers back towards the river and into the current. He's pushing up on Jinx's chin and she pops loose with a mouthful of skin and gristle.

Pushing her head back till her hold on him is broken. As she falls into the river, he's coming down on top of her. Now, he's beating her in earnest. Slamming her head with one fist, then the other.

The current starts to push Jinx away from Erik. He lets her go, figuring the cunt is his-tor-ee . . . . Trying to get himself out of the water and up to the fire . . . . A half-million dollars and the fuck of his life . . . . And letting her go.

She can hear the splashing waters; even see the frothy water tongues wagging at the starlit sky. And, there's a shooting star. She knows she's seeing the North Star, and leaving on a navigation of her own. There's Venus, the magna cum laude of the nighttime sky. The frogs and the katydids, clear as Gabriel's horn, clearly through the current's hungry growl.

Then, she's under. Beaten badly, too badly, and she knows it. She's got her eyes open, but now there is only blackness. Without any reason, she is holding her breath. The instinct not to breathe underwater outweighs her pain from running out of air. Her carbon dioxide is skyrocketing and oxygen plummeting. As her oxygen is depleted, she feels the darkness coming in on her.

So, this is how it ends. Drowning in the river.

A strong sense of embarrassment engulfs Jinx.

She passes an image of a little girl with a flower on the bank of the river, shaking her head over this senseless death.

Grasping the pendant between her breasts. Fist wrapped around the silver shark and dolphin . . . barely conscious and losing ground fast.

Passing into an unpleasant dream.

She is a great man-eating shark, far out to sea, coming in like a torpedo, led in by smell and the lateral line system, to kill a man.

The cartilage and smell sense of the shark is washing away it seems. Then, there is something else . . . .

It's said we learn and remember 10% of what we hear—15% of what we see—20% of what we see and hear—40% of what we discuss with others—80% of what we experience directly and 90% of what we teach others.

Jinx is experiencing an 'unloading' of all she's learned . . . what she's heard or seen or discussed with others and all she has experienced. Except for love. She loves Catcher. Never to let go of this . . . . He married her. Catcher Riley married her.

Becoming a swift and graceful dolphin. Skimming across the surface of this tranquil turquoise sea stretching ahead to the horizon where it meets a very blue sky.

She is engulfed with a here-to-before unknown sense of security. Slowly floating away. Her body washing unevenly down the river.

Behind, Erik is stumbling toward the fire . . . looking like he should be spooned into a jar.

CHAPTER XL

About ten percent of the people drowning undergo laryngospasm. That is to say, about ten percent of the people drowning, never inhale water into the lungs. These people die because of suffocation caused by their body's refusal to accept water past the vocal cords. When this ten percent quit holding their breath, and gasp underwater, the water hitting the vocal cords causes a contraction of muscles around the larynx. A person with laryngospasm has overcome the breathing reflex.

When Erik is holding him underwater in the Little Niangua, Catcher has an involuntary laryngospasm. And, when Erik is forced to release him, during Jinx's assault, Catcher drifts down the river. And, he begins to breathe again, his face barely above the dark waters.

Down river, there is a long sycamore tree laying horizontal across the channel. It's bent over from the roots in the riverbank, and very much alive. The river waters pour underneath and over the tree trunk and dissevers through the bough plopped out in the center of the channel. This is where Catcher comes to rest, pushed up into this clump of branches and leaves, rushed around by the dark swirling waters. And, this is where Jinx's body comes to catch also, nestling next to Catcher.

At first, he's aware of the sound of the river's current; then the sensation of being in swirling water; and on into a consciousness that details his immediate perch in a sycamore tree bush in the river, in the night, next to Jinx's body. His evolving consciousness catches here, and he's pulling what's left of Jinx's face up to his, with his right hand. He keeps his left arm hooked over a branch, but he can't get his left hand to work. Her face is pulverized. He's feeling no breath.

Catcher gets the body over a branch, so she can't wash away, then goes back to an 'old brain' recollection of his situation. 'Old brain,' in that it's more like an autonomic response than a calculated one.

It has been presented that human beings have an older clump of brain tissue atop the spinal column, and that the post primordial brain developed around this; that this 'old' brain functions in a pre-civilized, autonomic manner—instinctually—in many ways requiring suppression by the surrounding 'new' brain, in civilized situations. Tonight, Catcher's 'old' brain is in command, overriding the 'new' brain. In ancient warrior fashion, Catcher is taking assessment.

It is the early hours of the Fourth of July. He's hurt. Was hit by someone at the cave entrance. Fell. Broke his left wrist, and maybe more. Jinx was over by the campfire, and he was nearly unconscious from the fall. Someone held him underwater.

The only light is the moon and the stars. Scanning the river, he sees a small fire on the bank upstream. The killer-warrior locks on the fire—maybe his own campfire. Probably his own campfire.

Moving his feet and legs and head around. They are leadened, but movable. Feels over his own head; finds a bloody cut over a bump above his ear. Aware of his own trembling and an incoming coldness. Must get out of the river. Catcher pushes Jinx's body further up on a branch, and begins a traverse down the tree trunk towards the riverbank, same side of the river as the campfire upstream.

About this campfire upstream: it is Catcher's and Jinx's campfire. And, a brutally mangled redheaded man is moving around up here. It's Erik Starr. What's left of him. He's come up here by the fire, trying to recollect himself, following the fight with Jinx. He's spooked. Lost the 'BORN TO HUNT' hat and his .357 MAGNUM. He's in excruciating pain, rummaging through the backpacks. He finds Jinx's pain pills and Catcher's loaded .45 COLT. Sags down next to the fire, opening the Darvon. Pushing four of them into his battered mouth and washing them down with a beer from 'Jar Head's' pack. Just laying here, in extreme pain, against 'Jar Head's' pack, looking over his body. His left hand has a couple of bloody broken fingers, and he winces when he moves his shoulder blade. He's got a throbbing agony reaching upward out of his testicles into his lower stomach. Waiting for the Darvon to kick in. His head is swollen on the side, and his ear is torn and bleeding. His vision is blurred out of one eye and his forearm and neck are bleeding heavily. There's the burning pain from his neck, and this is unrelenting. His face radiating pain, and he's trying to push a loosened tooth out of the gum with his tongue. A lot of blood runs from his mouth, and he can taste it, and see it matting on the front of his undershirt. While he's sitting here, feeling the Darvon seep into his agonies, he's noticing the screwdriver handle protruding out of his thigh. Grabbing hold of the handle, he yanks the ice pick screwdriver out of his leg. Letting go of an inhumanly shrill scream that travels the up and down of the darkened river . . . . The animal and insect sounds stop.

The katydids are silent; no frogs or locusts. Cannot hear an owl or coyotes, or the rootings in the woods. Except for the river's rushing current, there is no sound. Even the fire is without the spitting noise. From out of the pain and Darvon stupor, Erik's getting the eerie sting of paranoia. Wincing while picking up the .45 COLT, and struggling to his feet. Still no fucking noise; what the fuck is going on? Where is the little hubby?

Erik limps down to the bank, looking for Jar Head's body. He wades out where he let go. Can't find the body. What the fuck? Where is Jar Head? Splashing back, up onto the riverbank, turning around to face the river, with the .45 dangling at his side, blood running down the grip. Where the fuck is my hat?

He cries out across the river. "Where are you Jar Head? I want you Jar Head . . . . Where are you?" Wondering where his 'BORN TO HUNT' cap is gone.

Colonel Catcher Riley has come up the riverbank to the edge of the gravel bar overlooking the campsite and Erik's backside. He lays down here, in the shadows. Getting his canvas military belt cinched around his forehead and eye, figuring to stay the blood flow from his head wound. Gets his t-shirt off, tears it and wraps his head. Gets this knotted and tied tightly, further slowing the blood flow. Laying back in the forest mulch, resting from the exertions; the warrior-killer brain clicking off the approximate distance across the gravel to the fire. Taking his boots off, then his socks. Gets a soggy handkerchief out of his pocket, folding it the size of his foot. With difficulty, he gets a wet sock over his foot with the handkerchief inside as a thin sole. He uses his pocketknife to cut a lower pants leg off. Folds this to fit his other foot, and pulls a wet sock over this foot and the folded pad. He's thinking he can cross the gravel bar to his pack without much noise. Still watching Erik's backside, past the fire, down at the river's edge; calculating the jaunt to his pack—then to Erik.

Erik's yelling again. "Come to papa you Colonel fuck. I'm here waiting Jar Head . . . . Jinx is dead . . . . What're you doing about that, chickenshit?" Erik's patrolling the gravel bar, watching the river.

Catcher makes a last calculation, then he's crossing the gravel bar, towards the fire and his pack, out in the open, in the moonlight. There's no noise, but for the rushing river.

"Hey, Jar Head, 'fraid to come out motherfucker?" Erik's standing out there, facing the river, with the .45 dangling at his side.

Catcher comes up to his pack like a saber-tooth tiger. He reaches inside, unsnaps the scabbard and pulls out the USMC, KA-BAR knife . . . . Seven is a positive number throughout the Bible. The blade here is seven inches long. Enough for Old Testament justice.

Catcher is erect, and walking towards Erik in a careful unhurried manner. Has the knife ready in his good hand. He has become the predator.

The owl on the river is gone. The diamond strand of stars up and down the river are becoming cold points of fire. The timber tops overhanging the waters are black etchings framing this killing zone on the Little Niangua. The fire has burned low and thin layers of fog cryptogram the last act in the plan to kill an officer. The moon is low in the west, throwing dark shadows across the river towards Erik and the Colonel. Still, no sound but for the river.

Gone are the frogs, katydids, and locusts. There's only the current, and the warrior coming upon Erik with the knife. There is no breeze, just a dampness seeping onto the gravel bar.

Catcher is making a stealthy approach. Going slowly, the rags in the socks on the bottom of his feet, pads over the stones . . . . Then, a rock turns underfoot, causing a grate . . . . Erik turns his bloody form around, facing a saber-tooth bloodmaster with warrior status in the most powerful armed force on Earth.

Erik is bringing the .45 up too slowly, because of the pain in his shoulder. He's recognizing Catcher Riley, but it doesn't compute.

Catcher's got the knife in hand, back by his side, wrist straightened as an extension of the handle. He's bumping Erik's gun hand with his bad wrist, stepping up close.

The .45 COLT jumps off a wayward round.

Catcher stabs Erik to the left of his navel, sinking the blade to the hilt, trying to hold him in close with his bum arm. Erik's bulging blues are telegraphing surprise from out the Darvon and pain.

Catcher's standing here, about three inches from Erik's face, trying to hold him up, with the seven-inch blade planted in the entrails.

"Colonel Catcher Riley, U.S. Army," those saber-tooth eyes probing Erik's.

Erik can still see, waiting for Catcher to bite him or sink fangs into his neck, feeling the searing pain burning through his center.

"It's you," Erik slurs. "It's you. Riley . . . the guy with the boat?"

Bumping the .45 out of Erik's loosening grip. Withdrawing the knife. Stepping back. Wracked with confusion, as he recognizes Erik Starr. "You!"

Erik slowly sinking to his knees, blindly holding his arms out feeling for the floor.

Catcher's holding his bad wrist to his side, gripping the knife in his good hand. Squatting, to stay in Erik's face. "Why? What are you doing here? Tell me," he rasps. "Talk to me."

Erik's got the whimpering look coming over his face, blood and phlegm sopping around his mouth. A lot of little bubbles foaming in the blood/phlegm. "She's my girl, buddy." Flopping face forward onto the rocks.

Catcher leaves him lay. Gets himself up and back to the fire. Seeing the Darvon bottle laying outside the fire ring. Picking this up and opening it. Swallowing the pills with water from a bottle. Thinking he won't die, and he's got to get Jinx's body . . . . What the hell happened? What's Erik Starr doing here? Why is Jinx dead? Why is Jinx dead?

CHAPTER XLI

The sound of the gunshot, fired by Erik, carries the up and down of the Little Niangua. Jake and Big Track come up short, standing in the dark shadows cast over the river by a westward moon.

"You hear that, Tracker," Jake half-whispers.

"There's blood in the waters," and Big Track forges ahead, across a mud bar alongside the main channel.

"Hurry, Tracker." Jake's slogging along behind.

The two of them are in and out of the moonlight, sloshing ahead, following the current. All the time in the continuous rush of the river.

"Fucking cowboy boots," Jake is muttering, trying to pull his boot out of a mud slick.

Gets in some sticker branches from a locust tree on the bank. Pulling through these, keeping Big Track in sight, trying to keep up with the huge Indian.

Big Track is weaving back and forth, crossing and re-crossing the main channel, trying to stay on the open gravel bars, going in and out of the shadows. Coming to a stop and holding his hand up. Jake comes up beside him.

"It is over," Big Track says.

Jake's looking across a broad ripple in the river, to the campsite.

"There's two men," Jake says, huffing from the rapid hike down the riverbed.

"Yes. One is dead, by the river. The one by the fire is putting boots on!"

"Go, go," Jake is pushing Big Track ahead, then alongside him, crossing the shallows.

They come up to Erik's body first. Big Track stands here, looking down, while Jake rolls the body over. Keeping an eye on Catcher, and he on them.

"It's Erik Starr," Jake's saying, standing up, looking around. "Where the hell is Jinx?" He kicks the .45 across the gravel.

Big Track is headed towards Catcher, up towards the fire. Jake is just behind.

Catcher's been watching them since they crossed the river. Sitting here trying to get his boots tied . . . . Figured them for friendlies.

Jake kneels over, taking a good look at Catcher. Trying to figure the turban style head bandage. "Catcher. Catcher Riley . . . . Remember me?"

"I remember you," there's a lot of blood running down his face and neck, and his left forearm is swollen.

"Jake Boss." Cleaning around Catcher's eyes. "Where's Jinx?"

Catcher's staring. "She's dead."

"Where?" Big Track looking down the river.

"Where is she, Catcher?" Jake's still squatting down, in Catcher's face. His voice is unsteady.

"Help me up," and Catcher is trying to push up.

Big Track and Jake help him to his feet.

"Give me the knife." Jake's got his hand out, but Catcher isn't giving the knife up.

"Friend or foe?" Catcher is facing Jake.

"Friend. And Big Track," motioning towards Big Track.

"It's Erik Starr." Pointing with the knife at Starr's body.

"Yes. Erik Starr," Jake says, standing still, listening to the river. "Where is Jinx?"

"Erik Starr . . . Erik Starr . . . The river rat marijuana grower!" Catcher's stumbling over this computation. Can't figure it. Blood seeping down the side of his neck, down his chest and back.

"Yes," Jake definite. "Where is J . . ."

"Her body is down river," looking Jake over. "What are you men doing here?" Holding the bloody knife down at his side.

"We came to warn you," squarely facing Catcher, muddy and wet from the crotch down. "I heard Erik was coming out here. I knew you and Jinx were camping here . . ."

"WHY is he out here?" Catcher's warrior, bloodmaster eyes peering out of the blood and dirt.

"Erik Starr dated Jinx before you married her. I figured he was dangerous." Standing here, facing Catcher in a candid way.

No one says anything. The three of them: Big Track, looking down the river; Catcher and Jake at each other. The fire's burning lower, and the river's current is the only sound.

Catcher throws the knife down beside the pack, "Let's get Jinx."

"OK, Catcher. Where is she?" Jake pleading.

"You men follow me," and Catcher starts off down the river. Jake and Big Track fall-in behind, following his lurching form.

They reach the horizontal sycamore, extending out over the river. Catcher, without turning around, "She's out here." Holding his bad arm up, indicating out toward the tree bush in the middle of the channel.

"I'll go get her," Jake stepping forward. "C'mon Tracker."

"No, I'll get her," and Catcher wades into the water, following the tree trunk outward towards the downed treetop.

Jake and Big Track stay behind in the darkness. Once, when Jake starts to follow, Big Track puts his hand out and shakes his head 'no.'

In time, Catcher's coming out of the inky blackness, towards them, with Jinx's body draped over his shoulders, like he's carrying a dead puma. A huge owl swoops down, letting go a piercing screech.

As Catcher reaches the bank, Jake comes around behind him, hunching down in Jinx's face. "My God, what'd he do to her?" He's trembling hard . . . "Catcher, I think she's alive." Feeling upside her neck. "She's got a pulse. She's alive."

"Is she bleeding anywhere?" Catcher waiting for Jake to check her out. Still has her draped over his shoulders. "You sure she's alive?"

"She's not bleeding much." Jake letting her head down. Got the deep down tremors . . . . "She's definitely alive . . ."

"We got any cell phones that work down here?" Catcher's still holding Jinx.

"It's a no-service area, Catcher. We'll have to hike out," Jake offers.

"We should go down river," Big Track, taking off in that direction.

"Follow Big Track, Catcher. There's a low water bridge and road ahead." Jake's got a hand on Jinx's back, waiting for Catcher to move. Shivering.

This is the way the four of them come down the river: Big Track way out in front, in the lead; Catcher with Jinx over his shoulders, wobbling and lurching; and Jake just behind. The moon is no longer visible, and the muted light of the stars is how they see. At difficult crossings, Big Track waits for the others to catch up, then leads across. Before dawn's light, they reach the low-water bridge.

Catcher lets Jinx off his shoulders and gets down on the ground, leaning against a tree, just off the end of the bridge. Pulling Jinx's body into his lap, holding her, trying to keep her warm. Hoarsely, "You men get help. She needs help now."

"Tracker, you go. I'll stay here," Jake panting. Without a word, Big Track stomps away, up the gravel road.

Jake's sitting down, leaning against a tree opposite Catcher and Jinx. "You know what happened, Colonel?"

Catcher staring from out the blood and mud. "We made our camp at the cave . . . after dark. I went up to see the cave. When I got up there, someone pushed me. I guess Starr. The fall about knocked me out . . . and then he came down and tried to drown me. When I came to, caught up downstream, Jinx was pinned on this tree beside me. I thought she was dead." Catcher is coughing, blowing blood out ahead of him. "Starr was really messed up. Jinx must have put up a hell of a fight."

"He tried to kill her." Jake mutters . . . . "You killed Erik?"

"Erik Starr is the marijuana grower!" Catcher can't put those two together. Jinx and Erik Starr?

"Yes. Runs the OMP. They plant it up and down the Sac River, I think."

Catcher's coughing. He has no shirt and is soaked with water and blood. "If I don't make it, have the sheriff bust the OMP . . . . You understand me," looking towards Jake.

"They will Catcher, they will," Jake nodding.

"Someone at the OMP took a bead on me awhile . . ." coughing hard. "Awhile back. I saw them."

"I'll make sure the sheriff knows," Jake answers. "He'll bust them alright."

"Make sure!"

"I will Catcher, I will." Jake's getting up, trying to tie the bloody bandage tighter around Catcher's head.

"Why was Starr on the river, Jake?" Catcher asking softly, out of half-consciousness.

"Sour grapes, Catcher. You took his girl . . . . You need to keep still."

"How'd he know . . . we were out here?"

"I don't know," and Jake's looking up the road, wanting help, now!

"She told him, Jake."

"Maybe, Catcher."

"She smokes a lot of marijuana. Where'd she get it, Jake?"

"Probably from him." Jake's got his hand on Catcher's shoulder, looking up the dark road. He's praying.

Catcher's barely audible. "Came through on a Hail Mary . . . . She did."

"You gave her a second chance, Catcher."

Catcher's looking down on Jinx's disfigured form, moving his fingers over her busted face, "I think she did well. She chose."

"Hold on Catcher, hold on. I hear a siren."

There's a hint of morning's first light.

"What day is this, Jake?"

"It's Wednesday, Catcher . . . the Fourth of July."

CHAPTER XLII

Sunday, August 2001. It's coming up on noon hour and it's hot. Jo Ann, Catcher, Jake, Big Track, and Marco are gathered together out here at Hattie's old farmhouse. Banded together in the insouciance of the Ozark backcountry. At least, in this moment of time.

Church is out, and Catcher is wearing a suit, as is Jake. Both of them on the porch, in the shade. Catcher with his back to the house, where he can keep an eye on Jo Ann.

Jake leaning against a post with his back to the yard. "Is she going to be alright?"

"Yes!" Catcher's standing here with his good hand in his pants pocket, and the wrist with the cast in a sling around his neck. He's perspiring heavily. "She's going to be just fine." He's not telling about the loss of the baby; coming off the opiates; the clonidine patches, chloral hydrate and muscle relaxants; the mix-up with Ultram, whereby the doctors got her on a synthetic opiate; the sleeplessness accompanying withdrawal; the loss of hearing and peripheral vision on her left side; the nose having to be broken again; the permanent scarring on her face; the repetitious questioning by law enforcement agencies; the repeated trips to the military hospital in St. Louis; the intricate dental procedures; the 'iffy' prognosis concerning her larynx; and so on and so forth . . . . But, the truth is, Catcher does know, she's going to be 'fine.' He's watched her comeback. Observed the rapid shrinkage of prescriptions. Tracked her interest in the Twelve Step program of Narcotics Anonymous. Encouraged her through the excruciating regime of daily exercise. Received the grim 'bona fides' of her life and accepted her soul wrenching remorse. The shame and remorse came early on; along with the suicide watches.

Catcher's watching Big Track, Marco and Hattie, sitting out in the mowed yard, fraternizing with Jo Ann. Besides kindness, there's this curiosity at work. And, Jo Ann is sitting in the lawn chair, bobbing her blonde mane and tolerating their perusal with her electric blue eyes. Even from the porch, Catcher can discern the red veins of scar tissue crevassing her face; this more endearing than disfiguring, to Catcher. The bandage is loose from her throat, but she's still mute, nodding her head to stay in the conversation. She too has her 'church goin' clothes on, and this flowery cotton dress has a wide, round neckline showing off her slender neck. The dress is sleeveless, her shoulders broad and the curves of her deltoids are pronounced. She's pushing her shoes off and is resting her feet in the grass . . . . He sees her glance his way.

It's a clear day with blue skies to match her eyes, and the temperature is climbing. Turkey vultures are riding the thermals overhead, and Catcher's glancing back up the driveway. Seeing the chalky roadway dust cloaking the overhanging foliage. He can smell the dust. The sound of a distant chainsaw is reaching here, and every few minutes, the shrill of a hawk.

Jake's twisting and looking up the driveway after Catcher, then coming back to hold Catcher in view. "You probably know more than I do, but they picked everyone up at the OMP," straightening up to take his suit jacket off. "They found the cave with grow lights, maps pinpointing marijuana plots on the Sac River . . . ."

"I've been meaning to ask you, Jake. Where'd you get the name R4?" Catcher's switching subjects.

Jake draping his jacket over his arm, "There are four things most important to me, Catcher," leaning back against the post. "God, myself, the club, and Jinx, Jo Ann. When I started the nightclub, I figured every temptation under the sun would present itself. I promised myself I'd remember four things: God, my integrity, the club, and . . . Jo Ann. I'd repeat to myself: remember four, remember four, remember four . . . . I named the club R4 to remind me to remember."

"Like an acronym. Interesting . . . . You know, I don't think anyone here owns a computer."

Jake studying Catcher in a quizzical manner . . . . "It wouldn't be worth the cost to some . . . . Maybe we don't need it."

Catcher, flat like, "Back in the day, I jumped into the jungle with more technology on my person than I now have in my house." Then, with more interest, "Any non-human predators around here bigger than a coyote or bobcat?"

"Eagles . . . . And a few mountain lions."

Catcher's looking at the bright blue sky. "Good." Studying the turkey vultures. Seems they're always up there, somewhere. Reaching up with his taped arm to shift the bandage around his head.

Hattie's coming up on the porch. Standing here in her knee-high navy dress, hair loose over her shoulders and shoes in her hand. "You men goin' to eat?"

"We're coming," Catcher's moving past Jake, down into the fresh cut grass.

Out on the lawn, eating fried chicken and potato salad. Trying to stay in the shade. Big Track is standing. Has his hair braided down his back, a bright yellow bandanna around his forehead, and a blousy red shirt tucked into baggy jeans. Marco's wearing a clean, faded pair of denim overalls and a white, short sleeve collared shirt. Hattie's sitting beside Catcher and Jo Ann, barefooted like Jo Ann. A light breeze diffusing the languid heat.

Hattie firing a diamond match and lighting a Camel. "Things'll be getting back to normal now," taking a drag off the cigarette. "Workin' folks don't appreciate the likes of the OMP." She's looking over at Jo Ann, watching her sip the ice tea.

Big Track is looking up at the sky, holding his plate out in front. "I think we will have rain."

"How do you know that, Big Track? The sun's shining." Marco using his fork to scrape up a last bit of potato salad.

"The Osage people came down from the stars and carried certain gifts through the generations," Big Track lifting another piece of chicken to his mouth.

"I'd say, I know what planet you came from Big Track," and Marco lifts the last bit of potato salad towards his face . . . pausing. "Your people cannot only forecast the weather, they can also change shapes . . . . They are shape-changers from a planet in another galaxy . . . ."

"I'm getting ready to change into a little bird," Big Track staring over at Marco, "and then I'm going to fly into your ear and build a big nest in your empty head." The hint of a smile crossing Big Track's face as he returns to eating chicken.

"You can joke all you want, Big Track," Marco still holding his potato salad on the fork, "but, fact is, you are the generations-old offspring of a half-breed alien with extrageneous powers . . . ."

"You're a character, Marco," Catcher winking at Jo Ann.

Jo Ann smiling back, the retainer visible for just that second.

"May be, but all great visionaries were characters," Marco getting a little defensive.

"I am not a half-breed. I'm hundred percent Osage," Big Track trying to set Marco straight . . . .

"Hattie, you have anymore coffee?" Catcher's interrupting.

"Me too," Jake's got the dumbfounded look, still grinning at Marco.

"I'll get it," Hattie's stabbing her cigarette out in the ashtray.

"You don't know the star I came from," Big Track in a serious tone.

"OK . . . OK, Big Track. So, maybe I don't. No need to get mad about it," Marco standing up, stretching his pudgy form.

"Tracker isn't mad," Jake grinning. "He just doesn't think white men know much," laughing. "Isn't that right, Tracker?"

"They don't know much," Big Track shaking his head.

"They never did Big Track," Hattie laughing, pouring Catcher's coffee. "The two of you goin' to get some cattle?" Looking over at Jo Ann.

Catcher, placing his hand on Jo Ann's knee, "Not till we take a little trip."

Hattie's moving over to get in the shade, still standing. "Well excuse the nosy neighbor, but where might you be going?" Smiling towards Jo Ann.

Catcher's looking at Jo Ann with a tight-lipped grin, not saying anything.

Big Track, Jake and Marco are looking at her, sideways, with heads down, like she can't tell they're looking. Hattie still standing here, with the coffee pot in hand.

"She can't talk for a few more weeks, folks," Catcher patting her knee, still watching her face.

Jo Ann, setting her tea glass in the grass, motioning in the air with her left hand, like she's writing. She's sitting forward in her chair.

"I'll get ya some paper and pen," Hattie heading back towards the house.

While they're waiting, Marco is hitting Catcher up for more work. "I could get started on your fences, while you're gone, Catcher . . . . You could pay me when you get back."

"I can put more fence posts in, in a day, than any white man." Big Track serious, talking mostly to himself.

"I've already been working on the place," Marco looking from Big Track to Jake, then back towards Catcher and Jo Ann. "How long y'all going to be gone?"

The shade is shifting, leaving Jo Ann staring into the sun. Catcher's standing, ready to help her move, when Hattie comes huffing back with the pen and paper. Jo Ann is motioning to leave her be, sitting back, allowing Hattie to drop the tablet in her lap. Lifting her face, smiling briefly at Jake, Big Track, Marco and Hattie, the spidery veins of scar tissue burning purple in the sun.

Taking the pen in her left hand, her wedding rings and the TAHITI charm flashing in the sunlight, she pens the following in childlike printing: TAHITI—LOOKING FOR DOLPHINS.

Edwards Brothers Malloy
Thorofare, NJ USA
May 27, 2014